WHO DO YOU THINK YOU ARE?

MALCOLM BRADBURY is a well-known novelist, critic and academic. He set up the famous creative writing department of the University of East Anglia, whose students have included Ian McEwan and Kazuo Ishiguro. He is the author of seven novels: *Eating People is Wrong* (1959); *Stepping Westward* (1965); *The History Man* (1975), which won the Royal Society of Literature Heinemann Prize; *Rates of Exchange* (1983), which was shortlisted for the Booker Prize; *Cuts* (1987); *Doctor Criminale* (1992); and *To the Hermitage* (2000). He has also written several works of non-fiction, humour and satire, including *Who Do You Think You Are?* (1976), *All Dressed Up and Nowhere to Go* (1982) and *Why Come to Slaka?* (1991). He is an active journalist and a leading television writer, responsible for *Porterhouse Blue* (Channel 4), *Cold Comfort Farm* (BBC TV), many TV plays and episodes of *Inspector Morse*, *A Touch of Frost*, *Kavanagh QC* and *Dalziel and Pascoe*. He lives in Norwich, travels a good deal, and was awarded a knighthood in the year 2000.

Also by Malcolm Bradbury in Picador

FICTION

Eating People is Wrong

Stepping Westward

The History Man

Rates of Exchange

Cuts

Doctor Criminale

To the Hermitage

NON-FICTION

All Dressed Up and Nowhere to Go

Why Come to Slaka?

Malcolm | Bradbury

Who Do You Think You Are?

STORIES AND PARODIES

PICADOR

First published 1976 by Martin Secker & Warburg Ltd

This edition published 2016 by Picador
an imprint of Pan Macmillan,
20 New Wharf Road, London N1 9RR
Associated companies throughout the world
www.panmacmillan.com

ISBN 978 1 509 837724 4

A CIP catalogue record for this book is available from
the British Library.

Typeset by SetSystems Ltd, Saffron Walden, Essex

Visit **www.picador.com** to read more about all our books and to
buy them. You will also find features, author interviews and news of
any author events, and you can sign up for e-newsletters so that
you're always first to hear about our new releases.

To Michael Orsler and Barry Spacks

who helped me to start writing

ACKNOWLEDGEMENTS

'Voluptia' was jointly written with Michael Orsler, and I am indebted to him for his permission to reprint it.

I should like to thank the editors and publishers of the following magazines and newspapers where these stories and parodies first appeared: *The Transatlantic Review* ('The Adult Education Class', 'A Breakdown', 'Dodos Among the Elephants' and 'Fritz'); *Encounter* ('A Goodbye for Evadne Winterbottom', 'Nobody Here in England' and 'Composition'); *Guardian* ('A Jaundiced View', 'Tough at the Top', 'Voluptia' and 'Room at the Bottom'); *Punch* ('An Extravagant Fondness for the Love of Women' and 'On yer Bike!, Or, Look Forward in Togetherness'); *New Review* ('Last Things'); *Nova* ('Who Do You Think You Are?'); *The New Statesman* ('Miniature Golf') *Ideal Home* ('A Very Hospitable Person'). 'The Adult Education Class' is, in modified form, a chapter excluded from my novel *Eating People is Wrong*.

CONTENTS

A Goodbye for Evadne Winterbottom

I

PERHAPS I SHOULD begin by saying that in all that follows I write, if a little frankly, as a professional man.

From time to time, then, in my capacity as a welfare psychiatrist, with a special responsibility for the young people in this provincial city, I am approached by people and asked what else there is one can do with sex besides have it. That's to say, there are, I find, many people, perfectly sensible people, who have a very natural desire to know in just what way the climate of sexual permissiveness and anti-chastity which is now our culture may be said to benefit them, give them something, enlarge their beings. 'If we live in a more permissive age, that may be our good fortune,' say the advertisements for some new monthly magazine in endless monthly parts, with a nude family on the cover, devoted to the topic of you, and me, and mankind; middle-aged ladies in the suburbs, shopkeepers down at the crossroads, clip this out, or things like it, and then ring me up, usually in the late evening, to ask just what it is that they mean. How? What good fortune? It isn't easy to answer, and I have to respond very carefully. *Very* carefully; for, of course, these night-callers might equally well be avid, punitive, radical ladies, devoted readers of *Forum*, enlisting my support for experimetal sex-play in the nursery schools. In my position, one is always walking such a delicate line. And what, then, can one do with sex besides have it? Well: one can make a personal politics out of it, change and be changed by it, earn

3

a new self and a new consciousness. Or so Evadne Winterbottom says.

Perhaps I sound a trifle uncertain; the truth of the matter is indeed that I'm beset by a good liberal ambivalence. I have hopes for us all; I have fears for us too. And in any case, as a professional man, one is caught. Take, for example, one quite important part of my duties, which is to visit the local schools and give small sex education lectures. These usually take place in an atmosphere of high solemnity, invigilated by the headmaster or headmistress and a surprisingly large contingent of other staff who happen, they say, to have a free period. I have no doubt that some of them also have enough change in their pockets and purses to ring their local MP, while others are in close touch with the local chapter of Women's Liberation. The delicacy required of me! How do I act? What do I say? I come in a dark suit, carrying a small brown briefcase. I look authoritative. I point out to the children the location and character of their genital organs, and say a little about their multifarious uses; I comment that some stimulation of these properties or appendages – which are not, I carefully stress, novel to the possessor but are common attributes in mankind – by their very owner will not lead to blindness or hideous tragedy; I divide these physiological attributes into two distinct classes, or as we say sexes, and point out their complementarity and potential conjunctiveness; I remark on the fact that that conjunction, when actualized, can have highly productive consequences; I speak of the need for forethought and scruple; I indicate, gently, that there are means and instruments by which the productive aspect of the process may be by-passed. Over the whole I cast, a little sweat standing on my upper lip, an atmosphere of humanism and enlightenment. It is, I explain to them all, more than crude practical information I am trying to give them, not a description of an abstract, primitive technology but a species of human feeling and human wisdom. Ignorance is, I say in my crescendo, blindness and folly; but knowledge and managed emotion is mastery. On the other hand, in deference to the

4

newer spirits in the audience, I add a few touches about the desirability of the fullest self-expression, the power of passions fulfilled. There is no aspect of the rhetoric that is not charged, no phrase that can go unconsidered. The teachers round the walls whisper among themselves and make extensive notes; afterwards they have post mortems with me over tea and buns round the staffroom table. 'You mean you try to please everybody?' demands Evadne Winterbottom. 'Oh, you're a fink. Maybe a kind-hearted fink; but a fink.' 'I'm a fink deep down, too: in my unconscious, and even a psychiatrist can have an unconscious, I'm a fink,' I say to Evadne Winterbottom, who understands.

Why do I feel guilty? Of course one reason is that, inevitably enough, quite a few of the children feel compelled to put the knowledge I have conveyed to them to the test: project-work connected with the class. They think, and in this they are simply sensing the obvious contradiction, that what I am offering them is not description but advocacy. Perhaps, in a sense, I am. This in turn frequently brings them back to see me in different circumstances. ('But I thought, Dr Denison, I thought you said it was abortion that came first and contraception was what we might fall back on?' 'Do you habitually reverse things in other areas? Telephone numbers, for instance?' 'But, Dr Denison, we only had half an hour; and then there was a French vocabulary test. There's so much to learn in schools these days.') I make some arrangements over the telephone; they go; I sit back in my chair, behind my desk, and squirm. I ought not to have a desk, which is an alienation device, but it's there in the room and the room is so small that I cannot but use it. Why do I squirm? They are learning and growing and becoming the newer, freer people. As a psychiatrist, I have naturally learned and come to venerate the good news out of Vienna; I know what a contorted hothouse all that old repression creates. After all, it was the hothouse I grew up in myself, not so long ago. I believe it took me about eight years of desultory – and highly anxious – curiosity before I was able to put two and two together about how you put one and one together, though of course it was largely this state of ignorance, along with the fact that it appeared to be shared by all my peers, male and female, that maintained me in a state of virginity until my late teens, when I acquired both the knowledge and a bicycle and was able to ride out and mend matters. My young have been spared all that; has it made them better? 'Of course they're better; they're not hung up about it. You're the one who's hung up, still; and you're supposed to be a psychiatrist, correct me if I'm wrong,' says Evadne Winterbottom.

It may be so; and a good man ought to know himself. But, as a professional man, one's aims are practical: to get on with the day-to-day work of welfare. ('Welfare? Ill-fare,' says Evadne Winterbottom.) Twice a week I set off from home, kissing my wife, and attend my small clinic, which is held in a nonconformist chapel not far from the centre of town. The chapel itself is early nineteenth century, but has modern – which is to say prefabricated – addenda. There is a large hut, split up into several rooms, large and small, which is the focus of all kinds of communal activity. I am in it now, writing these notes. A playgroup meets here in the mornings, bringing the neighbourhood three- and four-year-olds from their limited home backgrounds into this larger world, where they can urinate on the radiators and aid adult helpmates stick coloured paper onto toilet rolls, and so fashion figures of what they call man. And maybe man it is; who is to say not? I look now at a row of these artefacts, sitting there on the window-ledge, and ask myself, why trust Michelangelo, finally, more than these? On most afternoons there is a children's clinic, issuing orange-juice and inoculating babies; on one, by a kind of strategic obverse, a Family Planning Clinic, issuing diaphragms and creams, at first to the neighbourhood married women but more recently, after a brief sit-in, to the neighbourhood single too. I am on the committee, and so is the chapel's Minister, a most helpful and enlightened man who also runs a Youth Club here in the evenings, and who on FPC days patrols outside, looking out for the occasional young girls who peer in through the windows, a little hopelessly, and asking them kindly if they would like to come in and, as he puts it, get fitted. There is a modest modern heroism in all this, a putting right, a making possible. 'Impersonal bureaucracy,' says Evadne Winterbottom; 'We're devoted,' I tell her.

And so here I come in attendance, two days a week, with a nurse, Miss Rickett, advising on emotional and mental health problems, especially for those at school. The desk in the little office, the desk at which I write, is the same one used by the female doctor who attends the FPC, the male uncle-doctor who does the children's clinic. Their detritus is in the drawers; and the uncle-doctor, for pacificatory purposes, or perhaps for some profounder iconic need, keeps a toy rubber Noddy on top of the desk – an object I always want to move during my own sessions, though for some odd reason I have never had the courage to do so. It gives its rubbery nod to me now. I, of course, have my own distinctive supplies: bottles of ink for inkblot tests, pictures for free association games, etc. It may sound dull and routine; I may sound a dull and routine person. But the mothers in the terraced houses, the children who play in the condemned property up the street, the bootboys who meet on the waste ground, the middle classes up past the traffic lights, have all come to depend on us, know we are here and ready to spread our professional skills through the immediate universe of anxiety, tension, social problems. Most of the cases I see are straightforward and familiar: boys and girls who steal, or vandalize, or wet the bed, or fail unaccountably at school, or run away, or are found by their teachers or doctors or parents disturbed or highly strung. Miss Rickett has one approach: a large, healthy lady who is also on the local council, she inclines to the view that, as she puts it, 'God gave them bottoms to be smacked on.' I have another, more professional and I hope more generous. Even so, people and problems are problems and we usually manage in our way to agree and, more important, to alleviate. Only on occasion is there a more complicated, more challenging, even more threatening case. Let me take, for instance, to choose an example purely at random, the case of – as I had better call her to preserve the confidentialities of the consulting room – the case of Patient X.

II

Patient X is unusual among my visitors, in that she has now left school (she took A-levels last summer and has spent the last six months 'dropping out, hanging round, trying it all,' as she puts it) and also in the fact that there is, in a sense, nothing whatsoever wrong with her. She does have a marked manic-depressive cycle, with periods of high elation followed by periods of considerable depression, usually relieved by tranquillizing drugs which she gets from a variety of sources, none of them me; it is also true that she forms unusual, disturbing relationships, runs away from time to time, and so on. However, her problem is basically that she has a need to consult professional people, men older than herself but not too old, who can understand and explore her situation. In fact she had seen quite a large number of advisers of various kinds, in different areas, before she came to me, having initially succeeded in persuading her doctor that such consultations were the only thing that made her feel good. Obviously, in order to obtain such consultations and maintain them over a period, she has to have problems; but the sort of life she lives is such as never to leave her short of material. She frequents storm-centres and disaster areas: breaking marriages, communes, nightclubs with two-way mirrors. 'I've always had problems,' she told me on her first visit, when she was still in the sixth form. 'If I didn't have problems I wouldn't know I even existed. The odd thing is that they've never sent me to see *you* before. Why do you think that is? I mean, aren't I just the sort of patient you need?' The early sessions, while she was still at school, were fairly straight-forward, and largely taken up by a discussion of the previous consultations she had had with others. Now I ought at once to explain that I am, naturally enough, highly committed to the ethics of my profession, and it is cetainly not my custom to probe into treatments prescribed by my professional peers. In this case, however, I immediately struck upon an unusual dilemma: that her previous consultations and the problems she now had were intimately associated. The problem, simply, was this: she had developed an emotional pattern of intense dependence upon her advisers and then acquired a syndrome of rejection, or psychic hurt, when the professional context – as well as the fact that most of these advisers were married men – had cut short the development of that emotional set. I immediately told her, of course, that this was familiar enough in all forms of psychosomatic treatment, in that patients became excessively dependent on their doctors; the one unusual feature was the startlingly high degree of recurrence, the same pattern having occurred seven times. Naturally, I made it quite clear that mine should be the final course of treatment, and that the same pattern should not be allowed to repeat itself. 'Well, I think you've really managed to work your way round to the heart of the problem,' said Patient X, very admiringly. 'But do you really think we can do it?'

I explained to her how we should proceed. 'I want to lay down some guidelines from the start,' I said. 'The important thing is to have the atmosphere firmly defined, without soft edges. So the treatment must always remain completely impersonal. It must always occur in this consulting room.' I waved my hand at the room, the Noddy on the desk. 'Well, that's what they've all said,' said Patient X, leaning forward in her chair with an anxious look, 'but how can treatment be completely impersonal, when it's about me, and my feelings . . . and when in any case you'll want to ask me all sorts of very intimate questions about my sexual behaviour, and I'll have to acquire personal confidence in you for the treatment to be effective?' 'We can manage all that from here,' I said firmly, 'and let's be clear about this. You must never, for example, telephone me at home – unless, of course, some serious emergency, of a genuinely psychic kind, occurs.' 'Maybe you'd better write down your telephone number, then,' said Patient X. 'Just to reassure me on that.' As I say, one occasionally gets this kind of more complicated – though in fact not unfamiliar – case. 'Another point,' I said, putting down my pen. 'One of the dangers in this type of treatment is that the patient has always a vested interest in prolonging it. I've had, for example, patients who severely resent the fact that I have other patients to see. For that reason the sessions must be exactly timed. You must arrive here promptly, and leave promptly when I say they've ended.' Patient X rose to protest, putting her hands on my desk. 'But how am I to get to know you well enough to trust you?' she asked. 'Please sit down,' I said. Patient X seated herself and grew calmer. 'The trouble with this sort of professionality, and don't forget I'm used to it, is that it stands in the way of my ever getting help,' she said. 'But you must ask yourself what, in your case, would really constitute help? What would satisfy me would be for you to go away not needing any further treatment from any source. Isn't that what we're after?' Patient X nodded. 'Very well, then,' I said, 'the problem is therefore for me to overcome your feeling that you must always *have* help, to break the syndrome of dependence. It's three thirty, and you must go now.' 'You're just like all the others,' said Patient X. 'You don't trust me, you don't care about me. I'm just half an hour's worth of problems to you, straight in, straight out, so you can get paid.' I see from my notes on this case, which are out on the desk in front of me, that on that occasion Patient X left at four fifteen; and that a similar difficulty prevailed throughout all the early sessions, until we developed a more effective routine. Throughout those early sessions I noticed Miss Rickett getting more and more irritated with the patient; that, moreover, she never once left the room during these consultations. This was unusual, for the sessions were, as I say, prolonged, and Miss Rickett, like many heavy tea-drinkers, has to visit the lavatory quite frequently. In fact I often noticed her wriggling uncomfortably. But Miss

Rickett, stern in her way, has my best interests ever at heart, and once even ejected Patient X by main force when her too-lengthy presence put at risk my attendance at an important meeting of the FPC committee.

Well, as I say, the case of Patient X is simply an instance of my work, chosen utterly at random; and you would hardly want me to bore you with further details. Suffice it to say that the treatment was, inevitably, extended; the file in front of me is thick with scribbled notes. As time went on, and we got into the elaborate details of Patient X's life story, actions, feelings, explored at the most prolonged, over-detailed length, Miss Rickett took to falling asleep in boredom. This, curiously, alleviated the atmosphere considerably. We got onto new levels of frankness, even of interest; Patient X stopped resisting the conventions of the situation; the treatment began to go well. I also on the odd occasion did see Patient X outside the consulting room. Once, after a particularly trying afternoon with a mature nine-year-old caught making obscene telephone calls to our Lady Mayoress, I slipped into the Windjammer bar of a local pub, the Pineapple, and leaned against an old ship's wheel drinking sherry and puffing my pipe. 'Hi,' said a girl with a very large hat and a very small dress, with long black hair; it was Patient X. 'Take me somewhere,' she said. 'You're with some-one,' I pointed out. 'He can wait till tomorrow,' said Patient X, 'he won't mind.' 'My wife's cooking steak for me,' I said. 'See you,' said Patient X, and went out of the door with her companion, a young man with long hair dyed silver-grey. I went home and ate steak. Another such occasion, rather more sub-stantial in nature, occurred rather late at night, when someone who said she was her flatmate telephoned me at home to advise me that Patient X was talking of suicide, and was in a serious condition. It shows the awkward conditions we have to work with; perhaps I should briefly report it.

I went to the flat, at the top of a small house not far from the clinic, a cavernous wreck of a Victorian building which had been turned into cheap rooms, mostly occupied by students.

I found the numbered room, tapped on the door (there was no bell), and was admitted by the flatmate. Patient X lay in the living room, groaning on a rather broken and hideously patterned old sofa, of a type picked up for a few shillings in the junk shops. I looked at her and it was immediately clear that she was extremely drunk; in fact an empty bottle of Scotch, which the flatmate told me she had brought home full that evening, stood on the floor beside her. 'Has she said anything?' I asked the flatmate. 'Just that she was going to kill herself,' said the flatmate, 'and that I must call you and tell you so.' 'He left me, he left me,' said Patient X from the sofa. I had no great difficulty in guessing who 'he' was, since we had had a consultation the previous day, and she had told me, with some enthusiasm and a great deal of specific detail, about her latest boyfriend. It was, I had known for some time, Patient X's habit to frequent the cocktail bar of the most expensive hotel in the city centre and be constantly taken away from it, in sports cars, for adventurous purposes, by rich young men who had horses or yachts and were about to inherit the family business. The ones who seemed to interest her most were usually either married, or engaged to be married, or divorced: the ones who, as she put it, cried in bed, and were usually in the middle of some enormous, tangled, emotional contradiction, the ones she could help. It was a very familiar syndrome with Patient X; indeed it was virtually the story of her life, and, of course, the basis and foundation of her capacity to have problems requiring advice, treatment, and solution. The latest boyfriend – who was divorced, engaged to be re-married, and also sleeping with Patient X's best friend – had promised to take Patient X to Corfu with him, on a business trip, at the weekend; clearly, for any one of a hundred reasons, all predictable, this had collapsed. 'Has he been here?' I asked the flatmate. 'Yes,' she said, adding, by way of explanation, 'he's decided to become homosexual.' Patient X put a languid hand out in my direction and said, 'You must help me.' I resolved on a cool course of action. 'I think you ought to be put to bed,' I said. 'And then you must come and see me tomorrow afternoon.' I should explain that threatening suicide is a means frequently used by patients to obtain supplementary treatment.

'Yes, put me to bed,' said Patient X. 'You know, I was just going to suggest that.' The flatmate and I carried Patient X, not a small girl, from the sitting room into her bedroom, her long black hair hanging down nearly to the floor. 'There's my clock and there's my radio and that's my mirror,' said Patient X, dropping down heavily into the bed. The long mirror in the ancient wardrobe, equally junk-shop, had been described to me in many long sessions while Miss Rickett had slept, along with many practices that Patient X had performed before it. In fact, there were few details of the room that had not been portrayed to me in some circumstance or other; I felt I knew it utterly already, being surrounded by a corroboration of the erotic and emotional evidence. 'Where are her night-things?' I asked. 'You know I don't wear any,' said Patient X, and I felt almost embarrassed, for that too was a part of this scene and setting as it had been told to me. Between us, the flatmate and I undressed Patient X, who giggled, caressed the hair on her lower stomach affectionately, and asked the flatmate to fetch her some Horlicks, an improbable touch in the situation. 'Now you must go straight to sleep, and come and see me at the clinic tomorrow afternoon,' I said, pulling the duvet over her big naked self. 'For Christ's sake, it may be too late,' said Patient X. 'How can I possibly get through to tomorrow afternoon? How can I get through the night?' 'You're not so bad, just drunk and upset,' I said. 'Go to sleep.' Patient X sobbed and said, 'Why won't you help me? How can you leave me like this? Impersonal bureaucracy!' 'We're devoted,' I said. 'Devoted,' said Patient X. 'You're so stuck being a doctor you can't be a person and do something for me when it really matters.' 'I will, tomorrow,' I said, patting her arm. 'Help, help, help,' cried Patient X, grabbing my arm and moving over to one side of the bed. 'How can you care about me there, with that fat nurse slobbering in her chair? Care for me now.' I then had a discussion about the impersonality of treatment, of a type already reported, and hardly worth detaining you with; and it was some long time before I was able at last to get away. Nonetheless, the entire episode gave me a vastly deeper and more personal insight into the problem with which I was dealing, and a new comprehension of my utter lack of success. I brooded on it as I tottered down the stairs, dank and, at this hour, unlit. 'Traitor,' shouted Patient X, a long, white, naked, unsteady figure framed in her bedroom window as I walked, with only one glance back, down the path to my car, to go and report myself in at home.

III

Well, there you have it, then, just one among the many hundreds of cases I have to deal with: one with its exceptional features, yes, but typical enough in its way. Perhaps I should just add, to alleviate any anxieties, that, as I had expected throughout, Patient X did come to see me the following afternoon. She stood in the doorway, still a little unsteady, a big yellow hat on her head. I sat behind the desk, with its wobbly Noddy, and said, 'What are your symptoms?' as she stepped inside. Miss Rickett took one look and promptly fell asleep, a conditioned reflex if ever I saw one. Patient X looked at me. 'Some people say "How are you?" and not "What are your symptoms?" she said. 'Let me ask you, "What are *your* symptoms?"' 'I had carefully planned out beforehand what I was to say to Patient X on her arrival: I intended to point out to her that her problems were self-induced, that she put herself in their way, and that simply by changing the pattern of her life and expectations, looking for different people and different situations, she could avoid them. I began to say this, but Patient X said again, 'What are your symptoms?' Then, looking at me, speaking quickly, she pointed out what she said were some of the most obvious: a nervous twitching of the limbs, heavy smoking amounting to an obvious oral fixation, a marked tendency to withdrawal from human contact, and emotional regression. She observed that I was highly communicative in my professional function, because here I could work within abstractions, institutionalized modes of conduct and address, and pre-determined situations managed by myself; but that I used my rôle as a disguise for my obvious inadequacies and problems. I was apt to shelter away from normal emotional situations and demands; I vacillated and ran with prevailing opinion, either because I had no inner convictions or, rather more likely, a lack of will which would enable me to formulate and assert them; I compromised with life; and I subordinated and internalized all my expectations and desires. I was old, she said, more than thirty, which was a difficult time; I was married, and ten years married, which was a dangerous period; and I had assumed the rôle of an envious observer of others, a posture which enabled me to release energy and need by fixating it in the lives of my patients.

Realizing that Patient X was taking advantage of the situation arising from our out-of-hours contact, I stood up behind the desk, knocking over the Noddy, and said angrily: 'Look, I reserve the right to make all the diagnoses here.' The noise disturbed Miss Rickett, who started awake, looked around nervously, and mumbled, in another conditioned reflex, 'God gave them bottoms to be smacked on.' 'Go to sleep, Miss Rickett,' I said. 'Is this really what you want to do, really?' cried Patient X, gesturing at the tiny cubicle of a room. 'Is this what you wanted your life to be? Is this your final conception of a satisfying existence?' 'It's a job,' I said, 'a calling. One gets one's gratifications, helping people.' 'Well, there's the difference between us,' said Patient X, taking off her hat. 'I can explain my problems. I have problems because I expect everything. I expect people to take all they can: me, and everything else. I expect them to cut through the hang-ups and the limitations, and leave their lives and their dull wives, and throw up their careers, and take me to Corfu, and see what they've missed.' 'I see,' I said. 'I can explain your solutions too,' said Patient X. 'You have solutions because you think people should make do

15

with anything, just the way you have, and hold themselves tight, and not ask for more. But, really, *you* have the problems, and *I* have the solutions.' 'You may be right,' I said; as I remarked earlier, I suffer from a good liberal ambivalence. 'All right, look, I dare you,' said Patient X. 'Get up from that desk. Put away your pipe. Take me to Corfu. We'll sit on the beach and we'll write a book reforming psychiatry and we'll go to bed a lot and you can see all you've missed. That's what I've been trying to tell you; that's the only way through this absurd, empty situation.' 'He's not going to Corfu,' said Miss Rickett. 'He's going to a meeting of the Family Planning Committee. Time's up.' And, ever having my interests at heart, she bundled Patient X to the door. 'Fink,' said Patient X in the doorway, and then she was gone.

Of course, such disturbances are an absolutely normal and routine part of the professional life of those who devote themselves to helping others. One expects it. Nonetheless there is more to life than context; there is an inner me. (As Evadne Winterbottom says: 'A public self is all you are. What about the universe within?') There are times when I suspect that too much psychic self-awareness does not save a man; it impairs his ability to function. Of course, given my job, such a view leads to ambivalence ('*Mauvaise foi*,' says Evadne Winterbottom, who is an intelligent girl, and has read Sartre); even so, I feel I have proved it myself in the way I have maintained the workaday competence of my own professional life. But one *can* be disturbed by such events, such irruptions, shaken in the self; and I have to confess that on this particular day I was less than usually devoted to the affairs of the FPC, and that I went home in a considerable state of depression. The exact nature of my malaise was not clear to me; nor would self-analysis dislodge it. The phrases of the afternoon, the invitation, dwelt in my head. I considered talking it all over with my wife, Laura, but that seemed less than feasible. She is an attractive, positive, and understanding woman, a point of good sense in life, but the stability of our relationship is based, like most relationships, on compromise, on things left unsaid, dissatisfactions unarticulated. In any case, my wife is pre-Freudian; she lives mentally in the nineteenth-century vision of man, and above all woman, as separate, cloistered, impenetrable, chaste. If our ideas of selfhood are emblematized in architecture, Laura belongs not to the picture-window, open-plan era, but the period of the servant-guarded entrance, the long corridor, the inner sanctum. I say she is pre-Freudian, but that's inaccurate. She is anti-Freudian, and puts Freud in his place. 'The politics of desire,' says Evadne Winterbottom. Laura does not believe in such things for a moment. She simply makes it clear, as an intelligent, inner-directed woman, that Freud's view that sexuality is the basic human drive is a local problem, an obsession appropriate only to the heated frenzies of decadent, bourgeois, turn-of-the-century, provincial Vienna, and not to the modern England of today. Laura has gazed on sex; but she has found joy and release in other things. I realized this soon after our marriage, when I made Laura write down her dreams; they were wild sexual frenzies but they defied interpretation, until, one day, I grasped that they were a displaced symbolism reflecting suppressed anxieties about her deficiencies as a cook. Since then the pattern has become clear. In sex and orgasm Laura is willing and competent, but rational and controlled; however, she expresses a violent unconscious life of passion and will, a vital energy of self, a frenzied Lawrentian merging assimilativeness, in the production of, for instance, *canard à l'orange*. No, I came home, looked at her dark, hard, preoccupied face, and did not speak to her of my upset with Patient X.

Yet, I have to confess, a quiet agony persisted; and, if only to show you how professional life does inevitably spill over into private, to show, in a way, that we are human, I must tell you that what followed was an interlude of strange behaviour on my own part. That night, sitting in my small study, in fact the converted rear portion of our garage, driven heady, I suppose, by the temper of the times, the conversation of the day, the feeling of the overwhelming modern merging of the public and the pubic, I found myself compelled, somehow, to draw Laura's attention to a certain sense of incompleteness, of want, that I found coursing through me. What I did I did, I think, with delicacy: not wanting to disturb a valuable, valued harmony. That night, after Laura was in bed, I left a number of small cards around the house, under vases where she cleaned, in the medicine cupboard in the bathroom, in the refrigerator. The cards were simply inscribed and unsigned: they said things like *Shudder more*, *Try other positions*, and *Biting is not wrong*. Two days later I checked: the cards were all gone. Thereafter in bed I was devoutly analytical, looking for signs of a change, a change that would change me; and yet, too, in a state of fearful trepidation, horrified that I might have upset the form and order of our relationship. But nothing different or untoward or notably exciting happened, in bed or as we passed each other in corridors, and I gradually assumed that Laura had not read the cards or that, if she had, she had simply not understood them. By this time I was secretly rather pleased, since the entire matter had brought me to the heights of nervous tension; I am not the kind of man who makes intolerable demands. But then one day it dawned on me that she had indeed both read and understood the messages: the lack of understanding was mine. I was looking for change in the wrong place: the food had improved, enormously. It was a change – perhaps a rebuke, perhaps a surging, vital outlay of love, an exposure of Laura's most intimate self. We all give love, what of it we have to give, in our own way, and so try to serve. As for me, my sense of deep feelings unconsummated, of corners of self untouched and unexpressed, continues. I have no great expectation of ever, now, expanding my senses or my sensibility, though I sometimes feel signals in the air, vague promises. On the other hand, I have put on half a stone.

IV

I might add that I now feel that the whole experience with Patient X was of the greatest professional value to me. For, if part of one's professional duty is to be the man detached, another part is to be the man in a certain sense involved, the man who is following where consciousness is going; and if I am just slightly more competent in the latter aspect of my rôle because of Patient X, and if I see more clearly than I did where our culture and our history are moving us, and what they ask of us, and also what I myself am really like, and why, indeed, it may well be that what I am like is not really what anybody ought to be like, then perhaps we are getting somewhere. Or, at any rate, that is what Evadne Winterbottom says.

For I have, actually, seen Evadne Winterbottom a certain amount, in informal circumstances, since she ceased to be my Patient X. I gather that she has always tended to maintain this sort of relationship with some of her former advisers, dropping in on them now and again for a chat and a drink, meeting them in town, taking weekends with them, even while fresher consultants are considering the problems that are arising from just that situation. Even the young man with dyed grey hair was, I gather, a lecturer in sociology at the local polytechnic. We can talk freely now, since she is not my patient (she's now going to a very well qualified man of Laingian persuasions in the next town, where they have a teaching hospital and vastly superior facilities all round); and she is in fact an intelligent, articulate girl, with a persuasive belief in the value of her own liberation and a perfectly carefree attitude to the troubles and dilemmas that we were familiar with, conditioned by, in the pre-Pill world of our youth. We talk about her and we also talk about me. It is her theory that she is my natural complement: she claims that if she needed my solutions, I needed her problems. 'The modern symbiosis,' say Evadne Winterbottom. 'I agree,' I say. As she says, we each had our professional rôle to perform, mine

19

of adviser, hers of patient: she was dependent on my theoretical abstractions, and I was dependent on her freewheeling actions. But rôles wear out, become dysfunctional, and, for both our sakes, a new one was needed. 'You can be more than you think you are,' says Evadne Winterbottom, standing in front of the mirror in the junk-shop wardrobe. 'Impersonal radicalism,' I say. 'We're devoted,' says Evadne Winterbottom.

Actually, I have not seen her now for a couple of weeks. A young man who has his own plane, as well as a wife and seven children, and who is curiously enough a doctor, has taken her off to Malta for a bit. I met them in the Windjammer bar at the Pineapple, one evening when, after an awkward day's consultation with a twelve-year-old female arsonist, I went in for a sherry. He looked about two years older than I am, more tanned, lither, with more obvious money and more obvious brightness. He talked in a slightly hippy way, using words like 'man', which I thought affected; but then, on the edge of going to Malta, one probably changes style a little. 'Take me somewhere,' she said. 'You're with someone,' I said. 'He'll wait till tomorrow,' said Evadne Winterbottom. We slipped round the corner to the Stagecoach bar at the Goat and Compasses. 'A last consultation,' she said. Then she told me all about it, her doubts, the ups and downs of her feelings; she said she doubted whether she would be back in the district again; but then, in one of her characteristic absurdities, she said that if I needed her, if things became intolerable, I was to write to her, simply saying, 'Come back,' and she would come. 'Remember that,' she said, 'but only if some serious emergency, of a genuinely psychic kind, occurs.' What, of course, she doesn't realize is my position and my nature. I am old, more than thirty, and it is a difficult time; I am married, ten years married, and that is a dangerous period; the inclination of my character is to be recessive and not to impose my will, my needs, or my values on others. The result is a liberal ambivalence, a state torn between the claims of the past and the claims of the future, the desire for stability and solid, separate selfhood, the desire for its opposite.

But this is the human condition, and for it there is no treatment. I sit here now, in the surgery, looking at the Noddy on the desk, awaiting the next case, simple bedwetting, and write these notes. They are tentative, even muddled, and I am not sure for whom they are being written, or what they say, or ask. The place, the state of mind, the feelings, are not, I suppose, quite where I meant to end up. Somewhere, it is possible, there might have been another fulfilment, a greater self-celebration. But that is not given to most of us. Perhaps it is really and truly, for all that's said, given to none of us. With, I suppose I ought to add, the possible exception of Evadne Winterbottom.

I should like to end by hoping that this, in its way, answers the questions of those of you who have been kind enough to ring me up on the telephone, usually in the very late evening, and ask about the present historical state of man. I am, of course, at the surgery twice weekly, in the afternoons; and I am always available there, in my professional capacity, to answer queries or treat cases – to the best of my ability – such as may arise in these times of what I think we all recognize as considerable strain.

A Very Hospitable Person

THE NATHANS were together in the kitchen, doing a few last chores before their dinner guests arrived, when the telephone rang. Glenn Nathan had just got the trays out of the freezer compartment to empty them into the ice-bucket; he put them down in the sink and, still carrying the bucket, went out to take the call. Catherine, his wife, followed him out in her hostess apron, and stood in the hall to listen; and as soon as she heard Glenn say, 'Oh, hi, Leo,' she knew exactly what was coming – the Tuckermans were not going to be able to make it. Glenn listened on the receiver for a moment and then said, 'Sure, don't worry, we quite understand, Leo,' with his usual unperturbed politeness. 'They're not coming?' asked Catherine. Glenn looked at her, shook his head, and frowned. 'Oh, well, Jesus,' said Catherine, in a loud voice. 'Isn't that just dandy?' Glenn quickly put his hand over the mouthpiece, but couldn't have done it quickly enough, because the next thing he said was, 'No, sure, Leo, Cathy knows *just* how it is. We had to miss an invitation to the *President*'s house because one of our kids was sick. So we make it another time.' 'So we do *what*?' cried Catherine. Glenn looked at her angrily and went on being affable into the phone. 'These things happen, Leo,' he said. 'The kid will probably be as right as shine when he wakes up in the morning. We'll see you soon.'

Glenn put down the telephone and walked right by Cathy to take the ice-bucket back into the kitchen. Emptying the cubes into it, he said, with his back to her, 'Can't you wait till I get off the phone?' 'Unconsciously they didn't want to come,' said

Catherine. 'Yes, so they give their kid a fever,' said Glenn. 'Oh, I know those convenient fevers,' said Cathy. 'Look, they wanted to come,' said Glenn, 'Leo even drove over to the college dormitory to pick up the babysitter. She was right there when he phoned. They were coming right up to the last minute. And I could hear the kid *screaming*.' 'Well, they certainly loused up our evening,' said Catherine. 'Now it's just you and me and the Lawrences. And what do I say to the Lawrences? I only even met them once.' Glenn, still not looking at her, took the ice-bucket and carried it through to the living room to put it on the drinks table. 'You'll find something, Cathy,' he said, 'you're a very hospitable person.' 'I am with my friends,' said Catherine, following him through and plumping a couple of pillows on the sofa, 'but these guys aren't even American. And you know British people don't talk. They sit right there on their asses and look in the fireplace.' 'Bring them out,' said Glenn, taking a pretzel out of the dish. 'You invited them.' 'To meet the Tuckermans,' said Catherine. 'That's why I invited them. Look, just leave those goddam pretzels alone, will you?' 'All right,' said Glenn, putting the pretzel back in the dish. 'When they come, tell them they got the wrong night.' 'Jesus,' said Cathy, 'eat it now, you fingered it.' 'Don't be dirty,' said Glenn. Cathy began to laugh and Glenn came over and slapped her on the rump; and when the doorbell rang a couple of minutes later she had as good as forgotten about the goddam Tuckermans.

The two Lawrences stood on the porch, kicking the snow off their shoes. Lila Lawrence was wearing those heavy, 'sensible' British ones that made Englishwomen look what she called top-heavy at the bottom; Richard had acquired American over-shoes which he had taken off and now held in his hand, clearly uncertain what the natives did with them. 'Hi,' shouted Catherine. 'Drop them right there and come on in, friends.' The Lawrences smiled and stumbled inside. 'Did you know your *Welcome* mat's the wrong way round?' said Richard, grinning. 'Here you get welcomed going,' said Cathy. 'No, seriously, you're very welcome.' Glenn came forward and with a buzz of

26

activity took their coats, asking, 'How's the weather out there? Watchman, what of the night?' 'In England the country would be at a standstill by now,' said Lila, taking off her shoes and putting on slippers. 'Why, it's just a sprinkling,' said Glenn, hanging up the coats. 'Oh look, a fire!' said Lila, turning to see into the living room. 'That's very jolly. We don't even have a fireplace in the house we're renting.' 'Perhaps it's as well,' said Richard, 'the central heating won't go down below eighty. We have to keep going outside to bring our blood-heat down.' Cathy looked across at Glenn and winked; then she said, 'Come right in, come right in,' and led the way into the living room. 'How cosy,' said Lila, as the two Lawrences moved over together to a corner, by the wall, and stood close together as if they had to protect one another. 'Well, make yourself at home,' said Cathy. 'What can I get you to drink? In this crazy mixed-up household, I mix the drinks.' 'And I sew,' said Glenn. The Lawrences both laughed for an equal length of time and Cathy said, 'What's it to be? Take a spin along those bottles and think of something.' Lila, not looking, said, 'Have you a dry sherry?' 'Sure,' said Cathy. 'I'd very much like a Martini, actually, if it's not too much trouble,' said Richard, looking scrupulously at the bottles, a serious guest. 'No trouble, Richard, I make a wicked Martini,' said Cathy. 'Just a small glimpse of vermouth.' 'Very nice,' said Richard. 'Don't drink too much, will you, darling?' said Lila. 'We've got to drive back in the snow.' 'Oh, relax. You could stay here if you like,' said Cathy. 'We have plenty of room.'

Cathy went over to the drinks table and started to mix. 'Yep, Cathy's a whiz with Martinis,' said Glenn, sitting down. 'I never did learn how to do those things. I guess I was too studious. Why, Cathy was making them for me even before we were married.' 'Hey, you Lawrences, sit down,' said Cathy. 'None of that old British politeness.' 'Oh, thank you,' said Lila. 'Yes, she really did everything I couldn't do.' 'I really ran that apartment like I lived there,' said Cathy, stirring the Martini. 'Well, hey, for a while there you did,' said Glenn. 'Oh, that was a fun time,' said Cathy, laughing about it, 'You know, he couldn't do a thing? Not a *thing*. I had to teach him everything. From how to sew to how to screw.' 'That comes naturally,' said Glenn. 'It didn't, kid,' said Cathy. 'It did not. How's *your* marriage?' 'Fine,' said Richard. 'Where was all this? Where did you meet?' Cathy carried the sherry over to Lila, who was looking inside her purse, and said, 'Oh, this was out in the Middle West.' 'Champaign, Illinois,' said Glenn, 'I was in graduate school out there. And teaching a course in freshman composition. You don't have that form of slavery in England, do you?' 'No, thank goodness,' said Richard. Lila said: 'And what about you, Cathy? Were you in graduate school too?' 'Me, no, I'm stupid,' said Cathy, pouring the Martini out into the glasses, 'I'd never have finished college if I hadn't had Glenn to write my term papers for me.' 'I thought all faculty wives here were graduates,' said Lila. 'It's such a relief to meet one who's not. I had no university education at all.' 'That's not so bad,' said Cathy, 'if you've got something else . . . character.' 'Cathy was in my composition class,' said Glenn, 'I guess she was the worst person in the class.' 'I was,' said Cathy. 'That was why I moved in with Glenn. It was the only way I knew how to get a B.' 'Only a B?' asked Richard, laughing, 'What do you have to do in Champaign, Illinois, to get an A?' 'I couldn't give her an A,' said Glenn. 'Someone might have come along and re-read her themes.' 'Those shitty themes,' said Cathy, 'all about "My First Day in College" and "Is My Education to Broaden My Mind Or Train Me for a Job?"' 'They're even harder on the guy who's teaching the course,' said Glenn. 'He has to read them.' 'I don't believe it,' said Cathy. 'You just gave the best grades to the kids who talked in class. I talked in class, all the time.'

The Martinis were all fixed, and Cathy took them round: one for Glenn, one for Richard, one for her. She looked acutely at Lila and Richard and decided that the party was going just fine; it served those Tuckermans right. After Richard had sipped his Martini, she said, 'How does that go down?' 'Very good,' said Richard, 'I love Martinis but we can't really make them.' 'Well,' said Cathy, pulling up a pillow and placing it near Richard's feet, where she sat on it, 'you've got to have something, if you want to stay an interesting person.' Lila was looking at her and said, 'What do you do during the day, Cathy? Do you take courses?' 'No, I'm through with all that,' said Cathy, 'I've got these three kids holding me back.' 'I always think academic life's a bit unfair on wives,' said Lila. 'It's all right for the men, they have their work. Richard's having a wonderful time here, having seminars with all these elegant nineteen-year-old girls. Meanwhile I'm stuck in the house reading and shopping and trying to think of something bright to say about the utterly splendid day I've had.' Cathy addressed herself to the problem and said, 'Start a baby.' 'A baby takes nine months,' said Lila, 'I'd be back home in England by then.' 'I told you I was stupid,' said Cathy, 'I couldn't even figure that out.' 'Maybe we could do something with hormone injections,' said Glenn. 'Hey, are they still as backward about childbirth in England?' asked Cathy. 'A friend of mine came back from there with her vagina all ripped up. That kid's three years old now and intercourse is still painful for her, isn't that right, Glenn?' 'That's right,' said Glenn. 'I'm sorry,' said Lila. 'Look, do you mind if I smoke?' 'Oh, please do,' said Cathy. 'It's your evening.' 'Is there an ashtray?' asked Lila. 'I'm sorry,' said Cathy, 'we don't either of us smoke so we never think about those things. Glenn, get some ashtrays out the kitchen, will you?' Glenn got up and Cathy shook her head and said, 'Yeah, that's three years and it's still painful every time she does it.'

Richard got up to light Lila's cigarette; when he sat down again Cathy moved the cushion closer to his feet, slightly to the side, pulling her skirt down over her raised knees. The fire was burning brightly and it was a pretty cosy party; they ought to have more parties with four. 'So,' she said to Richard, 'you're really liking it here.' 'I am,' said Richard, 'Lila not so much. But I find it in lots of ways more exciting than at home. I think people are more experimental – intellectually and in the way they live.' 'Oh, here they're *stuffy*,' said Cathy. 'You really ought to go out to the Middle West. The kids here are so stuffy, they all come from these well-bred homes. And the faculty's stuffy too.' Glenn, who had come back with the ashtrays and was sitting on the sofa talking to Lila, said, 'Not all of them.' 'Yeah, all of them,' said Cathy. 'Still, I suppose it is sort of like England.' 'Is England stuffy?' asked Richard. 'No, I dunno, I've never been there, but what I mean is, this is a very Englishy section of the country. All the States isn't like this. You see, I'm from the Middle West myself and I'm used to things being more free and easy.' A bell rang in the kitchen; 'That's the timer,' said Glenn. 'I heard it,' said Cathy, but she was very concerned to make sure that Richard didn't think that New England was the whole of America, so she said, 'You have to admit people are kind of formal round here.' 'I suppose they are,' said Richard. 'You don't make friends like you do in other parts of the country. I wish I could take you back home and show you.' 'How about that stove?' said Glenn. He was right; you couldn't spoil dinner, even for a really interesting conversation, so Cathy got up and fluffed her hostess apron. 'Why don't we go through and eat,' she said.

They all filed through into the dining room, and when they got there Cathy suddenly noticed they still had places laid for the Tuckermans. 'Take out these two chairs, Glenn, will you?' she said. 'The Tuckermans were going to come, but they rang at the last minute to say they couldn't make it.' 'I hope there's nothing wrong,' said Lila; the Lawrences had known the Tuckermans in England. 'No, their kid's sick,' said Cathy. 'Well, they're sure going to miss a really nice evening.' 'Yes, indeed,' said Lila. Cathy sat Lila and Richard at either side of the table; it looked a good deal too long for four, so she made Richard move off-centre nearer to her, and had Lila move down nearer Glenn. 'There, that looks fine,' she said, and went through into the kitchen. Richard looked down the table to Glenn and said, 'What about you, Glenn? Are you from the Middle West too?' 'He isn't, I am,' said Cathy, appearing at the kitchen door wiping a knife. 'He's Baltimore, I'm small-town Illinois.' She disappeared out of view again, and Glenn said, 'That's why she's so outgoing. That's a different kind of girl from the ones round here.' 'Yes, I see what you mean,' said Lila. 'You see,' said Glenn, 'it wasn't until I went out from Baltimore to be a graduate student at Illinois that I knew what people meant when they talked about Middle-West hospitality.' Cathy, pouring out the soup, shouted: 'It sure did show you, Glenn.' 'That's right,' said Glenn, 'in all my life I'd never met anyone like Cathy.'

It was good to have a husband who appreciated what you had done for him, how you'd changed him, thought Cathy, listening to every word in the kitchen. She picked up, very carefully, the chafing dish into which she had poured the soup, and carried it through to the table. As she sat down she ruffled Richard's long dark hair – it would have looked effeminate on an American boy, but it was great on an Englishman – and said: 'One day I came into his office. We were supposed to have these consultations, you know, about once a semester. And I figured I had to do something about these low grades I'd been getting. Well, all the kids were going in there and asking him to raise their grades . . .' 'They'd come in and cry,' said Glenn, 'or send their fraternity president or the football coach.' '. . . so I went in, and Glenn had this chair for students to sit on, way across the other side of his office from his desk. So I picked up this chair and carried it across the room to right next to his and I said, "Okay, Mr Nathan, now you and me are going to have a really good talk." Well . . . it scared the pants off of him.' 'That's right,' said Glenn, 'I'd never even noticed her before that.' 'So you know what he said? "You and *I*, Miss Swenson, you and *I*." I can still see his face. I guess he thought I'd seduce him right there in his office.' 'And did you?' asked Richard. 'No, that was just to get him interested. I made him date me for weeks before he even got a hand inside my dress.'

'I say, isn't that a lovely chafing dish,' said Lila. 'You have such pretty things.' 'Glad you like it,' said Cathy, pleased at the way Lila noticed things like that. 'Know how I got it?' 'No,

31

how did you?' asked Lila 'Green stamps,' said Cathy. 'You ought to keep them. Glenn, sometime we ought to take Lila and Richard to the Redemption Center so they can see the kind of things you get there.' 'Yeah, we should,' said Glenn. 'And you make marvellous soup,' said Lila 'Well, I'm stupid so I cook good,' said Cathy. 'Everyone needs a skill. You know, we just had an offer to go back there?' 'To the Middle West?' asked Richard. 'Yes, Bloomington, Indiana,' said Glenn, 'I don't know what to do about it.' 'Take it, I told you,' said Cathy. 'It's not so easy,' said Glenn. 'It looked easy to me,' said Cathy, 'it's more money.' 'And more hours,' said Glenn. 'He ought to have taken it,' said Cathy to Richard. 'Wouldn't you have?' 'I don't know,' said Richard. 'These things are always hellish difficult to decide. And whatever you do, you always regret you didn't do the other thing.' 'I think he likes it round here because it's a women's college and he impresses himself talking to all those girls.' 'Well, that's nice enough,' said Richard. 'Yeah, but I'm sure they'd give him tenure out there. Here they don't give anybody tenure.' 'Anyway, there's a lot to keep you in the East,' said Glenn. 'There's so much going on.' 'But we don't go to any of it,' said Cathy. 'In Bloomington you go to more because that's all there is.' 'That could be right,' said Glenn, 'Anyway, I have to think about it some more.'

Cathy got up and stacked the soup plates and carried them through into the kitchen. 'This is going to take a minute,' she called, 'Why don't you Lawrences smoke?' 'I'll just get the ashtrays,' said Richard, 'We left them in the sitting room.' 'Fine,' said Cathy, 'Then bring them in here so I can wash them.' 'They're okay,' said Richard from the other room. 'Sure?' said Cathy, 'I'm a kind of neat-and-tidy person. Bring them to Cathy in the kitchen.' Richard came through into the kitchen and gave Cathy the ashtrays; she looked at him and said, 'It's been really nice for us having you over here with us this year. All the kids just love you.' 'Thanks very much,' said Richard, 'It's the funny accent.' 'Yeah, and that floppy hair,' said Cathy, '*And* you give good lectures. Our babysitters tell us.' Suddenly

Lila was in the kitchen too. 'I thought I'd better get the ashtray before I dropped anything on your lovely green carpet,' she said. 'There we go,' said Cathy, wiping out the ashtray with a paper towel and handing it to her. 'Well, I guess the meat's just about right. Lila, would you ask Glenn to come through and get the wine?' The Lawrences went back to their seats. When Glenn came into the kitchen, Cathy said: 'How do you think it's going?' 'Fine,' said Glenn. 'I really like them,' said Cathy, knowing they could hear, 'They're real nice people.' Glenn took the bottle back into the dining room and went around filling up all the glasses. As he was reaching over Lila's shoulder, she said to him: 'But you must get a lot of offers.' 'Oh, some,' said Glenn, 'but we're not too badly fixed up here.' 'He's the youngest assistant professor here, did you know that?' shouted Cathy from the kitchen. 'Very good,' said Lila. 'And he had the most publications last year of anyone on the faculty. I just don't understand why they're so stuffy about promoting him.' 'Cathy thinks I ought to be President of the United States,' said Glenn. 'Well, don't tell me you couldn't do that better than Johnson,' shouted Cathy.

She put the meat on the board and carried it through. 'That looks marvellous,' said Lila 'Well, thank you,' said Cathy, 'I'm going to have to carve it myself. That's another rôle Glenn doesn't play.' The red meat fell away into bleeding slices and she put it out on the plates. 'I'm reading your book right now, Richard,' said Cathy, 'I think it's great.' 'That's very good,' said Lila, 'I can't make head or tail of it.' 'When I like a person I like to read what he writes,' said Cathy, 'I think you learn more about them that way.' 'You ought to come to my course, Lila,' said Glenn, 'I use it as a required text.' 'Well I did, didn't I?' said Lila, 'but I'd feel rather odd sitting there with all those young students while you talked about my husband.' 'Here we are again, talking about work,' said Cathy, 'I sometimes think it's the only thing Glenn's interested in. Apart from going to bed with me. Which after eight years he still seems to appreciate.' 'Did you get the meat at the Safeway?' asked Lila. 'No,' said Cathy, 'we go into Boston to the meat market for it. We have a big deep-freeze.' 'That explains why it's so much better than mine,' said Lila, 'But of course you're such a good cook anyway.' 'There are a lot of places to shop I ought to show you,' said Cathy. 'Well, it's not worth it really, Richard takes the car every day,' said Lila. 'Make him shop,' said Cathy. 'Not likely,' said Richard, 'I've enough to do as it is.' 'That's another thing about this place, it's so inconvenient,' said Cathy, 'I'll swear we got better food in Champaign-Urbana than we do here.' 'What made you pick this college, Richard?' asked Glenn. 'They offered me money,' said Richard. 'You know,' said Cathy, 'what you ought to do is take a trip out West.' 'Oh, we mean to,' said Lila. 'Great, we must put you in touch with some people,' said Cathy, 'I mean real people. Not these stuffed shirts out here. How do you bear it?' 'Perhaps we're a bit stuffed shirt ourselves,' said Lila. 'Oh no you're not,' said Cathy, 'If there's one thing I really know it's people. You're not like them. You're alive.'

A warm geniality bathed Cathy, as it often did around this time in the evening, and she began to rejoice in her guests. 'If only there were more people like you around, maybe I wouldn't mind staying here,' she said, 'But I don't know. I really think everything's more real out there, don't you, Glenn?' 'What's real?' said Glenn. 'I mean people express their feelings more properly. They don't skate around everything that's important. You know what a difference it made to you. I mean, tell them, it released you sexually. He was practically impotent when I first knew him; and you know what it was? It was his environment, the East. That's all changed now. Well, I tell you, we have three kids.' 'I didn't know geography was so powerful,' said Richard. 'It's not geography, it's culture,' said Cathy, 'You've got to have a healthy view of your organs, is what it amounts to. It's a matter of being able to enjoy yourself and others, express your needs and desires. Well, I had to teach Glenn how to do that.' 'I know you did, but that was because you were highly sexed, not because you lived in Illinois,' said Glenn, 'And I was blocked because of those experiences I had as a teenager,

34

not because I lived in Baltimore.' 'I guess England's gotten very advanced in those things, according to the newspapers,' said Cathy. 'I think it has, to a point,' said Richard, 'but it's been a good deal exaggerated.' '*Very* much exaggerated,' said Lila. 'Well, no,' said Richard, 'I think sexual attitudes have been changing pretty fast and pretty radically. I can see that in my students for example. Their sexual habits are much freer now than they were even eight or ten years back when I was at college.' 'But isn't a lot of it talk?' said Lila. 'Not so much as you think,' said Richard. 'That's great,' said Cathy, 'You're quarrelling. Now we're really getting to know you.'

She got up, collected the plates, and went into the kitchen to fetch the dessert. Richard and Lila were busy defending each of their views to Glenn, and Cathy congratulated herself on how well she'd been managing the conversation; everyone seemed to get a look in. Bringing in the dessert, which was pumpkin pie, she asked: 'How do they feel about wife-swapping in England?' 'I never encountered it,' said Lila, 'Well, not as a formalized thing. I gather it is formalized in some places here.' 'There was this bunch of faculty at one place we were at, wasn't there, Glenn? What they did was to go to parties and throw all their doorkeys in a pile on the floor. Then everyone scrambled for them and whoever's key you got you had that wife.' 'It sounds rather a gamble,' said Lila, 'Did you make the pie-filling yourself?' 'Well, it seemed to me it sort of went against a woman's nature,' said Cathy, 'I think a woman likes to know who she's getting.' 'How do you explain the fact that the wives seemed to go for it just as much as the men?' asked Glenn. 'Well, that's true, I guess,' said Cathy, 'but I think these things can be done in a more dignified way. If God had meant us to have group sex, I guess he'd have given us all more organs.' 'Dignified, sure, that's what you say now,' said Glenn. 'It was all linked up with people getting their promotions and trying to put on a big show with the people that really counted,' said Cathy. 'It was not,' said Glenn. 'Well, one day you figure it out how you got to be an instructor,' said Cathy, 'It certainly wasn't all those brilliant articles you wrote.' 'The pie was really delicious,' said Lila. 'I thought I'd make one dish that was really American,' said Cathy. 'You have to try all these American things while you're here.' 'That's right,' said Glenn.

Cathy got up and suggested they move through to the sitting room for coffee. When she brought it through on the tray, she found that Lila and Richard were sitting together on the sofa and Glenn was isolated out in another corner of the room. 'Why don't you take that chair near the fire?' said Cathy to Lila wanting to make things more friendly, 'You're out in the cold there.' 'Oh, no, really,' said Lila, 'I'm as warm as toast.' 'How do people get jobs in England?' asked Cathy. 'They're advertised in the journals,' said Richard. 'Oh, well, that's another way,' said Glenn. 'I guess Glenn would really like to teach in England for a few years,' said Cathy. 'I'm told jobs are very hard to get there,' said Glenn, 'Is that right?' 'There just aren't so many of them,' said Richard, 'But you can always apply. There are a lot of Americans teaching in English universities now.' 'Milk and sugar?' asked Cathy. 'Thank you,' said Lila. 'Not for me,' said Richard. 'But I guess you really need to know people,' said Cathy. 'I suppose it helps,' said Richard. 'So, we know you,' said Cathy. 'Yes, so you do,' said Richard, 'Would you like me to send details of vacancies?' 'Great,' said Glenn. 'You must know most everybody in England who teaches philosophy,' said Cathy. 'I suppose we do, really,' said Richard.

'You know, Glenn, what we ought to do is go where the Lawrences are. Then we could all get together again.' 'That's a lovely idea,' said Richard, 'The only problem is that we don't seem to be taking any new staff just now. Philosophers aren't in such great demand. Now if you were a sociologist.' 'I don't mind changing,' said Glenn.

Cathy got her pillow and put it on the floor near Richard. 'Serve the brandy, Glenn,' she said, 'Glenn always does the brandy bit; it isn't a mixed drink.' 'Fine,' said Glenn, 'For everybody?' The Lawrences said yes and Glenn stood at the drinks table and poured from the bottle into their best balloon glasses. 'Well, that was a lovely meal,' said Lila. 'Yeah, but the nice bit is sitting down after,' said Cathy, 'You know, I really feel we've gotten to know you. You always hear how hard British people are to know, but I don't feel that way about you at all.' 'It's very nice of you to say so,' said Richard. 'I guess people are just the same all over the world. Except for these stuffed shirts round here.' Cathy, watching Richard sip his brandy and thinking how composed and charming he was in his very English style, suddenly noticed something: his hand shook, very slightly, as if under that confident and amiable veneer he suffered from nerves. That brought out the maternal instinct in her, and she said, 'I hope you're not going to let an American barber spoil that marvellous English haircut.' 'It's about time he did,' said Lila, 'It's disgusting.' 'Oh, no, you mustn't,' said Cathy, 'It's part of your charm. Why don't you let me cut it? I cut Glenn's hair.' 'No, I'll go to the barber,' said Richard, 'When I've saved enough to afford it.' 'Oh, come on,' said Cathy, 'I have these special electric shears. I'll go get them.' Lila laughed and said, 'He hates having his hair touched.' 'Oh, boy, does he?' said Cathy. 'That's really significant.' 'I shouldn't have thought so,' said Lila. 'I like the British,' said Cathy, 'but they really are kind of ignorant. Aren't you into body language?' 'Not really,' said Lila. 'Well, that's body language, baby, and it's bad,' said Cathy. 'You know what? We ought to psychoanalyse him. What was that psychoanalysis game we used to play in Urbana, Glenn?' 'You mean the free association game?' asked Glenn, 'It's just like it sounds. Everyone says a word to you and you have to say the first thing it makes you think of. I say "Mother" and you say "Screw" and we know you've got an Oedipus complex.' 'Oedipus complex,' said Cathy. 'Glenn,' said Richard. 'What made you say Glenn?' asked Cathy. 'He just talked about an Oedipus complex,' said Richard. 'That's somehow not quite right,' said Cathy, 'but so what? Glenn.' 'Impotent,' said Richard. They all laughed except Lila, who had got up and gone to the window to raise the drapes. 'Actually we mustn't be too long, Richard,' she said, 'It's snowing like mad.'

'Mad,' said Cathy. 'Comics,' said Richard. 'Superman,' said Glenn. 'Nietzsche,' said Richard. 'You have a too philosophical mind,' said Glenn. 'Why don't we try it with Lila?'

'No, thanks,' said Lila, 'I like to keep my neuroses well under cover.' 'Try it with me,' said Cathy. 'Cover,' said Richard. 'Bed,' said Cathy. 'Bed,' said Richard. 'Richard,' said Cathy. 'Ah, now, it's really going,' said Glenn. 'Going,' said Lila, 'That's what we really ought to be doing.' 'Oh, you can't go now,' said Cathy, 'This is a really fun evening.' 'That's right,' said Glenn, 'It's not so often you meet a couple you really take to.' 'It's been lovely,' said Lila, 'but Richard really isn't used to driving in thick snow.' 'Then stay the night,' said Cathy, 'Really. We can make any arrangements you like.' 'That's right,' said Glenn, 'Good old Middle-Western hospitality.' 'It's most kind,' said Lila, 'but Richard has a nine o'clock class tomorrow morning.' 'Oh, so I have,' said Richard. 'Oh, we'd get him there for that,' said Cathy, 'Now come on, *we* won't hurt you.' 'No, we must go, really,' said Lila, 'but many thanks for a lovely evening.' 'Well, we're disappointed, we really are,' said Cathy, 'but we'll see you.' 'You must come out to us,' said Lila. 'Fine,' said Cathy, 'Fine. And we mustn't forget about that trip to the Redemption Center.' 'Oh, no, quite,' said Lila.

They went out into the hall; Glenn helped Lila on with her coat and then the Lawrences both sat down on the bottom step of the stairway and put on their outdoor shoes. 'Many thanks,' said Richard and, going out, he bent down and turned around the *Welcome* mat on the porch. 'That seems more appropriate,' he said. 'Good night,' said Lila, and they disappeared out into the snowfall. Cathy watched at the door as they put on the lights of their borrowed old car. It started up, skidded a little on the turn, and then spluttered off into the curtain of white. Cathy went back into the living room to tidy up. Glenn was already stacking all the dirty dinner plates in the dishwasher and starting up the cycle. She packed the pretzels away into a cookie jar, emptied the ashtrays into the fireplace, and then got the vacuum cleaner from the hall closet and ran it over the rug.

Then she aerosoled the room with deodorant spray because she never liked the smell of cigarette smoke. When that was done she went upstairs and ran water into the tub. Then she undressed and got in, and there, lying back, looking down at her well-shaped body, her big firm breasts and her stomach flat as a board after three kids, she thought back on the evening. Then Glenn came in and ran his hand very deliberately down her body. 'Hi, stud,' she said, 'Think they enjoyed it,' 'Yeah, they loved it,' said Glenn. 'A pity they had to go,' said Cathy. 'Sure is,' said Glenn, 'Still, for Britishers they seemed very outgoing people.' Cathy suddenly remembered the sweet little gesture when Richard turned round the *Welcome* mat. 'I think they really liked us,' she said; Glenn's hands were getting her excited and she stood up in the tub. 'Well, thanks to you,' said Glenn, 'I guess everyone appreciates a really hospitable person.'

Who Do You Think You Are?

EDGAR LOACH was a thrusting, bustling social psychologist, his wife Rita was a bouncy physiotherapist; and they both lived together in what was called a town house in an inner residential district of the new Birmingham. They were liberal, responsible people, which meant that, when they looked around, they felt a certain social guilt about their rather comfortable circumstances; but they had to admit that, in view of the rôles they performed in society, the house suited them very well. It was quite tiny and very efficient, with a fitted kitchen, underfloor central heating, and a groundsman who looked after everything except a tiny patch of garden at the rear, their own garden, most of which they had paved. There was a communal television aerial, and the house was painted for them every three years in the standard colours of the estate. As the brochure which had tempted them to the house had said, it was an environment for exciting modern living; and the small estate, with its advanced exterior design and its compact interlocking of modular blocks, high density but with a true illusion of space, frequently appeared as a glossy photograph in the architectural reviews. Of course, as with most modern living, there were snags; as Rita sometimes complained, at cocktail parties, the only place you were really entitled to hang out washing was in your car. But it was ideal for a young, busy couple who were out at all hours; and the Loaches, being responsible professional people, always were. One thing about the house was that it was very conveniently placed for the kinds of social problem that, over the last few years, had become Edgar's stock-in-trade. There were squatters two streets away, and a hippy commune nearer still; there was a handy abortion clinic, and a twilight area with a severe problem of immigrant overcrowding within walking distance, and an active Sinn Fein group accessibly nearby. Birmingham had been taking an advanced line in the field of sexual expression and counselling, and the Loaches were into that, in an advisory capacity; Rita was fairly active in Women's Lib, which was also going very strong. Involved as they were, they were not in the house a great deal; Edgar was active in so many causes, so many types of social advising, that he was out until the early hours, nipping back and forth across the city, Yardley and Nechells, Aston and Stirchley, in his Mini. Rita, too, often worked irregular shifts at the hospital, and then taught natural childbirth classes on spare evenings.

So they really only seemed to come together in the house, and properly use it, at weekends, when they put on their casual clothes and sat in the living room or, on sunny days, on the patio, having late breakfasts, reading the Sunday supplements and the new paperbacks, drinking Campari, and listening to Edgar's avant-garde tapes – South American protest songs, sound effects tapes with French cries of orgasm – through a hi-fi system for which the house itself provided the perfect speaker. But it was good to be near the city centre, to see the new skyscraper blocks rising, the neon flashing, the ambulances roaring, the rattle of terrorist explosions, the pulse and throb of modern urban living. They moved through the new Bull Ring, the new underpasses, the multi-storey car parks, the concrete complexities of New Street station; Edgar was frequently at New Street station, because he had constantly to travel up to London, on the Inter-City, to sit on committees, see his publisher, advise reform groups, take part in a demo, do a television programme. He was not a narrow academic; and he had arranged his teaching timetable at the university so that he could have one free day a week, to keep up in the world. Today there was another such trip, a rather important one; he had to be on the mid-morning train. It was convenient that Rita was on late shift, because this meant she could take him down in the Mini and drop him in the forecourt, saving him the problems of parking. Rita drove very neatly; she got through the jams in no time, and when he got into the bright New Street concourse he was early. He bought his ticket, and then took the escalator down to the underground platform, humming a little to the music on the loudspeakers. Before he descended, he bought *New Society* and a packet of throat mints from the bookstall, and so was equipped for the train. Down on the platform he knew, an experienced traveller, just where to position himself for the first-class coaches – for he was on expenses. The electric wires crackled, the loudspeakers boomed, the train came in; Edgar was the first to bounce aboard and find himself a desirable seat in the air-conditioned coach, next to the window. The train moved off, into the tunnels, and then emerged to pass the Birmingham sprawl, the freight container yards, the canals, the motorway support pillars; there was a glimpse of the Rotunda.

But it was a familiar view; Edgar already had his head down into *New Society*. After a while, like any good sociologist, he began to grow restless and felt the need to do something. So he rose from his seat, leaving *New Society* to mark possession, and walked down the train, counting the number of coloured persons on it. There were forty-three altogether, two of them in first class, one of them, an Indian, smoking a cigar. It was a rather desultory exercise, since he wasn't writing on the matter; but then a sociologist is, like a policeman, always on duty, and his duties demand an attention to everything, to the mode and detail of everyday life. This little enquiry done, he went back to his seat, picked up *New Society*, and read it, down to the endless pages of job advertisements, through the countryside bit of the journey, the data-less wastes of agriculture and woods. Presently the dining-car attendant, in his red coat, came along to announce that early lunch was being served, so Edgar folded up his journal and placed it on the seat again, and went along to the restaurant car; he noticed on the way that the Indian in first class had finished his cigar, and was now reading the business section of *The Times*. He had steak-and-kidney pie, and by the time he was finished the train had reached the outer sprawl of megalopolis: the service was marvellous now. Middle-income low-density postwar housing units began to appear by the line-side, and notes of social tension obtruded – someone had daubed ABORTION IS MURDER on a railway wall, and you could see the aerosoled slogans of the teenage gangs on the walls and fences of the older suburbs. There were posters for confidential pregnancy testing on the boards of the stations they now began to flash through. Edgar went back to his compartment and from there on to Euston he watched carefully the various stages of urban expansion and change, the hints of shift and turmoil his practised eye could grasp, stopping only to bend down and clean his shoes with the back page of *New Society* as the train slowed down in the tunnels just before the terminus.

The new Euston still confused some of the people getting off the train, but not Edgar. He was the first of his influx to get in the queue for the taxis and was quick to find one. He told the driver to take him to the BBC Television Centre; the driver looked at him and said, 'Haven't I seen you on the box? Is it Mr Day?' but then he probably said that to anyone who happened to ask for that particular destination. Nevertheless, the faceless *Gesellschaft* of the great city, its web of impersonal relations, its well-known identity flux, was, Edgar thought, not inevitably the destroyer of personality; people could still emerge from the crowd. Edgar looked out through the darkened glass of the taxi and watched the urban display, the gear, the styles, the wild faces, the lights, the bursts of noise from boutiques and stereo shops. The taximan, presumabbly well knowing that people in television simply had to be on time, cut boldly through the traffic and it wasn't long before he was drawing up in front of the pole at the Television Centre. The guard there checked his identity; they had to be very careful, because of the bomb scares. But when he said he was doing a programme for Dennis Proddoe, they quickly let him through, and he was soon round the sweep and under the portico. 'What I like about you, Mr

Day, is you keep it frank,' said the taxi driver, as Edgar paid him and then, trying to do what Robin Day would do, tipped him generously. He carried his briefcase through into reception; the girl at the desk said, 'It's Mr Loach, isn't it?' and Edgar, while realizing that she must have a list of expected visitors in front of her, felt another moment of obscure pleasure.

She quickly contacted studio, and he only had to be seated for a moment in the glossy chairs of the foyer, glancing at the other visitors and reading a bit from a pamphlet listing the radio programmes to be transmitted to Bulgaria, when a programme assistant, a thin girl in a miniskirt and round steel spectacles, appeared. 'I'm afraid you'll have to check your bag,' she said, and led him round the corner, where the attendant made him write down in a notebook a description of his briefcase and its contents, and examined it before giving him a numbered slip. 'We're on high security,' said the girl, leading him to the lift. In the lift she said, 'Mr Proddoe's waiting for you,' while Edgar realized with pleasure that his bottom was against Shirley Bassey's. They got out, and the girl led him through the ship-like corridors of the circular building and to the teabar at Red Assembly. Here, amid the technicians chewing on buns at stand-up tables, Dennis Proddoe, the producer, was waiting to meet him, wearing a flowered shirt and white jeans with a purple stripe down each flared leg. He carried a white clipboard and a large blue paper flower. He seemed very pleased to see Edgar, whom he had produced before. 'Thank God you got here, old thing,' he said, 'I always worry about people coming from the provinces. I suppose it's silly.' Edgar shook hands with him, and Dennis said: 'Well, we must look sharp, we're all ready.' He turned and led the way down the corridor towards the studio, while the programme assistant walked silently behind. On the way, he said very solemnly: 'I think, you know, Edgar, this one's going to be a genuine breakthrough. For years I've been knocking out my brains to think of a panel game that had genuine relevance. Something that had entertainment values but transcended them. A show with a psycho-sociological orientation, plus meaning and concern. The sleepless nights I've had with it, Edgar, I can't count them. But I really think, don't I, Sharon, that this is the formula.' 'He does,' said the programme assistant. 'Good,' said Edgar. As if to alleviate solemnity, Dennis bounced rapidly three times from one side of the corridor to the other, and then they were at the entrance to the studio.

A uniformed attendant came up to Edgar, as though he were going to ask him about his bombs again, but all he said was: 'I'm afraid you'll have to put your cigarette out, sir.' 'I'm not smoking,' said Edgar, 'I don't.' 'Never mind, then,' said the attendant. They went through onto the studio floor. At first it was dark, high and gaunt, with wires and technology everywhere, and there were a great many very little people around the edges of the set. In the half-dark a thin, elegant man in a conservatively trendy suit and wearing mutton-chop whiskers came up to Dennis and said: 'Ho, Dennis, I dream about trousers like that.' 'I got them in Roma,' said Dennis, 'don't you think they're swish?' The man kissed the programme assistant very briefly, looked at Edgar, and said: 'Who's this, Den?' 'This is Edgar Loach, who's on your panel, and this is Jojo Brautigan, who's the chairman. Actually there's no need to give Edgar much in the way of a briefing. He's done the box no end of times. He taught me at university.' 'Ah, so you're to blame,' said the Chairman, 'Turned his mind for life, you have.' The whole party stepped over cables onto the set. It was suddenly bright, and Edgar, who had a slight sight imperfection, was momentarily lost. A figure dashed up to him and held an instrument close to his nose, and someone pulled one of the cables under his feet. Dennis took his arm to lead him towards the long, curved table where the panel was to sit. There were name plates in front of the places, notepads and buzzers on the desk, and the chairs twirled to encourage movement. 'What do you think of the photo-montage?' asked Dennis. Edgar looked up and saw behind the table a large and imposing blow-up, composed of shots of a policeman, a slum tenement, Centre Point, a starving child, a well-heeled young couple, probably from an ad, drinking drinks with frost on them on a yacht deck, a chromosome, a judge's wig, and a deodorant ad, all overlaid with iron bars of a cell. 'Marvellous,' said Edgar. 'I'm glad you like it,' said Dennis.

Then something came over the speakers and Edgar was asked to sit down. He was introduced to his two fellow experts, who were already there. There was a modern culturalist named Giles Fussey, a young man with dark glasses and an Afro haircut; and an advanced psychologist who had studied with R. D. Laing named Flora Beniform, a vigorously healthy-looking girl. Both had the pre-programme look, that slightly strained expression on those of their features that hair and glasses didn't hide. Edgar felt a twitch of nerves in his own stomach too, but then there was no need. He was a professional, and an expert; he said a few brief words to his colleagues, especially Dr Beniform, whose work he knew and respected, and then briskly ordered the stuff on his desk in a form that appealed to him. 'Now listen,' said Dennis, standing in front of them all with his hands up, 'I'm going to disappear into the guts and machinery now and we're going to have a short run through. I hope you've grasped the principles of the conception?' There were murmurs from Edgar's colleagues and Dennis said: 'Well, if you haven't, this will sort of show you. But it doesn't matter if you make utter twits of yourselves, or just say rhubarb; it's really more for the cameras and make-up than you. Don't pick your noses, and do your best, as we always said in the scouts. All right?' Dennis listened to something in his own ear and said: 'Yes, right. After this we'll go and have some strong drinks and discuss the format, and the recording will be at five, or fünf for German speakers.'

A camera went up very close to the chairman and he smiled at it. Then there was a long pause, and various strangers passed across the set, ignoring the panellists and spraying things with aerosols. The chairman said: 'I take it Edgar will concentrate on the social rôles and the tensions, Flora on the psychological hangups, and Giles on the cultural referents. I'll just stir the

49

pudding and add mayhem. I think Edgar goes first, since he's had the most appearances, then Flora, followed by, guess who, Giles. Dennis left me one note, here it is, it says: Remember to alleviate professional expertise with entertainment value.' 'You mean tell jokes,' said Giles Fussey. 'That's right,' said Brautigan. 'All right, duckies,' said Dennis's voice from some remote, magnified source, 'Titles in twenty seconds.' The lights changed. On the monitor Edgar saw himself. Then the titles flirted across the screen – *Who Do You Think You Are?* – and the chairman began explaining the game to the camera. A girl from somewhere off at the side brought the first victim to a chair in the middle, between the chairman and the panel. These were fake victims, not the ones to be used in the real recording, and they were mostly Wood Lane secretaries and people hanging about after other programmes or waiting to be studio-audience for this one. Out of the corner of his eye Edgar once again caught his flickering self in the monitors: a stout, sage, fluent figure asking telling questions about class, income, and rôle. The victims could lie, which they would not be permitted to do in the real thing, and that led to some comic confusions; but it passed off neatly and Edgar felt he had set the right pace. Flora came in next and muffed it slightly, making rather heavy weather of the psychic hangups, but Giles came in strong at the end with questions about responses to cultural change. By the third victim, they were all on their toes. The half hour passed by like a minute, and then the titles came up again and the run-through was done.

The chairman whisked them off to the hospitality room, and there was Dennis, wheeling up the drinks cabinet. They had to wait a moment for an attendant to come and unlock it, and then Dennis made sure they all had stiff, full glasses of something and went through his notes with them. 'Well, you were all simply great,' he said, 'but a few quirks and caveats, more from the angle of presentation than content. Edgar, your nose. It's perfectly all right looking, but you seem to probe with it, as if you're trying to smell the answer. It sort of bobs forward like this, and I can't quite explain it but it fills the screen too much. Can you, so to speak, hold it in, jampot?' 'I'll try,' said Edgar, laughing with the others. 'Flora, well, if you're going to ask so many questions about sex I think you ought to tuck this dress down a bit and give us a bit more of your bubs. I know it's corny, but it drives home what we're talking about, so it's all gain and no loss for everybody, isn't it?' Flora pushed some frills down and said: 'How's that?' 'You could go on for ever for me,' said Dennis, 'But it is better, yes. And Giles. Well, simply, Giles, you're too dirty. I want you to go and have a wash. I didn't know dirt came over like that, but it does. Sharon, will you take Giles and show him where?' Dennis then got up and filled up their glasses, and then they sat around and talked over a few amendments in the format of the show. 'The main thing is, you've got the spirit of it, *made* the spirit of it,' said Dennis, looking pleased, and he filled up their glasses again.

By the time they went back down to the studio, just before five, they all had a slightly tipsy air and a beaming, comradely feeling. But, it seemed to Edgar, it made the show go extremely well. The first victim came on, in the dark blue Maoist-type uniform they all had to wear, and Edgar got his class, lower upper middle, and his socio-economic grouping within seconds, and was not much longer in finding, through a sequence of interaction questions, his work rôle. He explained, neatly and concisely, to the audience the indicators he had had to go on – accent, physiological movements, phatic response, and so on. He went on and was also acute on the rôle behaviour-patterns, and got some quick assents about the man's drinking customs and pattern, his ways of addressing superiors and inferiors, his expenditure on clothes and his fornication frequency (FF). Flora quickly got into his psychic map, too, and with three questions about infantile toilet training, attitude to parents, and the date of his marriage had the basis for a psychic map of an essentially anal personality which she elaborated brilliantly; the man in the chair nodded in amazement. Giles, with a quick question about hostility to what he called long-haired Jesuses like me, was soon right in the middle of his cultural responses and soon got into radical tensions that clearly left the man aghast at his contradictions. Some trouble came with the second victim, who broke down and began to cry when Flora pressed him about homoerotic feelings; but Dennis, accurately enough, had predicted that this sort of thing might happen and told them to regard it as good television material. The man wept a good deal through Giles's questioning, but it was sympathetic, and when Giles explained the troubles lay not in the man's own mind but in the perverse repressions of the culture, he said: 'Thank God someone had the guts to say that, for my sake and the likes of me.' This reminded them all that it was more than a game; it was really an extension of their professional humanism. A girl came last; Edgar, really treading here on Flora's territory, got her abortion in the first two minutes, and her entire mores structure in two more. Fussey was very good on her immersion in the pop scene, and how it had liberated her; and then it was all over and the closing titles were coming up on the monitors almost before Edgar felt they had got started. He remembered they had to keep chattering at the end, though he had to prod Flora's leg under the table; she thought everything was finished and had turned to the monitor, watching it agog, staring into the image of her own eyes. 'Oh, duckies,' said Dennis, though the speaker from the control room, 'that was a thing of beauty *and* a joy for ever. I'm pleased, I'm delighted, I'm delirious. Edgar's still naughty with his nose, so we'll remind him for next week. No retakes, a lovely job, so see you all in Red Assembly.'

They all went back to Red Assembly, and Sharon, who had met them in the corridor, went off to get a tray of tea for them. 'It's not only fun, it's useful,' said Edgar, 'I think we're really showing the moral service we provide, with our professional knowledge.' 'Ho, here he is,' said the Chairman, and Dennis came up and made a bright suggestion: he'd like to take them all out to dinner. Alas, the Chairman had to leave, because he was also moderator in a radio panel-game they were recording in an hour at the Aeolian Hall – a more old-fashioned affair, he explained, with buzzers and a mystery voice. 'Not this whizz-kid level at all,' he said. Dennis took everyone else under his wing. He asked the programme assistant, in the steel-rimmed spectacles, to go and call for a taxi. Then they all went and signed out their possessions from the cloakroom, and by the time they were ready in the foyer, with Flora in a big fur coat and Giles in a splendidly embroidered Afghan jacket, she had a cab waiting for them under the portico. Edgar sat between Flora and the programme assistant on the upholstered back seat, and Giles and Dennis sat and rocked on the two fold-down seats across from them. 'What did you think, Dr Beniform?' asked Dennis, 'You were suspicious at first, weren't you, love?' 'I was,' said Flora, 'but I think you've convinced me it's worth bothering with.' The programme assistant said: 'I booked Greek. Was that right?' 'They'll love it,' said Dennis. Soon the taxi stopped, outside a Greek restaurant in an area Edgar vaguely recognized as Knightsbridge; he knew his London, but it was a visitor's London, not a resident's. The people at the restaurant knew Dennis and were effusively pleased to see him. The restaurant had a fishnet ceiling and was staffed with waiters, who, for some reason, wore brief shorts and fisherman's sweaters and had neat little check gingham aprons of the same material as the tablecloths. The party from the programme sat down and had an aperitif at the bar, and Edgar asked Flora about her research work, on the family. 'It's a lovely field,' said Flora. 'Of course life, and Laing, have transformed it, between them.'

They got a table quickly, obviously because it was Dennis, and the waiter came and took their orders. 'I think they look smashing, don't you?' said Dennis, and recommended some things to them. Edgar decided to try stuffed vine leaves. When the waiter had gone, Dennis said: 'I can't wait for the crits in the Sundays. I just have this feeling it could run for ever.' 'I thought it was six,' said Giles. 'Oh, that's just for a start,' said Dennis, 'Of course, I mustn't raise any hopes. For one thing, it raises taste problems.' 'Oh, not these days,' said Giles. 'I bet Maurice Wiggin or someone will bash it and say it's an intrusion into personal privacy,' said Dennis gloomily, 'But I think personal privacy's a dead duck, don't you, Edgar?' 'I suppose it is,' said Edgar. 'It's gone, driven out by the modern world of today,' said Dennis, 'I mean, surely there's nothing about man now that can be kept secret or indefinable. We can probe him all ways.' 'Oh, that's true,' said Flora, 'I mean, Edgar, is man, sociologically speaking, any more than the sum of his rôles?' 'That's a good question,' said Edgar, starting on the taramasalata, 'If you define rôle carefully and fully enough, then it seems certain that he's not. Rôle here would mean, of course, every form of socially learned behaviour. There's the genetic factor, of course, which is a problem.' 'Well, yes,' said Flora, 'But we're increasingly coming to see the socially derived factor in that. No, Dennis is substantially right. Of course that doesn't mean that privacy doesn't matter.' 'Oh, no,' said Dennis. 'You mean there isn't really a me?' asked the programme assistant, a serious girl. 'Of course there's a you,' said Dennis, 'but there's nothing about it you can cover up.' Edgar lifted up the tablecloth a little to expose a view of the miniskirt, and said: 'It's symptomatic that you've virtually confessed that, in the style of clothes that you're wearing.' 'Long dresses are in too,' said the girl. 'Oh, come,' said Flora, laughing, 'They're only culturally comprehensible as an alternative to the mini. What I mean is, they conceal what's well known, not what is mysterious.'

Now they were all on the main course; the stuffed vine leaves made Edgar burp a little, but the others took no notice. 'I'm not so sure about all this,' said Giles, staring at them through his dark glasses, 'What about the puritan backlash?' 'Do you believe in the puritan backlash?' cried Dennis. 'Come on,' said Flora impatiently, 'the backlash is an invention of liberals with paranoia. It makes no evolutionary sense. You can't put into the bottle what you've already poured out.' Dennis said: 'It's a bore catching people up on their metaphors, but of course you can, Flora dearie.' Edgar laughed and pointed to the three retsina bottles that stood empty in the middle of the table. 'Try filling those up again,' he said, smothering a burp.

'Well,' admitted Dennis, 'you've a point there. Not if you've already drunk it.' 'I suppose it all proves the truth of what Freud told us,' said Giles. 'The thing is, of course,' said Flora, 'not that what Freud said was true, I mean about the primacy of the sexual instinct, but that we have chosen to act as if it were true. We may choose, one day, to act as if something else were true. But I think it will take us a long time to reach the new synthesis.' 'And in the meantime people ask for more and can get more, can enjoy and fulfil themselves more,' said Giles. 'But what selves are these that they enjoy?' asked the programme assistant. 'Oh, oh, deep waters, too deep for me,' said Dennis, 'Let's order some more retsina.'

When the meal was over, and they had had some spiritous Greek liqueurs, Dennis, who seemed to have greatly enjoyed the evening, suggested that they all might like to come back to his place. Edgar burped all the way in the taxi, and at one point thought of consulting the Birmingham railway timetable card in his pocket, but of course he was all right for hours yet. The serious girl said: 'I think the mini is quite modest really. Look how quickly they brought out tights.' 'We all know what's under there, dear,' said Dennis, 'Of course it interests some of us more than others.' The taxi stopped in an area Edgar roughly predicated as being near Sloane Square, and Dennis led the way upstairs to his flat, which was on the top floor of a very handsome Georgian property. On the stairs they all walked behind the girl in the miniskirt and laughed a good deal; the girl looked round and said: 'You're just as bad as they were when I worked at Esso.' 'Words like bad and good have lost their power,' said Flora, who had been laughing too. Dennis unlocked the door of his flat and they went in. It was remarkably elegant, furnished in a mixture of very modern and very antique, and Giles picked up some things, sculptures and bric-à-brac, and posed some questions, and suddenly asked Dennis if he had a private income. 'We're not on the programme now, duckie,' said Dennis, and opened up a cabinet filled with bottles, 'You're worse than Arthur Negus. Which all reminds me I've always meant to ask whether you do that sort of stuff on yourselves, or whether you sweeties feel you transcend these things, live in some place higher than history.' 'What sort of stuff?' asked Giles. 'That sort of Tavistock Clinic stuff you did for me on the programme,' said Dennis.

Flora had taken the fur coat off and sat herself down in an armchair. 'I've been through analysis,' she said, 'That's part of one's training.' 'Have you been through . . . sociologis, Edgar honey?' asked Dennis, serving out drinks to everybody. 'I think I can fairly say yes,' said Edgar, 'The sociologist has to see himself as just such another social animal.' 'Well, why don't you get to work on each other?' asked Dennis. 'In what sense?' asked Giles, laughing. 'I'm not sure it would be professional,' said Edgar. 'Who do you think you are?' said Dennis. Giles laughed and fell backwards into a chair, already occupied by the programme assistant, who pushed him onto the floor. He lay there and laughed more. 'After all, you do it to the victims,' said the programme assistant. Edgar said: 'Very well, then. But don't forget, we're experts dealing with experts.' 'That's what we want to see,' said Dennis. So Edgar started firing questions at Flora, who sat in her chair holding a very large whisky, her colour quite red, and looking most attractive in the half-lights of Dennis's big room. Edgar felt quite drunk and quite gay, now, and he was enjoying himself, just as he had on the programme, so he put on a clever performance. Flora parried and pushed, but he finally managed to prove to her – or at any rate elicit a confession from her – that she was vastly more rooted in the concepts, attitudes and lifestyle of her upper middle-class origins than she had really cared to believe. 'Hypocrite!' cried Dennis. 'A perfectly acceptable contradiction,' said Flora, 'It is through psychic action against one's origins that most innovation occurs.' 'Well, now you can get your own back,' said Dennis, 'Wait a minute, though. I want to see the dress tucked down a bit more, the way it was on the programme.' 'I thought it was wonderful when he made you go and wash,' said the programme assistant to Giles. 'I should have protested,' said Giles, 'It was radical dirt.'

Now Flora was on her mettle; she was very high-powered, and Edgar realized at once that she must have had her eyes open all night for his ego-deficiencies. She quickly got at the insecurities in his authority rôle, and a few minutes later she was into his marriage. 'Your first?' she asked, as if that showed lack of ambition. She went into his aggressions, and Rita's resiliences; his dependencies, and Rita's competences. 'Do you talk to her?' she asked, 'How truly can you speak?' It was like an expert cook carving a turkey, and she was soon down to the carcase of it all. The endless cycle of business that had become their mode of life, the work at all hours, the silences of Sunday morning over the colour supplements, the infrequencies of their intercourse: it only meant one thing. 'Can you describe to me the nature of this sensation of love you say you feel for her?' asked Flora. 'No,' said Edgar, 'No, I can't.' 'Because you're inarticulate, you, Edgar Loach; or because all this activity hides the fact that it's a worn memory – in fact, simply isn't there?' 'I don't *know*,' said Edgar. 'Think now, rest, dig for emotion,' said Flora, 'It's important, we know it's important. Recall your feeling for your parents, your mother. Use it as a test. Is it there, is it?' 'No,' said Edgar, 'No, Flora, it's not.' The perception seemed so utterly true that Edgar began to cry. 'I think he'd better lie down,' said Dennis, and they took him and put him on the coverlet of Dennis's gorgeous double bed. After the sobs stopped, the burps continued, and then the door opened and Flora came in. 'I'm sorry,' said Flora, 'I think the only way out of this impasse is for us to make love.' 'I'm a naked spirit,' said Edgar.

Flora took off her red dress and laid it carefully on a chair at the bedside. 'It's not a bourgeois hang-up,' she said, 'I'll be wearing it again later in the series.' She took off her scraps of underwear and soon her big essential self was onto his in a psycho-sociological union. But then Edgar felt, suddenly, a kind

57

of terror; it struck him all at once that making love with an advanced Freudian was the biggest test of his career. The frank intimacy of the revelations about his make-up that he was putting before her appalled him; he groaned and tucked his head in the coverlet. But she knew what that meant too. 'Relax,' she said, 'Forget my Reichian bias. Think of me purely as an anatomical woman. Just act naturally.' 'What, in your terms, is natural?' asked Edgar. 'What you feel impelled to do, if, of course, you can distinguish impulses from routine marital habits,' said Flora. 'You see everything,' said Edgar. 'It's what always happens,' said Flora, 'At first I attributed it to myself as a person, but then I realized that the rôle dimension was crucial.' Edgar tried to summon his energies, but he could not forgo the analytical dimension he knew they shared in common; in the end he had to say: 'I'm sorry, but as a sociologist I find it impossible to make the distinction.' 'The rôle from the person?' asked Flora. 'The rôle *is* the person,' said Edgar. 'But you're hypostasizing my rôle only in one direction,' said Flora. 'You mean that of the woman is primarily and that of the psychologist secondary,' said Edgar, hopefully. 'Well, that suggests that the rôle of a woman is not culturally conditioned, which it clearly substantially is, but for the moment let's propose the answer yes,' said Flora.

The hypothesis proved, for the occasion, remarkably satisfactory, though when Edgar came to think about it again, a few days later, he recognized that it was not, intellectually, a tenable position. 'You know, it's wonderful, those burps of yours have stopped too,' said Flora, 'We can see the origin of those now.' A moment later Edgar was fast asleep. Flora looked at him, dressed again and went back into the living room. Dennis freshened her drink, and they had a good talk. An hour later it occurred to them all that they ought to go and look at Edgar and they took their drinks through into the bedroom to inspect him. He was on his back, mouth wide open, in the deepest of sleeps. 'He was going to catch a late train back to Birmingham,' said Dennis. 'I think it would be unwise to disturb him,' said

Flora, 'It's quite clear that sleep is serving a therapeutic function.' 'He's on my bed, duckie,' said Dennis, 'Who does he think he is?' They all began to laugh, and then Flora said, 'Ssshhh,' and they went back into the living room, where Giles offered to make some soup for them. 'Ought we to call his wife?' asked Dennis. 'Well, given the underlying condition of that ménage, I doubt if it makes much difference,' said Flora, 'Of course, there's one thing, he may have classes in the morning.' In the end, the girl with the steel spectacles tried Edgar's home number, but there was no reply. Rita was out at a meeting of the Women's Liberation group, and she did not get back to their modern town house with the Mini until the very early hours.

The Adult Education Class

ALL THROUGH the winter, once a week, on a Tuesday, Stuart Treece, a professor of English, left the university and went out on a mission; he taught an evening class at the Adult Education Centre, a large, grimy building set, not as the university was, on the urban fringes, but right in the centre of this provincial town. It was a building in civic gothic, of redbrick towers and pointed windows, and its rooms, heavily invested with Victoriana, were the haunts of the more unsettled of the community: evangelizing vegetarians, bleak apocalyptics, seasoned protestors with the stains of Trafalgar Square on the seats of their jeans, young teachers with solemn ambitions, secretaries hoping for deliverance through acquiring speedy reading techniques, walked nightly in through its portals. Tonight it was a wet cold evening as Treece mounted his motorized bicycle, his books in the saddlebag, and set out on his mission through the almost empty streets; wind whistled in his ears, cold blurred his eyes. But the building – it was one of its greatest attractions – was warm, a haven. Treece walked in the door, past the book display – 'ALL ARE available for YOUR WINTER reading' – and down the corridor to his first destination, the men's toilet. Here he stripped off his oilskin cycling suit, washed off, under the tap, the dust on his hands that had flapped up from the books he had been working on all day, sat on the edge of the sink quickly reading through a page of notes, his preparation; then he set forth along bleak corridors, as ready as he could be for the fray.

In the common room, when he looked in, there was a fire,

the new *New Statesman*, and an elderly lady wearing a *vol-au-vent* hat, one of the students in his group, which was devoted to the topic of modern poetry. 'What's a nice book to give for a Christmas present, Professor?' she asked, looking up from her knitting, 'You know all about books.' 'Oh, I never read *nice* books,' said Treece, 'only rather nasty ones. Isn't it safest to give a book token?' 'Oh dear,' said the old lady, putting away her knitting, and following him along the corridor to the room where the class met, 'I think they're so tasteless and impersonal. I give books because they're personal. That's why I come to this.' 'Quite,' said Treece, entering the bare room, with its long table and uncomfortable chairs. They were the first there. On the blackboard was a diagram, left over from the night before, of what Treece realized, a little belatedly, to be the female sexual organs; he began rubbing it out just as the class jostled in and sat down. There were about fifteen of them: fat motherly ladies who counted how many pullovers Treece was wearing, and worried about him; little men with small Grimsby moustaches, who were furniture salesmen, bus inspectors, newsagents; two nuns; a few bearded local Bohemians, who, after the fashion of these radical times smoked black cigarettes; and, baldish, nodding, smiling, Louis Bates, that strange man, one of Treece's students from the university. Here was the group he must fire; he turned to it, in welcome. 'What do you think of this, for a sofa?' asked one pleasant lady, sitting down at the oblong table, and producing a piece of ornately flowered furnishing fabric from the shopping basket she carried with her. Treece looked at it, fingering it dutifully. 'Yes, I like it,' he said. 'Here, did you see Connolly's bloody review on Sunday?' asked one of the Bohemians, 'I've written to them about it. Again.' A man who now owned a bookshop but persisted atavistically in calling himself a bricklayer – he was the class's worker – began selling copies of a little literary magazine called *Hooligan*, published at Leeds University. They all drew in their chairs around the oblong table, and waited for things to happen.

'Are we all here?' said Treece, sitting at the head of the table. The class secretary put ticks down the register. 'Mr Smart's not here,' she said. 'I expect it's too cold for him,' said one of the old ladies. 'Yes, that'll be it,' said the class secretary, 'but he is a tryer and he'll put in his attendances. He suffers with the cold a lot.' 'Well,' said Treece, 'we ought to start, because I want to finish on time this evening.' 'Going out, Professor Treece, then?' asked one of the ladies. 'Yes, I'm going to a party.' 'Lovely,' said the lady. 'We used to have marvellous parties when the children were young,' said a housewife, 'balloons, gingerbread men, everything.' 'Dr MacElwee used to have a class party,' said one of the insurance men, 'Meeting before Christmas he'd come in loaded up with buns. Everyone would bring a bit of something, cakes and such like. 'Of course,' said a housewife, 'we have to remember that Professor Treece isn't married like Dr MacElwee was. His wife was lovely. She often used to come and make comments.'

Dr MacElwee hovered over the class, a persistent ghost. He was the previous tutor. He had come up through the old tough days of the WEA and had a steadfast commitment to working-class culture and the critical analysis of newspaper advertisements. The middle-class housewives found him marvellous. Now he had been translated to higher things, running a liberal studies programme in a college of advanced technology; but Treece knew all about him, though he had never actually met him. He knew about the kind of ties he wore, and how he always lost the key of the book-box, and how he hated James and Proust, and how he and Mr Smart used to quarrel about the First World War; they seemed to Treece like possessors of an illness who were not satisfied with one, but wanted a second and a third opinion. And so they came along, year after year, to compare MacElwee's D. H. Lawrence and Potter's D. H. Lawrence with Treece's D. H. Lawrence, noting similarities with pleasure and differences with doubt, and building up great accretions around the one book, which they read time and time again. There were moments when Treece asked himself why they really did come. As week succeeded week, he grew to suspect that they weren't really understanding what he had to say, as he discoursed on and on about *The Four Quartets*, juggling subtleties of interpretation and differentiating between various states of visionary perception. The odd thing was that none of them *stopped* attending, save for one conspicuous defector who had objected to the inclusion of Eliot on political grounds and had been disliked by the rest of the class. On the other hand, the things they said seemed to bear almost no relation to the things *he* said. They appeared often to sit, on three sides of the oblong table, following out little private trains of thought in the interstices of his own observations.

Stuart Treece believed in education, and he was sure that it was all very profitable, all the same. But when he came here, out of the university, a special anxiety, a want of certainty, plagued him. For it was surely true that the only person who seemed to be following at his heels was Louis Bates. Bates was one of his undergraduate students, an odd persistent man in his first year, older than the others. There were, indeed, times when it seemed to Treece (and he suspected, to Bates too) that he was the *only* undergraduate at the university. Mrs Mary Baker Eddy once instructed her followers in Christian Science that they were forbidden to haunt her house or her drive; Treece felt the need of the same instruction for Bates. For Bates was a dogged pursuer, a man who popped up in the most unexpected places: at foreign students' weekends, at staff cocktail parties, in the bookshop, on the doorsteps of various faculty members. Treece had suggested to him, when he appeared at the first meeting of his class, that he had enough work on his hands with the university course without attending an adult education class as well. 'Well,' Bates had said, licking his lips thoughtfully, 'I do feel that in the honours course we do less than justice to the moderns – who are, after all, converting contemporary experience, for us primary experience, into literature. That's just a little belief of mine.' Treece had had to

66

grant some justice in this, and so Bates had come, and paid his fee, and solemnly sat there week after week, nodding his domed head at the better *aperçus*, getting angry with the weaker brethren. The rest of the class didn't quite share his view about primary experience. They were interested, but writers seemed to annoy them rather, critics annoyed them a little bit more, and though they respected everything Treece said, he sometimes thought they respected him mainly for two things – the fact that he got his cup of tea, served at midway point in the two-hour meeting, free, while everyone else paid fourpence; and the fact that he could actually earn his living doing this kind of thing.

In consequence of this analysis of his class, Treece in more recent meetings had changed his technique somewhat. Instead of working on line-by-line analyses of major works, referring back learnedly to Donne and Jessie Weston, he had curbed his scholarship and tried to apply what he called, rather pretentiously, the Socratic method. This meant that he read poems and passages of prose to the class and then asked them questions. Tonight he began with Auden's song, 'As I Walked Out One Evening'. He produced from his briefcase a wad of cyclostyled copies of the poem and pushed them to the people sitting nearest him. 'Would you pass these round the table?' he said. There was a good deal of fuss as everyone took the sheets and stared at them with blank fascination; they always enjoyed, to the full, any teaching aids, and there were hisses of awe and delight when he wrote words like 'free verse' on the blackboard. 'Would you like me to read it aloud?' he asked. 'Yes,' said the housewife nearest to him, 'and I'm going to mark bits with my pencil.' 'I did give you copies of this last week, didn't I?' asked Treece. 'Did he?' said a lady. 'Yes, I think you did,' said an insurance man. 'You asked us to *read* it,' said a Bohemian, 'for this class.' '*Did* you?' asked Treece. 'Yes,' said the Bohemian. 'No,' said everyone else. 'I didn't really,' said the Bohemian. 'Well, I think you're going to find this fairly easy and straightforward, after the Eliot. So just listen and tell me afterwards what sort of purpose the poem has; what it says and why it says it in that way. Watch the tone, the diction, the verse form.'

Treece then read the poem. It was followed by a silence. 'Well, what do you think?' asked Treece. 'I would say this,' said one of the class, a schoolmaster, after a moment, 'he's a real poet.' 'Why?' asked Treece. 'He's a technician, a consummate technician,' said the schoolmaster, 'he knows exactly what he's doing, where he's putting words and so on.' 'Yes, good. Well, what do you all think it means? How clearly is that meaning expressed?' 'Can you say what a poem means?' asked a Bohemian, 'Who was it said a poem should not mean but be?' 'MacLeish,' said Treece, 'but that doesn't indicate that it has no paraphrasable meaning at all.' 'I didn't like it,' said a lady. 'Why not?' 'It's cruel,' said the lady, 'and it isn't fair.' 'Why should it not be cruel? And to whom is it cruel?' 'I don't quite know,' said the lady, 'it just sounds cruel.' 'It must be cruel to someone.' 'Well, then, to everyone, I suppose. I think he's accusing me of wasting my life, and you can't say that sort of thing to people.' 'But surely there's a sense in which nearly all literature is saying that? Arnold once said that poetry is at bottom a criticism of life and surely we do expect literature to do more than entertain us. We expect that it should reflect upon the nature and responsibilities of man, don't we? And that it touch us at a very deep level of our experience? It's a form of high civilization, to produce and read literature; and all really great literature is a record of the worth of man, and a criticism of the deviations from the highest kind of living.'

'But writers are only other people, after all,' said the woman. 'But very dedicated and refined people who are really concerned with this question of quality,' said Treece, beginning to glow with excitement, 'What do you live for? What do you want life to provide you with?' 'Are you asking *me*?' asked the lady. 'No,' said Treece, hastily, 'I mean, that's what literature asks us.' 'Of course,' said Bates, 'some people just *live* life away.'

Treece laughed, and Bates looked very pleased with himself. 'But, but,' cried an insurance salesman, 'poetry needn't be about life at all, need it?' 'How can it avoid it?' asked Treece. 'Well,' said the man, 'some of the best poetry in the world is about birds, and flowers, and the wind. Look at Keats. Now there's a poet. I'd say that was pure poetry. Keats knew what poetry was about.' 'But isn't the question one of Keat's relationship to those things?' 'No, not really,' said the salesman firmly. 'Well, what you're saying sounds very depressing to me. I teach literature because I believe it does do those things, does have that sort of quality and concern. But doesn't that mean anything to you?' Treece looked around the room, suddenly puzzled and unacquainted; what he was saying was so much at home with him that he felt it odd that here might be people who did not think, deep down, in the way that he did. It was a matter on which he was persistently innocent, and he realized now, as he had been forced to realize on other occasions before, that here were assumptions that were not commonly shared. 'Well, of course, literature is about life in a sense,' said one of the housewives, 'but it's got to be pleasant and entertaining, hasn't it? Otherwise it doesn't interest you. What's the good of reading a sad, depressing book, like so many of these modern books, when you spend all your life trying to avoid those things? I don't know about you, but I have enough trouble of my own without reading about other people's.'

From the far end of the table a voice suddenly spoke. 'You people surprise me,' said the voice, which was Louis Bates's, in very loud tones, 'Here's a man telling you what literature is really about, trying to raise you up, and you don't recognize what he's saying.' At first Treece wasn't clear about whom Bates was talking, whether he meant Auden or himself; he *hoped* that he meant Auden. But then, as Bates went on to condemn the ingratitude of the class, he recognized with unease that this was a paean of praise directed toward himself. His first response, when he knew this, was one of fury. He was prepared to believe that Bates's comments were sheer flattery, spoken with the intention of bettering his own position as a student. But then he realized that this really wasn't true; it was evident from the flash of his eyes and the spittle flying from his lips that somehow what was said had violently engaged Bates, that he had, and in an extravagant form, values that he shared very exactly with Treece. Then Treece's reaction was shame – shame in his apologist, who, by behaving in this ridiculous way, by committing this solecism, was virtually guying all that Treece was trying to state and stand for. It wasn't enough to have someone say the right things; they have to be said by the right persons for the right reasons. And when he saw that, Treece became embarrassed by another kind of shame, shame for being ashamed of his apologist; the two shames existed together and were the same emotion. Bates went on, elevating and murdering Treece's case; he extended it and parodied it and made it absurd. He spoke for about five minutes and the view became not the view of Treece's commitment but of Bates's maladjustment. 'Here is a man who can teach you how to put depth into your lives,' said Bates, 'You're privileged to read these things with him.' Treece knew he had to stop Bates or destroy his class; Bates had to be sacrificed to preserve the cause he was arguing. Treece said: 'That's enough, Bates. This is my class, not yours. And I'm afraid neither you nor I will convince anyone with that kind of rhetoric.' Bates's round eyes grew large and sad and he stopped in the middle of a sentence. Treece expected he'd then go on to excuse himself; he had heard many such Bates excuses. But he dropped his head and said nothing. The class, already looking uncomfortable, looked more uncomfortable still. It would look to them like a private quarrel. To restore atmosphere, Treece said he would read the poem again. He did this. When he had finished, the housewifely lady who had spoken before spoke again. 'Well, I still don't understand it,' she said, 'I didn't before and I don't now. I wish someone would explain it. But it doesn't seem very poetic to me.'

'Well, let's talk about that,' said Treece, 'What is a poetic poem? Or to put it another way – aren't all poems poetic?' 'Oh, no,' said the housewife. 'Well, then,' said Treece, 'what is it that Auden is doing with language that gives you a sense that this isn't poetic?' 'Well, it's sort of the way everyone speaks,' said the lady. 'Yes, it is, to a point. What's different about it?' 'Oh, some of the words.' 'Pick them out,' said Treece. 'But shouldn't all the words be poetic?' asked the lady. 'Well, how do words become poetic? Doesn't a poet have to use the language of his time? And heighten it and sharpen it and concentrate it?' 'To communicate better,' said the lady. 'Yes, in part,' said Treece. 'Well, what I'm saying is that this poem doesn't communicate to me at all.' 'Does it to anyone?' asked Treece. 'Well,' said a bank clerk, 'this is by D. H. Auden, isn't it?' 'W. H. Auden, yes.' 'Well, what I was going to say was, wasn't Auden trying to use the language of the common man?' 'Yes, that's right, Mr Hope, he was,' said Treece, 'up to a point.' The class all looked pleased at this victory by one of their members; they now felt they were getting somewhere. The man smiled. 'Yes, well, if this is the language of the common man, why doesn't it communi-cate to Mrs Wilkins? That's the key question, isn't it?' Treece admitted it was. 'Well,' said the man, 'if I might suggest a few things, I think it's because the common man doesn't want poetry in his language.'

'Balls,' said a bluff man at the other end of the table. 'Mr Tinker, please,' said Treece. At once the class was in uproar; an old lady hit Mr Tinker with her scrap-pad. Mr Hope, in uncovering Treece's pattern of thinking, had endeared himself to all; whereas Mr Tinker, who was a Communist and smelled at the armpits, was not at all popular. Perceiving his isolation, Tinker, proud of it, rose to his feet. 'Ladies and gentlemen, I want to apologize to all you comrades for a momentary indis-cretion. Passion drove me to words I wouldn't normally have used before you, but what I meant to say was this: I think our friend is overlooking the significance of the whole working-class movement since the French Revolution. Fascist poets and critics have too long obscured the value of the language of the common man. Even in poetry.' Mr Tinker sat down.

Go on, Mr Hope, with your argument,' said Treece. 'Well, Professor Treece, what *I* was going to say, when Mr Tinker burst in like that, was that poetry has to delight us as well. Now, what D. H. Auden is saying here isn't difficult to see. I think he's saying that time defeats us all and prevents us from realizing our youthful hopes. But he doesn't say it to please.' 'Very good,' said Mrs Wilkins. Then above the heads Treece saw an arm waving; it was Bates's. 'May I speak?' said Bates. All the members of the class turned to see what fresh shock was in store. 'Go ahead, Bates,' said Treece. 'Well, I'd like to read an almost identical poem – that is, a poem of an almost identical subject. I won't tell you yet who it's by. If you do recognize the author, don't shout out. Then after I've read it, I'd like, if you don't mind, Professor Treece, just to ask the class and Mr Hope one or two questions.' Treece looked at this indestructible character with renewed amusement; Bates said, 'It's all very relevant.' 'All right,' said Treece.

Bates beamed and then read from a large tome, the title of which he obscured behind an immense hand, the song from *Cymbeline*, 'Fear No More the Heat o' the Sun'. The reading over, Bates turned to Mr Hope and asked him whether he thought the piece was any more delightful than the Auden song. 'Yes,' said Mr Hope firmly. 'Why?' demanded Bates. Treece watched his class slip away from him and with a tired hand plucked at the straps of his briefcase. 'Because it's more poetic,' said Mr. Hope. 'Well, then, I suggest the reason is not that Auden hasn't succeeded in his poem but because he hits home too hard.' 'That's right,' said Mr Tinker. 'It has relevance to your own life; he describes your own situation,' said Bates. 'That's it, comrades,' said Mr Tinker. 'The glacier's in *your* cupboard. *You're* in the land of the dead. He's pinned *you* down, hasn't he?'

Uproar was renewed. 'I think it's awful,' said Mrs Wilkins. Mr Tinker got to his feet again and shouted: 'Good lad, good lad.' 'I think Mr Tinker is drunk,' said the old lady. 'Please sit down, Mr Tinker,' said Treece, 'and please pay attention to me.' The class quieted down. Then Treece, cutting off any further comments from Bates, who was now well prepared to make some, went on to another poem. 'Perhaps this one seems more poetic,' he said. It was by Dylan Thomas. Treece read the poem, 'Lament', slowly, to give time for passions to subside. 'Well,' he said after he had finished, 'did you prefer that?'

'Yes,' said Mr Tinker. 'Why?' asked Treece. Mr Tinker preferred it because it was about sex, and said it would improve everyone present if their bedsprings squeaked a bit more often. 'Let's leave sex until after tea,' said Treece, wearily. Mr Tinker misunderstood this and said that in his view it was better in the afternoons and in the open if possible.

'I think Mr Tinker should be expelled from the class,' said the elderly lady.

Tea came in, and this restored some order. The two nuns, who had not been looking happy, revived. After tea followed a more controlled discussion of the Dylan Thomas poem, in which Treece managed to extract a sense of its meaning and design from various members of the class. At the end when Treece stopped the evening just on nine, Mr Hope stood up and said, 'Well, I don't know how the others feel, but I think this evening's been most instructive. I think it's shown one thing, though, and that is whether you ask of poetry what these ladies want, or whether you want it to be about life, Keats stands out above all the rest.' Everyone began to stand up and put on their coats. '*Don't* forget to avail yourselves of the book-box,' screamed Mrs Tubbington, the class secretary, 'and *don't* forget your tea-money please, to me or in the saucer by the door.' The two nuns took out separate purses: 'We each pay for our own,' said one of them to Treece, with a giggle. Everyone was filing out, except the few people who always stayed on a little afterwards to ask him personal questions, encourage him to get married, take up little points of discussion. 'I don't like to say this,' said the elderly lady, but I don't think Mr Tinker should be allowed to stay in this class. Several people are signing a little petition. He's spoiling it for everybody.' 'Wah!' shouted Mr Tinker, who was standing in the middle of the room, putting his coat on and scratching his crotch, 'It's a free country, you can't throw a man out. Ye all can't help envyin' a man wi' a spot of blud in his veins.' 'Mr Tinker's right,' said Treece, 'but I do hope you will control your language, Mr Tinker. We do have nuns here.' 'I've see them,' said Mr Tinker.

There were a few more questions, and then only Louis Bates was left, looming large by the doorway. 'I wondered whether we were going in the same direction,' he said. 'I've been wondering the same thing myself,' said Treece, putting papers into his briefcase, 'You realize you spoiled this class.' 'A number of people commented that it was the best class they've ever had,' said Bates, 'We certainly made them think, didn't we?' 'We?' asked Treece. 'Well, you and me and Mr Tinker,' said Bates. 'I thought you behaved rather badly, Bates,' said Treece, 'You certainly have a way with the dramatic gesture, don't you?' 'I suppose I did behave rather ill,' said Bates speculatively. 'You did,' said Treece, firmly. Bates looked enormously flattered at this; all attention was a compliment to him. 'Perhaps we could discuss it,' he said, 'Perhaps I could come round to your house one evening.' 'There's nothing more to say,' said Treece, 'except that I expect you either to act in a responsible way or not come to this class in the future.' Bates grew pathetic. 'But this class is the most rewarding thing in my week,' he said, 'it's the only time I get to hear you in detail. Someone ought to tell you that you're a most stimulating teacher.' But as he stood in the washroom, putting on his cycling suit, Treece felt only the deepest sense of failure. It seemed to him that the only man he could convince, the only man who shared what he most believed in, was a preposterous madman. To this man he was fettered; this was his own half-self; and he suspected that there was nothing in the world he could do to set himself free. He watched Bates walking ahead of him down the street, pacing out his strange long step, and his shoes seemed to fit in the same footprints. 'I wondered whether we were going in the same direction,' Bates had said. 'Perhaps we are,' thought Treece, getting on his motorized cycle, and riding off into the provincial city, 'Perhaps after all we are.'

Nobody Here in England

I

THE FACULTY CLUB on campus accommodated academic visitors for twelve dollars a night, in pleasant circumstances; and it was here that Leo Dennie, an administrative person, found a room, the very best room, for Mrs Prokosch, when at last the citadel fell, and the college acceded to her long-expressed desire that she should come and speak at it. On the early afternoon of her day of arrival, Dennie, an elegant young man, with a decent concern for making things go smoothly, and a mild pride in his capacity to do so, got into his car at the Administration Building, and drove, over the highway, through the campus, to the Faculty Club, just to check the reservation and make sure that all was well. As he drove, he began to prospect the visit, as people do, and a few uncertainties began to strike him. Mrs Prokosch, it was quite clear from the aristocratic tone and the European flamboyances of the letters she wrote, was a woman who would tolerate no hitches. He expected none, except that the whole visit was contentious, and a political man, a man of tact, a man of organizational ability, a man like himself, might well have thought it the wiser thing to make the reservation at the College Motor Lodge on the green; then, if anything did happen to go wrong, the college itself would be just a little less implicated. But then, again, not. Mrs Prokosch was, after all, coming to make a benefaction as well as give a lecture; indeed the latter had been the price exacted for the former. That put the college in the position of persuader; and the charm of the

79

place itself, and it had some, the charm of the people, was part of the persuasion. In any case, Mrs Prokosch was staying for only one night, which, in Dennie's view, based on experience, was just about the right length for any sort of romantic relationship; past that point the charm of novelty began to be replaced by the wrinkles of confrontation. Here was the Faculty Club, new, comfortable, and one of the best buildings on campus; it looked reassuring to Dennie as, smart in his hundred-dollar Burberry, carrying a cellophane-sealed bunch of flowers in one hand, he got out of the white Mercedes, and ran up the steps.

Inside the foyer, behind the reception desk, in a black dress that showed the top slopes of large tanned breasts, stood Mrs Schnodd, the resident manageress, smoking a small cigar, and counting keys. 'Aren't they beautiful?' asked Mrs Schnodd, leaning forward and peering at the flowers through the wrap, 'I'll find you my very best vase for them.' 'I have a desire to spread perfection,' said Dennie. 'You look like a beau,' said Mrs Schnodd, 'These are for the lady?' 'It's a welcoming touch,' said Dennie, 'Don't misunderstand. She must be eighty.' 'Well, I gave you this room,' said Mrs Schnodd, opening a door, 'I always think this one is our best.' Mrs Schnodd went to the window, and drew the drapes; outside stood a most precise view, out onto the rough lawns of the campus, with the white spire of the chapel poking up out of the elms, caught dead centre in the window. The little square of dissent, where the student protesters and the graffiti artists endemic to any campus operated, was hidden away round a happy corner; the scene was a vignette of the arcadian campus, the field of learning. There were trees with gently falling leaves, there were blue jays hopping in the grass; under a maple three students sat solemnly reading, while to the right a group of faculty in track suits euphorically practised football passes, beneath a stark blue sky. 'That's perfect,' said Dennie, 'Can we keep it like that?' He put the flowers down, went through into the sanitized private bathroom, and filled the vase with water. Then he posed the vase on the table in front of the window, and began arranging the flowers, dropping them neatly in in an elegant display. 'You know, you should have been some kind of artist.' said Mrs Schnodd, pulling the pleats in her hair straight with her fingers. A leaf dropped; Dennie punctiliously swept it up with his hand, and put it in his pocket. 'I'll just leave her a note,' he said. He sat down at the writing desk, took a sheet of college-crested paper, and wrote a brief message of welcome, giving his campus telephone number, asking Mrs Prokosch to call him once she had settled in, explaining that he would show her round and introduce her to the President, Dr Halpert, who looked forward to welcoming her formally.

It was one of several problems on Dennie's cool mind that, in fact, Dr Halpert did not really look forward to welcoming her at all. He rarely looked forward to welcoming anyone, not being a welcoming man; but Mrs Prokosch had, with her letters, already induced in him a severe trepidation, and all one could hope was that, despite this, he would remain on campus and not head off to his lakeside cottage on a sudden fishing call. For three or four years now, Mrs Prokosch's letters had been regular items in his President's mailbag. They all began 'Distinguished Scholar', a judgment on himself that Halpert, a modest man, did not share; they contained extensive literature on Women's Rights and the Feminist movement, not a topic of great interest to this man, President of a men's college; they also indicated that, conditions being right, Mrs Prokosch had conceived a wish to give the institution what she called, in her correspondence, 'a gift worth the bestowing', this being 'my singular collection of intimate letters and associated items of the late George Bernard Shaw'. It was the thought of the gift that raised the most trepidation; like all colleges, this one welcomed benefaction, but it was never a simple matter, a pure disinterested activity of the mind, and Halpert did not like the mind sullied. Benefactors had, after all, a taste for approaching as many colleges as they could, and raising the stakes of reward as high as possible; there were also forgeries, and problems of insurance; caution was necessary. Halpert was a sharp but simple man, a native Ohioan of Baptist background who had scarcely ever left his own state and believed himself perpetually vulnerable to East Coast deceit; caution took up much of his time. He always hid letters of this type for several months, or replied expressing interest but explaining that he was too infirm to meet the donor. First Folios went to Texas, Thackeray papers to Illinois by default; in this Halpert found an evidence of his basic integrity. 'These spooks,' he used to say, when the faculty increasingly began to indicate concern, 'I get a whole lot of letters from spooks like this. Oh, they've got the goodies, but what do they want in exchange? I'll tell you: academic honours superior to Einstein's, right?' It was Dennie himself who had rescued Mrs Prokosch, after coming on her correspondence one day, tucked away in a file about some quite different matter, where Halpert had put it. 'Straw was an incredible correspondent,' he told Halpert, 'His letters get high prices. And there must be thousands that haven't reached the dealers or the libraries yet. He just wrote so many.' 'Postcards to women,' said Halpert, 'A forger's paradise.' 'They were good postcards,' said Dennie, 'And a fascinating lot of women.' The thought of the sort of fascinating women Shaw might have known clearly brought new agonies to Halpert's mind; the letters went back into the files again, 'under review', and would undoubtedly have stayed there had the college not appointed as new head of the English Department Ethan Elbow, a young man from Princeton, who wore tennis shoes and was suave with passionate ambitions. He wanted a graduate pro- gramme, and was interested in anything remotely resembling research materials; he had made a public speech of thanks to a colleague who had returned from a summer trip to Europe bearing a toothbrush used by E. M. Forster. It was he who had suggested that the college set up a research resources committee. 'What about the spooks?' Dennie had said. 'Okay, show him the spooks,' said Halpert, 'But find out what they're all trying to shake us down for.' 'I ask but one recompense,' Mrs Prokosch had written, in reply to Dennie's delicate letter, indicating collegiate poverty and the rarity of its award of honorary degrees, 'It is my wish to address your young men on the subject of GBS, a much misunderstood genius, whom it was my pleasure to know very intimately.' 'One lecture?' Halpert had said in relief, 'What kind of a shakedown is that?' And so it was that Mrs Prokosch was coming, to this place, this room, this bed; Dennie checked the room out once more, and then left with Mrs Schnodd.

'But *how* is this lady coming?' asked Mrs Schnodd, as they walked down the thickly carpeted staircase toward the foyer. 'Mysteriously, Mrs Schnodd,' said Dennie, 'I offered to meet her at the airport. But she said she'd like to descend in her own way. I guess there's some divine agency that takes charge accounts from people like her.' 'This reservation is for one night, right?' asked Mrs Schnodd, as they reached the desk, from which Dennie took a packet of British Player's; it was the only place in town you could buy them. 'That's it, a one-night stand,' said Dennie. 'I asked because I thought maybe she was coming permanently,' said Mrs Schnodd, 'She sent us this great sort of valise by Railway Express. Take a look. It's right there in the cloakroom.' It was a big, old-fashioned, ship's cabin trunk, emblazoned with ancient labels from Cunard and French Line and Matson, strapped with leather, scraped with use. He looked, and it occurred to him, with a momentary sense of sin, that perhaps this was the point of it all, the thing itself, the all-too-beneficatory object. The Jamesian shivers ran over him, and the corresponding scruples; one didn't, one couldn't, possibly *touch*. 'She certainly doesn't travel light,' said Dennie, 'I'll drive back to Administration until she comes.' 'Okay, Mr Dennie, baby,' said Mrs Schnodd, 'And I'll give you a call right away she gets in, how's that?' 'Fine,' said Dennie, and ran down the steps into the slanting fall sun. His white Mercedes 220, the only one in town, an object of some pride, stood elegantly in the gravelled lot; he got in and drove out through the campus, towards Administration. Some scruple had separated

Administration from the main campus, setting it across the main highway to Columbus, so the old campus retained its ancient provincial dignity.

It was a beautiful Ohio fall day; the colours were good, the atmosphere sharp, almost tactile. The old redbrick college buildings, with their wooden detail, framed with white rail fences, overhung with reddening trees, made an elegant picture of American charm. There were Hallowe'en pumpkins in the windows of the dorms, and dead leaves had been blown into the wheels of the bicycles, which stood in slotted blocks outside them. It was a spared place; Dennie, though an administrator rather than a scholar, a man of files and secretaries, no intellectual, felt its virtue. It had tasted the troubles of the last agonized decade, when bombs and hate and blood seemed to have attended what before had been for Dennie, on the outside, the serene virtue of critical thought. Once some black students, urging non-negotiable demands, had retreated onto a roof and begun to strip it, throwing the shingles down on the student body below. But the Professor of Philosophy, a renegade Englishman from Cambridge, reputedly an admired pupil of G. E. Moore, had climbed to the roof, in a Norfolk jacket, and had reasoned with them, and discussed ethical imperatives, and the measure of good, and the mean of virtue, and they had come down, and reasoned, and duly graduated, and the community of intelligence had survived. The students challenged; there were always anguishes. But the faculty were generally revered, as they can be in provincial places, where there is some real paucity of wise men; and the general tone was of a virtuous mean. Politeness prevailed. Even if Mrs Prokosch's lecture tonight were to be terrible beyond belief, the critical wisdom would function quietly; no one would protest aloud, or sweep from the room, or ask the wounding question; it would be discussed briefly elsewhere, and forgotten. Dennie reached the main gates, ever open; he halted the Mercedes; he inspected for traffic.

An ancient plum-coloured Pontiac was battling on the main highway out of town, headed in the direction of Columbus, eighty miles away; suddenly, without showing signals, it came for the college gateway, and for him. He kept the Mercedes stationary as the other car, with a flamboyant desperation, took the curve. An elderly, white-haired woman, with a red face, was heaving at the wheel, at the same time glaring through the windshield and mouthing speech. Something lightly snicked the side of his car; the Pontiac swept past; inspecting his mirror, Dennie saw that the Pontiac had pulled off the road behind him, and stopped. The woman leaned from the window and waved at him imperiously. A traditional and ingrained wisdom told him directly: this was Mrs Prokosch. He backed the Mercedes into safety, got out, went across to the Pontiac. Mrs Prokosch sat firmly in her seat, big knees wide apart; she looked supiciously at him from the large red face, with considerable white eyebrows; she began to talk. Her window was wound up, so that it was impossible to hear her; Dennie tapped politely on the glass and indicated that she should wind it down. Proximate but isolated, they stared at each other thus for several seconds. Then, in unwilling concession, Mrs Prokosch opened the quarter light. 'I'm sorry. I couldn't hear you,' said Dennie pleasantly. 'I said you nearly hit me back there, young man,' said Mrs Prokosch, 'If I hadn't been a driving artist we'd both be dead now.' 'Are you Mrs Prokosch?' asked Dennie. 'How do you know that name?' asked Mrs Prokosch. 'I'm Leo Dennie,' said Dennie, 'I arranged your visit.' 'All right, I'll tell you,' said Mrs Prokosch, 'I am.' 'Good,' said Dennie, 'We're very pleased to see you.' 'So you drive into me,' said Mrs Prokosch, 'I've been driving fifty years and you're the first accident I've nearly had. Or that's my story.'

'Well, you're here,' said Dennie, 'Let me take you to your room at the Faculty Club.' 'Well, Dennie,' said Mrs Prokosch, 'you look like a nice, well-endowed young man. Why don't you do that?' 'I'll turn my car round,' said Dennie, 'If you'd follow me.' 'I'll be right there on your tail,' said Mrs Prokosch, 'Maybe even putting a little salt on it.' Dennie went back to the Mercedes, and turned it; he passed the Pontiac, which fell into line behind him, and followed him, uncomfortably closely, to the Club. Outside the Club, they parked side by side. 'Hey, Dennie,' said Mrs Prokosch, swinging one leg out of her car, revealing vast bloomers under her skirt, 'you know, you can drive quite well if you try.' 'Thank you,' said Dennie. 'How about bringing in my luggage, Dennie?' said Mrs Prokosch, handing him her trunk key. He opened the trunk: an abundant plenty, of suitcases and boxes, Safeway bags and baskets, met his eyes. He lifted out three suitcases and strung them around him. 'See that totebag there?' said Mrs Prokosch, 'Tote it for me, Dennie.' They mounted the steps; at the top, Mrs Prokosch turned, said, 'Ber-rump,' and pushed open the glass doors with her buttocks. 'I guess this must be your visitor, Mr Dennie,' said Mrs Schnodd, standing there in the foyer, smiling nicely. 'Did you get a trunk come for me?' asked Mrs Prokosch. 'It's right here,' said Mrs Schnodd. 'Well, I guess you opened it,' said Mrs Prokosch, 'They weren't there, were they?' 'Oh, no,' said Dennie. 'Show me the can, Dennie,' said Mrs Prokosch. When Mrs Prokosch had gone in, Mrs Schnodd and Dennie, draped in suitcases, stared at each other. 'I feel like an old, tired gigolo,' said Dennie. 'I guess it suits you, too,' said Mrs Schnodd.

II

'See that one right there?' asked Mrs Prokosch, cutting into a rare steak, 'That's one of him at dinner. The food before him is all nutritional. GBS was vegetarian, you know; he thought his diet gave him his vital energy. Maybe it did too, he lived to a marvellous old age.' 'You're doing fine yourself, Mrs Prokosch,' said Dr Halpert, his bright round face shining beneath his white crew cut; he was bearing it all splendidly. 'Seventy-eight, not bad for a steak buff,' said Mrs Prokosch, swilling wine. 'Who is this beside him?' asked Peter Luby, a young instructor, at the dinner with a purpose; it had been his designated task, for weeks, to read through the Shaw letters and memoirs in the library, and assess the truth or falsity of Mrs Prokosch. 'Oh, that's, hell, I don't know, H. G. Wells, one of that crowd,' she said, not bothering to look. 'May I?' asked Ethan Elbow, taking the photograph, and putting on a pair of spectacles that aged him instantly into a worn old scholar, 'Are *you* on this photograph, Mrs Prokosch?' 'Do I look as if I'm on it?' asked Mrs Prokosch, 'No, I wasn't even around then.' 'I see,' said Elbow, 'How did you acquire it?' 'How do you think, Perry Mason?' asked Mrs Prokosch, 'He sent it to me. He sent me many things. And if you can get those spectacles to focus down there on the righthand bottom corner, you'll see he signed it for me too.' 'To my Vera,' said Elbow, 'Is that your name, Vera?' 'No,' said Mrs Prokosch, 'I guess he just called me Vera, for some reason. It means truth.' 'Yes,' said Elbow. 'He had a remarkable beard,' said Halpert, 'A most impressive man.' 'I'll say,' said Mrs Prokosch, 'Oh, that wiggly, squiggly beard.' 'I guess you spent a lot of time in England,' said Peter Luby, detecting. 'Did I?' asked Mrs Prokosch, 'May I burn one of those Pall Malls? What makes you think that?' 'Of course,' said Luby, lighting the cigarette, 'Well, that's where he lived.'

'I like you fellows,' said Mrs Prokosch, 'I like you male chauvinist pigs. Now, England. Did I go to England? Well, sure, I was there this one time. That was in 1915. Henry James was dying. He wanted Wilson in the war. I don't know where Pound was. I don't think Amy Lowell was there. Gertrude Stein was in Paris, of course. There was nobody around. People say: what do you remember? After all, that was when it was all starting, American literature was starting again, in London. What I remember is absence. I went all over London, and I asked people: "Is there anybody here in England?" But there wasn't. They were all at the war fighting, or somewhere else. Many of them were somewhere else.' 'But Shaw was there,' said Ethan Elbow. 'No,' said Mrs Prokosch, 'not at that point. Or maybe he was and I've forgotten.' 'I see,' said Elbow. 'Of course there were women there,' said Mrs Prokosch, 'That was important, the new woman feeling. Harriet Monroe, Harriet Weaver, Gertrude Stein, Katherine Mansfield, Mabel Dodge, Marianne Moore. They weren't all there, of course. But that was the literature. Shaw knew women were the new literature. That was part of his greatness.' 'But somewhere, at some time, in some circumstances, you did meet him,' said Ethan Elbow, looking sourly into his coffee cup. 'We were on terms of the most considerable intimacy,' said Mrs Prokosch. 'You wouldn't like to tell us the story?' asked Ethan Elbow. 'It's somewhat personal,' said Mrs Prokosch, 'I'll tell you when I'm dead, how's that?' 'Oh, Mrs Prokosch, must we wait so long?' asked Dr Halpert. 'I don't believe in modesty,' said Mrs Prokosch, 'I've fought all my life for frankness. But what's a story once it's told? Where's my interest, after that?' 'But these items you have,' said Elbow, 'Can you authenticate them?' 'The time to tell all is not yet,' said Mrs Prokosch, 'Not yet is the time to tell all. But I will say this. GBS may have been witty and malicious, but he had a rare capacity for tenderness, *Tendresse*.' 'My,' said Dr Halpert. Mrs Prokosch stubbed out her cigarette on the dinner plate, reached in her very large purse, and took out another photograph.

'Look,' she said, 'this is one of him in his own garden. You see the tall, handsome lady in the white long dress? Who do you think that is?' Halpert stared at the flouncy flamboyances of the Edwardian photograph, shot in sunshine. His face brightened; he said, 'Why, it's *you*, Mrs Prokosch.' A snicker broke from Mrs Prokosch's red face; she took back the photograph and handed it to Dennie. 'How about that, Dennie?' she said. 'Very nice,' he said. 'Ellen Terry,' said Mrs Prokosch, 'I thought everyone knew Ellen Terry.' Elbow, who could be heard faintly groaning across the table, took the photograph.

'A mighty fine lady,' said Halpert, 'I remember my father sitting on our porch talking about Ellen Terry, when he came back from his European tour.' 'They all were,' said Mrs Prokosch, 'GBS loved handsome people. Women with the *élan vital*. Ones who stood up to him. Especially lying down.' 'Yes,' said Dr Halpert. 'I see this one's been signed too,' said Elbow, 'but I can't read the writing' 'No,' said Mrs Prokosch, 'that was his reformed spelling alphabet. He wrote to me mostly in that.' 'Can you read it to us?' asked Elbow. 'I can't read it,' said Mrs Prokosch, 'It was just a lot of kooky squiggles to me.' 'So you never understood what he wrote to you?' asked Elbow. 'There are other languages than words,' said Mrs Prokosch. 'So you did meet him?' 'All will be explained,' said Mrs Prokosch, 'or maybe it will be. It depends how you behave. What do you need to know for anyway?' 'There's an old saying, "Never look a gift horse in the mouth",' said Halpert, 'but we have to. Otherwise we'd never be able to shut the doors of our library. We have to evaluate and authenticate.' Mrs Prokosch's red face laughed; she pushed the photograph back in her purse. 'Halpert,' she said, 'Always trust the word of a lady.' 'Yes,' said Dr Halpert. 'How else are we going to get our lies listened to?' said Mrs Prokosch. 'Other languages than words?' said Elbow. 'Oh, yes,' said Mrs Prokosch, 'you should try them.'

'Well, Mrs Prokosch,' said Dr Halpert, 'You lecture in just over an hour. Do you wish to lie down, or would you like some brandy in the lounge?' 'Why don't we mix it,' said Mrs Prokosch, 'I'll lie down with the brandy in the lounge.' 'Oh, right,' said Halpert, waving to the waitress. She came over, a thin, despondent girl: 'Well, Leonora,' said Halpert, 'that was a mighty fine steak you served us.' 'It was good?' asked the waitress. 'Right,' said Mrs Prokosch, 'But when I say rare I mean rare, if you take my meaning?' 'It wasn't good?' said the waitress. 'It's okay, not your fault,' said Mrs Prokosch, 'You just carry the stuff, you don't cook it. Right, stick your arm out, Halpert. You're going to squire me out there.' Filing out of the dining room, Dennie noticed that Mrs Schnodd, in her black dress, was standing furtively behind a pillar, gesturing at him. 'Excuse me,' he said to Ethan Elbow, leaving the line. 'If you ask me,' said Mrs Schnodd, the pleat in her hair falling down, 'this lady ought to be out there in the funny farm.' 'I'm sorry about Leonora,' said Dennie, 'But she's a sort of *grande dame*.'

'Oh, you'd love anything,' said Mrs Schnodd, 'But I'd just like you to come upstairs and see her room.' A certain chaos was apparent even before they reached it; the corridor was filled with furniture. 'She had the maid move all this stuff out,' said Mrs Schnodd, and she threw open the door, 'And how about that?' In the short time since Dennie was last in the apartment, neatness had given way to utter disorder. The trunk stood by the wall, and its contents seemed to have been emptied liberally about the room: books were scattered about, paintings of small size by unknown hands, saucepans, cushions. It must have been the bulk of Mrs Prokosch's wardrobe over a considerable span of years that lay on the bed and on the chairs. In the wastebasket, Dennie's flowers were dumped, and a bright stark light filled the room. 'You really think she's staying for one night?' asked Mrs Schnodd. 'What happened to the drapes?' asked Dennie. 'Oh, those she took down,' said Mrs Schnodd, 'She told the maid she has to have some more.' 'Why did she take them down?' asked Dennie. 'She said they're transparent, and the students were leaning out of the dorm windows and looking at her in her knickers.' 'I see,' said Dennie. 'I just wondered what you were going to do,' said Mrs Schnodd, 'because I'm out of my little mind.'

'Can't we move curtains in from one of the other rooms?' asked Dennie. 'They're all the same,' said Mrs Schnodd, 'It's a uniform scheme of decoration. Or it was.' 'Do you have measurements?' asked Dennie, 'I have thick drapes in my apartment.' 'I can tell you that,' said Mrs Schnodd. 'There are seventy-five minutes before the lecture,' said Dennie, 'Come on, let's go.' In the Mercedes, as they drove through the turning paths of the campus, Mrs Schnodd began quietly to cry. 'I like the work,' she said, 'It's a great job. I'm happy. It's just the occasional kook you meet.' 'That's how it is with these *grandes* old *dames*,' said Dennie, 'They live in the past.' 'What's so special about her?' asked Mrs Schnodd. 'Well, on the one hand, she was Bernard Shaw's mistress,' said Dennie, 'and on the other she wasn't.' 'I don't believe it,' said Mrs Schnodd, sniffing, 'that great fat terrible flesh.' 'Perhaps she was wonderful and slim and sexual in her day,' said Dennie, 'Of course maybe she wasn't.' 'She acts like she wants to get laid now,' said Mrs Schnodd, 'How about it, Dennie, for the college?' 'No, thanks,' said Dennie, 'not for the Gutenberg Bible.' 'You know,' said Mrs Schnodd, crying, and putting her arm out straight across Dennie's neck, so that she could lean her head on it, 'That steak. It was as rare as they come. *Saignant.* Bloody.' 'I believe you,' said Dennie, 'I know.' 'I cooked it myself,' said Mrs Schnodd, 'I told the cook I'd do a real special.' 'It was great,' said Dennie, 'It was fine, Mrs Schnodd.' 'Why don't you call me Pippitt,' said Mrs Schnodd.

'Fix us a drink, Pippitt, and I'll get these down,' said Dennie, when they got to his apartment. 'Hey, you're a real aesthete,' said Pippitt, looking around, 'You're a collector.' 'I like beautiful things,' said Dennie, getting a chair and taking it through into his bedroom. His own curtains were velvet, very favourite curtains; he stood on the chair and unhooked them. 'You're a really interesting guy,' said Pippitt, coming in, 'I brought you a drink.' 'I'll get it in a minute,' said Dennie. Pippitt lay down on the bed and pressed the television selector; the big skinny head and bright teeth of Kojak bobbed on the screen. After a moment she began to cry some more. 'I don't understand it,' she said, 'I don't see what she's trying to do here. But if you think she's leaving tomorrow, you're crazy.' 'We'll fix it,' said Dennie, unhooking the last drape. He got down off the chair and found that Pippitt was standing in front of him with her clothes off, crying and squeezing her nipples with her fingers. 'I'm so unhappy,' she said. 'There's the lecture in less than an hour,' said Dennie. 'I know what you're telling me,' said Pippitt, 'I know you aesthetes.' 'It's not that,' said Dennie. 'It's great work,' said Pippitt, 'I love it in that place. But then, wham, you get one of these kooks.' The tear splashed off Pippitt's face. There were only fifteen minutes left before the lecture when they reached the Faculty Club, and carried the bundled drapes up the stairs. Through the glass doors of the lounge, they could see the dining party gathered together in the club chairs. A despondency was on Halpert's face, but in the middle of the group, Mrs Prokosch, her face very red, laughed with great brightness. 'Huh,' said Mrs Schnodd, 'will I be glad when she goes home.' 'Who says she has a home?' said Dennie. The tears began running down Pippitt's face again. 'I was just kidding, Pippitt,' said Dennie.

III

'Hey, Dennie,' said Mrs Prokosch, when he entered the lounge a moment later, 'Where have you been?' 'I got some new curtains for your room,' said Dennie, 'I hear the others were too thin for you.' 'That's right, Mr Dennie,' said Mrs Prokosch, reaching into her brassiere and feeling her left breast, 'One doesn't usually put an elderly lady in a room overlooked by a student dorm.' 'I don't think really overlooked,' said Halpert. 'So you went in my room,' said Mrs Prokosch, 'Get a good look round?' 'No,' said Dennie. 'Weren't there, were they?' said Mrs Prokosch gleefully, 'I'm no fool.' 'Perhaps we'd better start over to Old Main Chapel,' said Halpert, 'How about your lecture? Do you need to go upstairs and get notes?' 'Notes!' cried Mrs Prokosch, stubbing out a cigarette, 'I've given this lecture in hundreds of colleges. All over the world.' Halpert, struck by an anxious thought, glanced at Dennie. 'You have?' said Halpert, 'Well, it's my great pleasure to introduce you. Could you give me your title?' 'It's a briefie,' said Mrs Prokosch, '*My GBS.*' '*My GBS,*' said Halpert, taking an old scrap of paper from his pocket, and noting this, 'And a little biography about yourself?' 'I just want you to call me a leading Shavian expert,' said Mrs Prokosch. 'A shaving expert?' asked Halpert, looking blank. 'Shavian is how we adjectivize Shaw,' said Ethan Elbow, looking dour, 'Mrs Prokosch says she's a leading Shaw expert.' 'Great,' said Halpert, 'It's a pleasure to have such a distinguished person.' 'I'll just find the can,' said Mrs Prokosch, heaving her great body from the chair, 'and then we can let it roll.' 'Oh, boy, oh, boy,' said Elbow, when she'd gone, 'This is a real operator.' 'Is she a fake?' asked Halpert, anxiously. 'Maybe we'll know after the lecture,' said Elbow. Peter Luby, breathing hard, joined them; he had been sent on ahead to scout the audience. 'It's full house,' he said, 'We've been hauling them in from the library and cafeteria and the showers. There are some kids in bathrobes, but I put them on the balcony.' 'Good thinking,' said Halpert.

The door of the ladies' room opened; Mrs Prokosch came out. She had put the interval to good effect: mascara had appeared round her eyes, her nose was thickly powdered, and a large purple scarf was thrown over her white hair and then wrapped around her neck. 'How do I look, Dennie?' she asked. 'Fine,' said Dennie. They advanced, the distinguished party, through the foyer, past the desk, where Mrs Schnodd, in her black dress, stood watching them; down the steps, into Halpert's Dodge station wagon, where, along with two sacks of lawn fertilizer, they fitted comfortably. Mrs Prokosch sat in the front seat next to the President, who drove slowly and solemnly across campus to Old Main. All along the route, they could see figures flitting in the ill-lit darkness towards the chapel, and when they got there the entire auditorium of the old building was crowded, ground floor and balcony packed, with students perched, for want of room, on the window sills. In the reserved seats, a group of faculty, alerted several days earlier to their duty, had forsworn their dinner parties and their grading to let their grey hairs glimmer reassuringly in the old chapel roof-lights; there was even a small sprinkling of well-dressed faculty wives, leaning from row to row to report to each other on the neighbourhood pregnancies. The occasion had a solemn, even a reverential air, and Dennie, slipping in on the back row, next to Peter Luby, watched the heads turn as the eminent procession made its way down the aisle and towards the stage: Halpert leading, Mrs Prokosch centre, Elbow in the rear. They mounted the stage; they sat in a row; Halpert stood and made a moderately gracious introduction. Then Mrs Prokosch rose; she went to the central podium, white-haired, red-faced, in the black dress, the purple scarf. 'I sing the body electric,' she said, 'Energy, vitality, biology, the eternal woman.' This seemed very solemn, but the audience appeared interested and without malice.

'I want to take you all back to 1914,' said Mrs Prokosch, warming, 'Everything was happening. Consciousness was exploding. Woman was evolving. The new was about us. Old walls were collapsing. In Chicago, St Louis, New York, Boston, San Francisco, everywhere. Amid this is one wonderful, personal story. It is my story. I am going to tell it to you.' Mrs Prokosch leaned forward, in intimacy; Halpert looked uncertain; Elbow looked sullen. 'Come with me to a certain New York *première*,' said Mrs Prokosch, 'The opening night of *Pygmalion*, a new play by Mr George Bernard Shaw. A young beautiful girl, in white, sits in the audience, watching that glittering performance. 'Guess who,' whispered Luby. 'To the core of her soul she is overwhelmed. It has happened at last. The new truth is revealed. She runs up on the stage. She stands there before that well-dressed audience, clad in their jewels, worth many thousands of dollars. "We stand at the turning point of the world," she cries. People come from backstage to take her off. "Let her go," shout those brilliant people, "She speaks as if inspired." That girl was me, that occasion my first meeting with Bernard Shaw.' 'She met him there?' asked Luby. 'A spiritual meeting,' said Mrs Prokosch, 'He had spoken to me, across the wide Atlantic. I knew I must speak to him, tell him who I was, tell him I was the new heroine he wrote of. I wrote a letter, and at that moment began one of the most fascinating correspondences in history.' Dennie, looking around, noted that a certain scepticism seemed to have settled on the audience. But now Mrs Prokosch stopped abruptly, and unbuttoned three buttons of her dress. Reaching somewhere inside, with a hand that settled somewhere around her waist, she produced from the interior a thick flutter of paper. 'Here it is,' she said, sorting through the flutter, and plucking out letters she began to read them. There were fond letters and vain letters, letters from Mrs Prokosch; they spoke of the arrant female principle and the need of the new woman for the new man. Mrs Prokosch's face tilted upwards, like some pleading suffragette's, or some early innocent statuary. An occasional curt postcard from Shaw intersected. Now there were passionate letters, erotic letters; they said, I claim you, you shall have me. Halpert, on the stage, solemnly blushed, the red pouring up from his neck and into his cheeks. White-haired, red-faced, Mrs Prokosch read on, through the innuendoes, the genital references; and, as Dennie stared at her, the strange inhuman biology of the old body before him, the big veined legs, the heavy trunk, the oddity of the seamed old head, the opening lips, the staring eyes, the fanned hair, the entire cellular construct, began moving before him, absurd.

'But did they ever lay each other?' whispered Luby. The chapel bell rang the half hour; Mrs Prokosch read on, letter after letter, year after year. When it rang the hour, Mrs Prokosch stopped. 'That is the story of me,' she said, thrusting the letters back into her sagging big bosom, 'Relics.' In the amiable applause, Halpert crossed to her; she took his arm, and they came out through the crowd. 'That was mighty interesting,' said Halpert, as they drove back across the campus towards the Faculty Club. 'It was bloody fabulous,' said Mrs Prokosch, breathing hard in the dark. At the Club, they went back into the lounge, and ordered more brandies. 'Perhaps,' said Halpert, when the drinks came, 'we could discuss your . . .' 'Benefaction,' said Mrs Prokosch. 'That's right,' said Halpert. 'My mementos,' said Mrs Prokosch. 'Now clearly,' said Ethan Elbow, leaning forward, 'there were many letters from you to him. But are there many of any substance from Shaw to you?' 'We were intimate,' said Mrs Prokosch. 'Do you mind if I ask how?' asked Elbow, 'It was wartime, you were on one side of the Atlantic, he was on the other, there were German submarines in between. You say you crossed once, but didn't meet him. It takes remarkable equipment to bridge a gap like that.' 'He was a superman,' said Mrs Prokosch, rising, 'I'm tired, I'm going to bed. I've done my service.' 'Perhaps we could discuss it in the morning,' said Halpert, 'Are you planning to leave early?' 'I don't know when I'm planning to leave,' said Mrs Prokosch. 'Dennie could bring you over to my office,' said Halpert, 'Could we say at ten?' 'Let's say at ten,' said Mrs Prokosch, 'I'm a tired old lady. Dennie, bring me to bed.' Mrs Prokosch held out her arm; Dennie took it and led her out into the foyer, to the desk, to pick up the key. Mrs Schnodd, in her black dress, stared flatly at him as she handed it over. He led Mrs Prokosch up the carpeted stairs, and to the door of her room.

'Put the lights on for me, Dennie,' said Mrs Prokosch, when he had unlocked the door. 'There we go,' said Dennie, 'Goodnight.' 'Draw the drapes,' said Mrs Prokosch. When he had pulled them to, he turned, and saw Mrs Prokosch lying on her back on the bed, in her black dress. 'All right?' said Dennie. 'Put me to bed, Dennie,' said Mrs Prokosch. 'I must go now,' said Dennie. 'Here's a key,' said Mrs Prokosch, 'Open the red suitcase.' 'I ought to go,' said Dennie. 'Shaw, Shaw,' said Mrs Prokosch, 'There are two sides to every story.' 'That's right, Mrs Prokosch,' said Dennie. 'Open the case,' said Mrs Prokosch. Dennie knelt down, and unlocked it. Inside he saw several large girdles, and three bottles of J & B whisky. 'There's a tiny bottle in there,' said Mrs Prokosch, 'Bring it to me.' The bottle was in the bottom of the case, under more underclothes: a green glass bottle, in an old style, containing a small quantity of fluid. 'You know what that is?' asked Mrs Prokosch, 'My memento.' 'No,' said Dennie. 'Put me to bed, Dennie,' said Mrs Prokosch. 'The President's expecting me downstairs,' said Dennie. 'You don't want the letters,' said Mrs Prokosch. 'You must talk to the President about those,' said Dennie. 'They're relics,' said Mrs Prokosch, 'Old things nobody wants.' She dipped in her dress, and pulled out the letters; the paper scattered about the bed. Dennie looked. 'I'm sure they're of great value,' said Dennie. 'Maybe I'll just keep them,' said Mrs Prokosch, 'What could you do with them?' 'They'd be used for scholarship,' said

Dennie, 'They'd have historical value.' 'You know, that's me we're talking about,' said Mrs Prokosch, 'My body, my sex. You can go to hell, Dennie. So I'm a lump of old meat. This old meat made it with Bernard Shaw.' 'Yes,' said Dennie. 'You don't believe me,' said Mrs Prokosch, 'I never met him, Perry Mason was right. But he wanted me. Circumstances were not in our favour. But we made out.' 'I don't understand you,' said Dennie. 'Sit down, Dennie,' said Mrs Prokosch, 'I'll tell you.' Dennie sat on the edge of the bed; Mrs Prokosch lay on the bed, the bedside lamp shining on her red face. 'He wanted to father on me,' she said, 'He sent me his seminal fluid. This bottle is his seminal fluid.'

'He sent that?' said Dennie, 'Across the Atlantic?' 'You don't understand,' said Mrs Prokosch, 'We wanted to make a new race. I had the ideal biology for the future. You don't know about that. You don't know anything, Dennie.' 'No,' said Dennie. 'You and your dirty little modern sex,' said Mrs Prokosch. 'Goodnight,' said Dennie. 'Here, Dennie,' said Mrs Prokosch, 'I want the furniture changed. Dennie, I want a different room.' 'I'm sorry, there's nothing I can do,' said Dennie, 'Goodnight.' 'Go to hell, Dennie,' said Mrs Prokosch, as he pulled the door shut and stood in the corridor. Down in the lounge, under the lamps, Halpert, Elbow and Luby were sitting, in easy chairs, over another brandy. 'Here he is,' said Elbow, with a grin, 'We were worried about you.' 'Elbow says she's a spook,' said Halpert. 'What has she got?' asked Elbow, 'Three or four postcards from him to her. The rest is the gush of a sentimental woman. A lady angling for a little place in history.' 'I doubt if she'll give us anything,' said Dennie, 'I don't think we've pleased.' 'That's what I figured,' said Halpert, 'Give us the letters, how would she get to lecture at the next colleges in line? For some of these spooks, it's a living.' 'I suppose one college has to be the end of the line,' said Luby, 'Why not this one?' 'She'll find somewhere that serves her meat the way she likes it,' said Elbow, grinning. 'At least we had the lecture,' said Halpert. 'That's right,' said Elbow, 'She speaks like one inspired.' 'Time for shuteye,' said Halpert, 'Dennie, bring her over in the morning, if she stays.' 'Sure, I will,' said Dennie, getting up.

IV

With no drapes on his windows, Dennie slept very badly, and woke at seven, in discomfort, to find the early morning sun cutting straight into his eyes. He got out of bed, pulled on his bathrobe, and went through into the kitchen to make some coffee. As he was drinking it, the telephone rang. 'This is Pippitt,' said the voice, 'I'm sorry, I didn't have anyone else to call except you.' There was a familiar note in the voice, and Dennie recognized tears; he said, 'Hey there, Pippitt, is there anything wrong?' 'That kook,' said Pippitt, 'I told you she was a kook.' 'Mrs Prokosch?' asked Dennie, 'What's wrong?' 'She set her room on fire,' said Pippitt. 'What do you mean?' asked Dennie, 'She burned everything up?' 'She burned herself up,' said Pippitt. 'She's hurt?' asked Dennie. 'They took her to the hospital in Amber,' said Pippitt, 'I called the fire department, and they called the police, and they called a doctor, and he called an ambulance.' 'Who's there now?' asked Dennie. 'The fire chief,' said Pippitt, 'A cop.' 'Keep them right there,' said Dennie, 'I'm coming over.' Putting down the phone, Dennie found his body shaking. He pulled on a shirt and pants, and hurried down to his car. Driving across town, between the silent, white-painted houses, he began to groan with a sense of disaster. He groaned for his part in bringing it here, for the letter of invitation, the booking of the room. The big red face, lying on the pillow, in the light of the bedside lamp, took shape in his mind; he groaned for that. The campus was stark and empty, with heavy shadows on it; its peaceable air had slipped, and become absurd. In the plain morning light, the red bricks of the buildings were black, the white wood grotesquely white. The grass was frosted; no one moved. In the lot outside the

Faculty Club, there was a firetruck, and a police cruiser. He jumped out of the car, ran up the steps, and went inside.

In the foyer Pippitt Schnodd stood; she was wearing a silky housecoat, and her hair was out of pleats and down her back. She looked pretty and sad. 'Dennie, Dennie,' she said, 'I had to call you.' 'Of course,' said Dennie.' 'I knew it all the time,' she said, 'I knew she meant something.' 'Who found her?' asked Dennie, 'Did you?' 'No,' said Pippitt, 'One of the other guests. The Emeritus Professor from Michigan, he had the next room. But I went in there, it smelled like I can't tell you.' 'You come in the lounge and make yourself some coffee,' said Dennie, 'Who's upstairs?' 'There's the fire chief and Mr Pulowski from the Police Department,' said Pippitt, 'You want to go up?' 'I have to go up,' said Dennie. A hose lay along the corridor leading to the guest room. The door was open. In the room there was a smell as of burned meat. The carpet squelched underfoot. But otherwise the room seemed curiously untouched by the incident. The bed was badly singed and soaked in water; on it were the charrings of many pieces of paper. Clothes had burned, and a few books. But the red suitcase stood open as he had left it; the goods and the cases lay about the room. 'No sweat, Mr Dennie,' said the police chief, an elderly man in steel-rimmed spectacles, 'It's an open and shut. The lady must have fell asleep smoking a cigarette. There was a pack of Kents on the bedside table. This was a one-night paying guest, right?' 'That's right,' said Dennie, staring at the charred papers. 'Well, you had fire precautions,' said the fire officer, 'Her garment was one of those old flammable cotton nightdresses. Nobody wears them but this is an old lady. Get one of those items ignited, they burn up like paper. You can't play games with fire.' 'Is she very ill?' asked Dennie. 'Well, it's an old lady,' said Pulowski, 'There's a lot of burning lower down the body. They took her over to Amber, though, that's a hotshot hospital. And the doctor said this lady is a pretty tough cookie.' 'That's right,' said Dennie. 'This old guy from Michigan gets in someway and wraps her in a rug,' said the fire chief, 'That's who she has to thank. He must be seventy himself.' Dennie looked round the room again, at the charrings, the stains. He remembered Mrs Prokosch there on the bed the night before, old and enormous, the top of her dress unbuttoned, the big veined legs outstretched. 'If you're through,' he said, 'We'd better get this all tidied up.' 'We're through,' said Pulowski. 'There weren't any letters?' asked Dennie. 'You mean a note?' asked Pulowski, 'No, it's our routine, always look around for a note. This is accidental, no sweat.' 'I meant old letters,' said Dennie, 'She came here with a lot of old letters. She'd scattered them all round her on the bed.' 'That's right, that's what burned up,' said the fire chief, 'You drop all this paper round you, you light a cigarette, you fall asleep, what else do you expect?'

Pulowski came and stood near to Dennie. 'You saw these papers scattered?' he asked, 'You were here last night?' 'I was probably the last person to see her,' said Dennie. 'Is the room the way it was when you left?' asked Pulowski. 'Not quite,' said Dennie, 'She'd moved things around a bit.' He picked up a photograph from the writing desk, the one they had looked at over the steak: 'To my Vera,' said the Shavian handwriting. Then, glancing into the wastebasket, he saw, next to his dumped flowers, the green glass bottle. 'She threw that out,' said Dennie, 'It's Bernard Shaw's semen.' 'Maybe I should take that,' said Pulowski, opening the bottle and sniffing, 'You mean it's come?' 'Yes,' said Dennie. 'I'll test that out, I don't like bottles,' said Pulowski, 'Bernard Shaw?' 'A famous Irish writer called Bernard Shaw,' said Dennie, 'She had a lot of mementos from the past. She'd said she was going to leave them to the college.' 'She wanted you to have this guy's come?' asked Pulowski, 'I guess that's the intellectual life.' 'Instead she left you a load of trouble,' said the fire chief. 'It's a tragedy,' said Dennie. 'They happen,' said Pulowski. They walked out of the room and down the staircase. Outside the Club, in the cold fall air, some early-rising students stood, looking at the firetruck and the cruiser. 'Okay,' said the fire chief, 'I'll write you a report. Don't worry. The damage is mostly water damage. Your cover should cover it.' 'I'll call you if there's anything funny here,' said Pulowski. Dennie watched the two vehicles drive off, through the campus. Then he went back inside the Club. In the lounge, amid the stale smell of last night's cigarette smoke, Pippitt sat in her silky housecoat. She had made coffee in a silver pot; the pot was inscribed with the name of an alumnus who had done internationally well in transistor electronics. Her hair was fanned out loosely round her head; her eyes were puffy. Handing Dennie a cup of coffee, she looked up at him blankly. 'Oh, that kook, Dennie,' she said. Dennie sat down and stirred the coffee. 'It was an accident,' he said, 'You weren't responsible.' 'Sure,' said Pippitt, 'How do you think it is, to have that happen in my Club? Right by where I was sleeping?' 'I know,' said Dennie. 'She came here to do that,' said Pippitt.

Dennie looked at her. 'No,' he said, 'It was an accident. She was burning up the letters. We'd riled her, and she didn't want us to have them. She didn't want to leave us anything.' 'Okay,' said Pippitt, 'Why move house here? She brought everything. All her stuff, all those things, she brought them here.' 'I guess she has nowhere to live,' said Dennie. 'Sure she wanted to leave us something,' said Pippitt, 'She wanted to leave us her.' 'I don't believe so,' said Dennie. 'That's what she told the old guy from Michigan,' said Pippitt, 'He said, all she said was, "My benefaction to the college".' 'Pippitt, look,' said Dennie, 'That could mean a hundred different things. I mean, you think about it.' 'You think about it,' said Pippitt, 'She came here and you didn't attend to her properly. She was flesh, she insisted.' Dennie thought about it. In his hand he found the photograph he had picked up in the bedroom, Shaw and Ellen Terry; he turned it over and over. 'She wanted to kill herself here,' said Pippitt, 'in my Club. Well, I guess if she dies, she'll be useful for research. You could embalm her and Professor Elbow could shelve her in the library.' 'You could be right,' said Dennie. 'Is she going to die?' asked Pippitt. 'I can't believe it,' said Dennie, 'She somehow seems to be biologically eternal. Endless living tissue.' 'Tissue or not,' said Pippitt, 'that lady doesn't come back here.

I made a rule. I don't look after her.' 'There have to be relatives somewhere,' said Dennie, 'I'll have to find out all about that. I'll call the hospital soon.' 'Oh, you love it, don't you?' said Pippitt, 'Organizing things. What about all that stuff upstairs she left?' 'Can't you put it away in a closet somewhere for safekeeping?' asked Dennie. 'I guess,' said Pippitt, 'If you think it will stay there. You look kind of crumpled, Dennie. This is the first time I ever saw you without a clean shirt?' 'I'd better go back and clean up,' said Dennie, standing up.

Pippitt's hand slid forward, out of the silky housecoat, and held onto his sleeve. 'Oh, stay here,' she said. 'I have to fix things,' said Dennie, 'And you look like you could use some more sleep.' 'You think I'd sleep?' asked Pippitt, 'I can't even go back up those stairs without you, Dennie.' He looked and saw the tears running down the young flesh of her face, along the creases beside her nose, round the red rip of her mouth. 'That old woman, that meat burning, I saw her,' said Pippitt. 'I'm sorry,' said Dennie. Dennie looked at the slim plucked legs, the hard block of the trunk, the sharp, prodded breasts, the wet eyes, the red mouth, the fanned hair, the cells and the tissue. 'Don't you like me?' she asked, 'You liked me before. Come up with me.' He felt the sexual quiver in his loins, that binding grab. 'No,' he said. He went out through the foyer, down the steps of the Faculty Club, and got into the car.

A Breakdown

Miss Bean was a girl with a large face, a good figure and fat legs who, in the middle of her second year at the university, had a breakdown. The breakdown developed shortly after the end of the Christmas vacation, during which she had begun an affair, in her home town, which was Chesterfield, with a married man; it started then, the breakdown, but continued and developed, reaching its height towards the end of February and the beginning of March, when she started talking to everyone about the married man, and the affair, and its passion and its sincerity. Miss Bean had had affairs before, but this was, she said, her first *real* affair, and what mystified her, and upset her, and made her talk about it so much, was that she could not see what had gone wrong. The married man and Miss Bean had been, they both agreed, they both knew, very much in love; they had come to mean, in those weeks over Christmas, everything to each other; and so, on her part, it was natural for her to expect that he would leave his wife and four small children and come away to live with her. 'He wanted to,' said Miss Bean, 'He was the one who said it first.' Night after night, parked in the cold up on the moors in his car, they had talked about it, elaborated it. 'The trouble was, he wasn't sensible,' said Miss Bean, 'He didn't think about the necessary things, where to go, how to live.' But Miss Bean did; night after night, back at home in her parents' house, Miss Bean had filled it all out, given it a workable substance. Her idea was this: he was to leave his job in Chesterfield, where he was a chartered surveyor, working in a little office, and come to Birmingham, which was where Miss Bean was a student, taking her degree in French. In Birmingham there was good money in the car factories, and he could do that for a bit, and in a year and a half Miss Bean would have her degree. After that they could leave England altogether, and go and live somewhere on the Continent, in Spain or Majorca, or the South of France, or Venice. There Miss Bean could give English lessons; they wouldn't need much money anyway; and he could do what he liked, lie on the beach and swim, and they would talk all the time, and have parties, and make love where and when and how they wanted.

But for some reason, said Miss Bean, when she talked about it, it had simply not worked out. One evening the married man came for her in his car, and when they stopped it, up on the tops, looking down over Chesterfield, with the moors all round them, he had said, quite shortly, that he wanted the relationship to end. 'And he couldn't say why,' said Miss Bean, 'He just said he had to come to terms with his wife again.' Miss Bean had been very upset; she had called him a coward. 'He agreed,' said Miss Bean, 'He agreed.' So Miss Bean saw she had been used, had been just the fun you can't get when you're married, a bit on the side; and yet she knew, knew in her heart, he'd loved her, and still did. She made him drive her home, and the next day she sat down with her Basildon Bond writing pad and wrote a letter to his wife, telling her what had happened and trying to confront her with the devastating logic of the situation. 'You must set him free,' she said at the end of the letter. The man came to see her; he was angry; he told her she had done wrong. 'I was trying to rescue him,' said Miss Bean, after she got back to Birmingham, to the flat in Moseley she shared with five other girls. She sat down, she unpacked her books, she started to work on an essay, she thought about the whole episode, her mind stuck. She thought of his face and she cried. Her mind unstuck, stuck again; in February she started talking to people, desperately, telling the story over, looking for the weak point; then she cried for four days and the doctor, when called, said she was having a breakdown. The doctor sent her to a psychiatrist, who had long talks with her, and gave her tablets to take; but neither the talk not the tablets made her feel the slightest bit better. She couldn't work, she couldn't sleep, and neither people nor things appeared real to her any more. Nothing took on any shape or design, and no obligations seemed worth fulfilling. Even noises – the ordinary noises of traffic, people talking on buses, toilets flushing – began to violate her consciousness, shatter what grip she had, and the world came to seem to her like a shrill scream.

Then Miss Bean didn't want to take any food, and she began to cut her classes, or rather not remember that she ought to go to them. Her tutor asked to see her, and she went to him and told him, as she had by now told many people, her story. As she talked, she began, as she always did, to cry. The tutor's therapy was work: read more, write more. She looked at him blankly; she saw that it was hopeless. No one really understood; she was utterly isolated. 'No, I want to leave,' said Miss Bean, 'I want another start.' Her tutor sat at his desk; he told her how useful a degree would be to her, and offered to help her to work more effectively. 'I can't work,' said Miss Bean. 'Then it's really a psychiatric matter, I'm sorry,' said the tutor. Miss Bean stood in the doorway, with tears on her face, and told him she would not come back. The next day she had another appointment with the psychiatrist, but she did not want to go back there either. She decided that the tablets the psychiatrist gave her were placebos, and that his advice was the same. He was an old-fashioned moralist, telling her, like everyone else, that she was making unreal demands, that she had to face facts. 'I don't want more reality,' Miss Bean had said, 'I want a good and satisfying unreality.' 'That doesn't get us anywhere, does it, Miss Bean?' the psychiatrist had said, pushing his desk drawer open and shut. Clearly she was one of hundreds of cases, not worthy of detailed consideration; Birmingham itself was too big, and she felt ridiculous in the city. She stood in the Bristol Road for an hour, and counted the streams of cars. Something better, she said to herself. They're suppressing me, she said to her friends, at the flat in Moseley. She decided she had to do something for herself; and what she did was get on a bus, go to a travel agent in the Bull Ring, and buy herself a plane ticket for Barcelona. She took the plane at just about the time she was supposed to see the psychiatrist again; and, as soon as it was in the air, above Heathrow, she started to feel a little better.

The Trident flight was quick, and the airport bus gathered her up and dropped her in the centre of Barcelona in a few minutes. Although she had never been to Spain before, and was not sure why she was there, except that it was one of the places she had talked about with the married man, she was able, by speaking French, to find herself, by evening, a little apartment. It was up on the hill over the town; the sea was visible to the front, the mountains capped with a radio beacon behind. She had brought with her only one bag, stuffed with unwashed clothes; she washed them in the sink, and then draped them out over the balcony. She had no plans.

*

The next day she decided to take on the city. She tried it, at first, in very small, careful doses, riding on the bus down into the old town and wandering round in slow, considered sweeps of interest. She walked down the Ramblas, and looked inquisitively at the features of all the birds that, in their hundreds, were on sale there in little cages. She cut across through the big fish market, where ice dripped from the slabs. The stalls were brightly lit, with big, flaring lights, and the Catalan women who cut up and sold the fish stood high on plinths, shouting, performing like actresses in a theatre. The crowd jostled by, and Miss Bean walked tentatively in it. For the next few days she went back there, as if to see how much of the noise and the light and the people she could bear. When it became too much for her, she went outside into the street, where the smell of the drains struck through her head, and she was afraid for herself. But after two days the noise and smells stopped paining her; the parade of people ceased to be hostile, and seemed instead to take into itself as much of her as she could spare. She stopped thinking about the married man; and as for what she had done to his wife – and she realized that she had worried much about his wife – that now seemed quite remote. He was little; she was growing bigger. She wasn't quite right, but it felt as if only a small jump more were needed, and she would have her functioning self back again.

For three days she ate almost nothing, but then, feeling better, she sat down at an outside table of a café beside the cathedral, which she had also taken to visiting, and ordered some garlic soup. She thought about the dark place with the candles. The soup did not come. After a while, a Spaniard who had been sitting alone at another table crossed over to her, asking, in English, if she were an American. He was a man of young middle age, with bright black eyes in a pained-looking face; he walked with a faint limp. Miss Bean almost seemed to know that he was coming over to her; as soon as he moved from his table, she took her straw bag off the table in front of her, and put it down on the pavement beside her. 'No, English,' said Miss Bean. 'Ah,' said the Spaniard; he waved a hand at the opposite chair; he sat down in it, and whistled the waiter. He asked for a *cerveza*. 'Ask him to bring me my soup,' said Miss Bean. When the waiter had gone, the Spanish man lit a cigarette, and leaned forward, and said that he had heard that English girls were much more liberated than Spanish ones; he asked Miss Bean whether she considered it true. Miss Bean considered; she said she thought they were. It was odd, said the Spaniard, that the Spanish admired freedom so much, and yet the women were not free. Yet to the Spanish man, freedom and food were one. The waiter returned, carrying a round tray with the beer and the soup; he set it out on the table. After he had gone, the Spaniard leaned forward and offered to tell Miss Bean a confidence. 'Do,' said Miss Bean. 'I have slept with two English girls who have been on holiday at Sitges,' said the Spaniard. 'Did you?' said Miss Bean. From the pocket of his jacket, the

Spaniard took a wallet; from it he produced a small piece of paper. On this, he said, one girl, the nice girl, has put her address; can she tell him where this place is? The piece of paper had a name on it – Mary Braithwaite was the name – and an address, in Macclesfield, written in pencil in clumsy, bad capitals. Miss Bean stared at the paper. She examined the writing. She recalled she had been in Macclesfield once, four or five years ago; and she began to remember the place and describe it, very plainly, to the man. She said there were hills around, and chimneys in the valley; they made silk there. 'Silk,' cried the Spaniard, and expressed much interest, making Miss Bean explain things to him quite exactly; once, in an access of responsiveness, he reached across, under the table, and patted Miss Bean on the thigh.

They sat in the warm March weather; presently a shoeshine boy came along, and the Spaniard called him, in a rather imperious fashion, and put his foot on the block. While the boy knelt in front of him, he began asking Miss Bean about herself. At first she felt a little panic; the absurdity of her situation struck her, and for the first time she saw herself as planless; she had only a little money, an apartment to keep up, and no idea what to do next. But then she began talking about herself and to offer, tentatively, an identity; some of the things she said were true and some of them not. She said she was a graduate, from Manchester; that she had taught in France, which, briefly, she had; she said she had come to Barcelona to study languages and find a job. Especially, she said, she wanted to teach; did the man know how she might go about it? The man tipped the shoeshine boy; he solemnly considered the matter, and offered dismal conclusions. There were many permits needed before one could work in Spain; did she have the permits? It was not useful to teach French in Barcelona; people learned it too easily. As for teaching English, well, only the girls wanted to learn that; the men had to work to become engineers. The girls all went to the British Institute, on the Avendia Generalísimo Franco, and took the Cambridge Proficiency examination. There were many people who taught English in Barcelona. The Spaniard looked at her; she put her head down, and felt depressed. 'I am sorry I cannot help you,' he said, 'And now I must go.' 'Oh,' said Miss Bean. The Spaniard looked again at Miss Bean; he told her his name – it was Juan Rivera – and then suggested that they might meet again, that evening. He mentioned the name of a café near the harbour; he reached in his wallet again, took out a tiny slip of paper, and wrote down on it an address. 'You come there,' he said. Miss Bean watched him walk away, with his small limp; she thought about the little identity of herself he was walking away with. She called the waiter; he had paid for her soup. She got up, walked to the bus stop, and took a crowded bus back to her apartment.

When she got in, the room seemed very hot. She opened the shutters, and looked out of the window. Below, in the court-yard, two Catalan women, in black dresses and scarves, were beating and cleaning a carpet. It was very hard to tell their ages, because of their dress; it was possible that they were quite young. They were beating the carpet with a kind of furious acceptance, shouting and chattering with great energy and violence. Miss Bean watched them for a while; then she saw that she was letting mosquitoes into the room, so she closed the windows and sat down, in a chair. After a while, she went to the tiny bathroom, to take a shower. She let the lukewarm water pour over her, for perhaps five minutes, standing passively under its spray in the small tub. Then she dusted her thighs and underarms with talcum, and splashed some perfume, from a small bottle given to her by the married man in Chesterfield, onto her breasts. Then she lay aimlessly on the bed in her underwear, for perhaps another hour or so. Now the sun was down. It was nearly the time at which Juan had asked her to meet him. She was not sure that she had decided to go, but she found she had. She got up, and went down the stairs. It was much cooler outside. She took the bus down Balmes. Near the harbour, she got off the bus, and took a taxi, the only way she knew to find the café. Taxis were cheap, and she could show the driver the piece of paper. The taxi threaded between public buildings that looked stark and unfurnished; outside one of them, police jeeps were drawn up, in a long row. The town, now the sun was down, looked black, even menacing, bare of civility. The streets were busy with people walking in groups; beside a public monument in a *plaza* Miss Bean saw three dogs engaged in a copulation. The taxi driver was shouting through the window, telling people to clear his way in the narrow street; finally he stopped before a very little café, and Miss Bean got out.

Juan was inside the café, as he said he would be; he sat at a cloth-covered table, on a bench seat. Beside him on the seat there was a suitcase. He rose as she came in, smiled faintly, and handed her the menu as she sat down. 'Here is the card,' he said, 'But I have already chosen for you.' The café was quite crowded, but the waitress came quickly, and began to set the meal out for them. There was much noise and the food came, plate after plate, one after another; very good food, fish soup, a plate of seafood, a meat course at the heart of which was a steak. Miss Bean, who had hardly eaten for so long, felt a sudden restoration of the appetite; she ate voraciously through the courses, taking the veal steak, fresh strawberries, cheese. While she ate, Juan talked, in an elegant fashion with many politenesses; he talked about his childhood, about the tourist attractions of the region, the pleasures of the sea. At first Miss Bean replied, with careful responses; but after a while the rhythm of the conversation seemed to operate without her, and she concentrated on the food, turning it into a pleasure. A young man walked from table to table, playing an accordion; he stopped beside them, asked Juan a question, and then played a song which Miss Bean vaguely recognized as the British entry for the Eurovision song contest. He smiled; Juan, not ceasing in his long conversation, leaned across to him, and slipped some coins into the pocket of his jacket. 'That was nice,' said Miss Bean, 'Thank you.' 'He has played it for you,' said Juan, 'I ask him.' 'Yes,' said Miss Bean. 'You are sad,' said Juan. 'No,' said

Miss Bean. 'Oh, I think so,' said Juan. 'No,' said Miss Bean. 'It is a good evening,' said Juan. 'Oh, yes,' said Miss Bean, looking down at their empty plates, thinking, for some reason, about her empty apartment.

The waitress came to their table, in a black dress and white pinafore, with, Miss Bean saw, white gloves; Miss Bean watched the gloves while Juan said amusing things to the girl, very dark, very sparkling. When the waitress had gone, Juan leaned forward and looked at Miss Bean. He said, 'Now, you want to make some love?' 'Do I?' said Miss Bean, feeling in her shoulder bag, and taking out a packet of cigarettes and a lighter. 'It was a good meal?' asked Juan. 'Great,' said Miss Bean. 'Good,' said Juan, 'and you like me?' 'I think so,' said Miss Bean. 'That's good,' said Juan. 'Yes,' said Miss Bean, lighting her cigarette. 'We go?' said Juan. 'We ought to let the meal go down first,' said Miss Bean. 'Oh, waiting is so hard,' said Juan. 'All right, then,' said Miss Bean, 'I have an apartment.' Juan's eyes widened, and his lips pouted. 'No,' he said, 'We cannot go there. The night watchman will see us. You will lose your reputation. I cannot do that.' 'Where did you have in mind?' asked Miss Bean. Juan patted the suitcase beside him. 'We go to an hotel,' he said. 'Yes,' said Miss Bean. Juan picked up the suitcase; he smiled again at the waitress; he led Miss Bean out of the café. Outside it had begun to rain; people walked by in the street with newspapers over their heads. 'Wait here,' said Juan, 'I bring a taxi.' Miss Bean stood in the rain, beside the suitcase, half inside a doorway; the minutes passed, and people began to stare at her, to speak to her. Miss Bean began to feel anxiety spinning inside her again; but just then a black taxi came slowly along the street, and Juan was looking out of it, his head stuck out of the window. The taxi stopped; Miss Bean had to carry the suitcase to it herself. It was light and clearly entirely empty, though, when the taxi stopped in a narrow street, at a small hotel, Juan carried it into the lobby as if it were loaded with bricks.

In the lobby, Juan made Miss Bean sit on a bench seat near

a fern; she stared at posters, advertising a circus, while he went to the desk. He was there for a while; there was apparently something about identity papers, but the girl seemed to know Juan, and Miss Bean saw him pass her a banknote. The food she had eaten seemed heavy in her stomach; the rain splashed heavily in the street outside the doors. A bellboy walked towards her, to pick up the suitcase; but Juan, arriving first, picked it up and said something. The bellboy looked at Miss Bean; he said nothing; he led them up the stairs. which were uncarpeted, to a small room. He left the key; he took his tip. Miss Bean sat in an old chair and looked at the room; it was high and dark. Juan sat on the bed and looked at her. 'It is not the best, but it is enough, I think,' said Juan, 'There is a bed.' 'Who's fussy?' asked Miss Bean, sliding her shoulder bag off her shoulder, and getting up. As she undressed, she could smell the perfume she had splashed on her breasts. Juan stood and watched her. 'You are lovely,' he said. 'Not very,' said Miss Bean. 'Lie down,' said Juan. 'All right,' said Miss Bean. Lying on the bed, Miss Bean watched Juan undress; she saw him come towards her, she felt his mouth come against her. The window was open, and she could hear the rain outside. 'Lovely,' said Juan. Miss Bean's sensations, as they made love, were all passive ones, as if taking a lesson in a culture. Juan began to touch and kiss her with delicacy, almost in a formalized style at first. But then, perhaps because she was passive, he began to knead and pinch her. She looked at his eyes, looking at her body; she said, 'Too rough.' 'English women are so liberated,' said Juan. 'Don't believe all you hear,' said Miss Bean. 'I know,' said Juan, 'Bend like this.' 'All right,' said Miss Bean.

After it was over, it seemed very cool in the room, and Miss Bean began to shiver. She felt Juan warm against her and wondered why she was cold. Then she was asleep; but in the middle of the night she woke, and there were griping pains in her stomach. She pulled the sheet off the bed to wrap round her, and groped her way along the black hotel corridor, unable to find any switches, until she rediscovered the lavatory the

114

bellboy had pointed out. After a moment, she vomited all the meal she had eaten into the dark round of the bowl. She hung over the mess for a while, with tears in her eyes, until at last she felt better. Back in the room, Juan was awake; he guided her through the dark to the bed, and then, when she lay down, he began to touch her again. His hand came between her legs. She wanted to speak, but somehow language seemed powerless; how could you explain to a Spaniard that you were having a nervous breakdown? So she let his hands move, and hurt, and tried to respond with sensations, found herself reaching for all her adequacies, tried all she could to matter. The vomit was still a curdling taste in her mouth; but she moved, and groaned, and ran her hands about him. When she woke in the morning, it was because Juan was shaking her arm, and saying, 'Now it is time to go.' He was already dressed, a small neat person, with pained eyes. She smiled at him, and put her clothes on quickly. He stood politely, not touching her; she wondered if he would. When she had tidied her hair she turned, and he was sitting at the tired dressing-table, with a piece of paper and a pen in front of him. 'Here, please,' he said, 'write down your name and address for me.' 'My apartment?' asked Miss Bean. 'No,' said Juan, 'your address in England.' Miss Bean took the little ballpoint pen, and wrote the address on the paper. Then something struck her and she said, 'When am I going to see you again?' 'Ah,' said Juan, spreading his hands wide, 'I am very busy. I have many businesses.' 'Do you?' said Miss Bean.

He picked up the suitcase. 'I disappointed you,' said Miss Bean, 'I'm not very well.' 'No, you are very well, it was a great pleasure,' said Juan. 'See me again,' said Miss Bean, 'You said you were free.' 'I am free, and not free,' said Juan, 'English women are very liberated, but they do not know how to behave. I am a married man. I have sisters. If you see me on the street, you must not speak to me.' 'I see,' said Miss Bean. Juan opened the bedroom door for her. Going down the gloomy stairs, carrying his suitcase, he said, 'Walk from this hotel and find a taxi. I think you do not have much money, so I will pay this room.' 'Well, goodbye then,' said Miss Bean. 'At your apartment it is better to give the night watchman some *pesetas*,' said Juan, 'so he will not tell people you are a whore.' Miss Bean went quickly out through the hotel lobby. The same bellboy, the same girl at the desk, were watching her; she heard Juan's limping footsteps behind her stop, heard him put down the suitcase, and then say something as he moved towards the desk. She heard the girl at the desk laugh. In the street, Miss Bean felt very sick again; but she hurried, almost ran, until she reached the corner. She found herself on one of the main avenues, so she walked along it until she came to a café. The café reminded her that she was ravenously hungry; she sat down and ordered breakfast. One of her breasts hurt where Juan had pinched her. She ate the breakfast with pleasure. While she was eating it, a Spanish boy of about eighteen, in good clothes, got up from another table, and stopped by hers, and spoke to her; she did not look up. After she had finished eating she did not feel like going back to her apartment, and so she walked along the shopping streets, and went into some of the stores. The crowds did not disturb her. In one shop she saw some toy rabbits, made of real fur. For some reason they reminded her of the four children of the married man in Chesterfield, whom she had never seen; for some reason, perhaps because she had never seen them, she bought them one each, spending much of her money, and some paper to mail them home in. Then she walked all day, and went back to her apartment in the evening.

Two days later, Miss Bean was walking again by the cathedral, past the Roman ruins to one side of it. As she left, she could see the café where she had met Juan, and there she saw him again, sitting outside at one of the tables, talking to a girl. The girl was wearing a miniskirt and had on a denim cap; she was very pretty, and it was not hard to guess that she was English. Juan had a piece of paper in his hand, and was showing it to her, and this reminded Miss Bean of the piece of paper

116

on which she had written her address, as she sat at the dressing table in the hotel bedroom. Miss Bean thought how, if she was the English girl, she would describe Chesterfield, what one would say about it. Perhaps one would mention the spire, and the moors around. She wondered why she had put her real name, her real address, and what it looked like, to a stranger, on a piece of paper. Then Miss Bean turned and walked through to the Via Layetana, where she got a taxi. She told the taxi driver to take her to a BEA office, and there she bought a ticket to London. Then she returned to the taxi, and had the driver take her back to her apartment up on the hill. She found the owner and told him she was leaving; to her surprise, she discovered that she could say this in Spanish. She had always been good at languages. She went upstairs to her apartment and put most of her things in her case. Out of the window she could see the Catalan women, beating a carpet, free and not free. She went to bed early that night, and the next morning she took the bus out to the airport, and took the Trident flight to Heathrow.

When she got back to Birmingham, in the evening, she took the bus to Moseley and went to the flat she had shared with the five other girls. Another girl had come in, and taken her place, but she slept on the sofa in the communal living room, and in the morning made herself bacon and eggs for breakfast. Then she went into the University, and talked to the Head of the Department, asking him to let her resume her course. She told him that she had been away for a few days, because she had had a nervous breakdown, but it was over, and she was able to work again. He was sceptical, but Miss Bean was very positive and convincing, and during the day he made arrangements for her to be admitted to the course. A week later she went to a student party, and got drunk, and took her clothes off, standing on a table. Later on, a boy studying Electrical Engineering took her to his car, and made love to her in the car park. He wanted to see her again the following evening; Miss Bean refused. When she woke the next morning, on the sofa in the flat, she knew for sure that she was all right again. She sat down at the table and wrote a very good essay on Racine; and when, a few days later, her tutor handed it back to her, she found she had got quite the best mark she had ever had for it.

Miniature Golf

THE BELLAMYS were really very busy people, so that the only time they ever seemed to get together as a family was when they went abroad together, as they always did, for their summer holidays. He had a job, and she had a job; he worked in the county planning office, she in social work. He had a car, and she had a car; going on holiday, they always took his car, because it was bigger, and had a roofrack, and there were three of them, with quite of lot of luggage. What they did was to drive down to Southampton on the first day, and stay the night in a hotel, which Petra, in her efficient way, had booked months before; after all, everyone did the same thing in the summer. Then, after they had had breakfast, they would drive down to the docks, and join the long car queue, staring through the glass at all the other GB families, with their caravans or tents and their cars filled with petrol at the pumps on the docks, because in France it was, after all, more expensive.

This year the ship is a British one, and has the worn, overused air of having done too many of these cross-channel voyages too fast. Newspapers from previous trips litter all the passageways; the service at lunch is appalling, and for some reason, quite ridiculous on a voyage to France, the only red wine available is Argentinian; there are queues in all the public rooms, as people wait to change money, book return passages, buy duty-free cigarettes and perfume, rent tents. An air of irritability prevails, and it is quite a relief when the ship enters the harbour at Cherbourg and the passengers are called, through the loudspeakers, down to their cars.

The Bellamys go down to the car-deck, and get into the Maxi, looking through the glass at all the other families, waiting to start the ignition and get into France. The bows of the ship slowly rise. Joanna sits in the back, with her radio on, trying to get a French station, but there is much interference; Petra sits in the passenger seat, with the RAC route-finder she always remembers to send for on her knees, open at the street map of Cherbourg. The cars start moving off the ferry.

'Drive on the right,' says Petra. 'I was going to,' says John. They coast up to the passport barrier, where they are briefly checked; then they follow the line of British cars in convoy to the centre of town. Petra has a well-planned route, and when they are out of Cherbourg, and driving down the peninsula, she makes him turn off, to the right; it lets them drive down by the coast, and they lose most of the other British cars that way. Petra has her Michelin, and she has written to various Syndicats d'Initiative on the way; it is, as always with her, a very well-planned holiday. The sea splashes violently against the rocks near the road.

Petra talks to Joanna, who is uneasy about the holiday, being at the age when being with parents is as much an irritant as a pleasure. 'Why do we always do the same old things?' asks Joanna. 'Next year you can plan it,' says Petra. Listening to the faintly irritable chatter, John, excused by driving, wonders about holidays, and why we have them, and what we hope to learn. They repeat themselves; it is as if a conversation, dropped a year ago, is being exactly resumed.

They stop the night, as is planned, at Avranches, where they know a very good hotel, only marred by the number of British who stay there and try out their French on the staff, who speak English perfectly well. In the morning, they go on, round into Brittany, to Mont St Michel. They went to Mont St Michel last year, but it is a pity just to drive by it; as Petra says, it's one of those places that stimulate the imagination. They park the car off the causeway, in the official place, next to another British car. Joanna carries the camera, Petra the guidebook, open, and they walk in through the walls and up the steep little streets, between the tourist shops, one after another, filled with pottery and beach-toys and souvenirs. They do not, of course, buy anything. The crowds jostle; they climb up and up. At the top, they look down on the quicksands, glinting in the sun at low tide. Joanna sits on the wall, dangerously, one haunch over the edge; it is a long drop. 'Did you take a diarrhoea tablet?' asks Petra. Joanna says: 'I'm sick and tired of sights. Why do we always do the same things?'

Coming up the hill towards them are a party of spastic children, managed by two nuns. They struggle over the cobbles, through the thick crowds, some with crutches, splayed out, their blown out faces laughing. It is like some strange mortification. 'It's silly to bring them here,' says Petra. 'Have you finished?' asks Joanna, 'I'd like to go to the beach and swim.' 'I don't know,' says Petra, 'Why does one do it?' 'Do what?' asks Joanna. 'Come on holiday,' says Petra, 'If no one really enjoys it.' 'I'd enjoy it if you'd let me,' says Joanna. So they go back to the car, drive to Dinard, and find the beach. Joanna changes in the car, and runs into the water in her two-piece swimsuit, looking very white and thin. Afterwards they oil themselves and sun. Joanna lies tummy-down on the sand, and looks enviously toward a beach-club, where some teenagers are playing volley-ball. 'I think we ought to stay here,' she says. 'I think we'd better get on,' says Petra. 'After all, we want to get down there before the Partridges.' The Partridges are old friends; they met them on holiday last year too.

John lies and stares along the beach at a French family, father, two teenage daughters, a younger son; they are playing *boule* on the sand. The father is fat, moustached, patriarchal, in bikini-style shorts that fit grotesquely just under the bottom curve of his belly. Authoritative, he gives orders to his children about how to play the game. There is a shout; someone has won; the father goes over to his older daughter, who has long dark hair. He slips his hand under the lower part of her bikini, along the haunch, and squeezes the buttock. The girl looks up at him and smiles. Petra's hand comes down on John's back; he twists his eyes to look at her. 'I think we ought to be getting on,' she says.

They have lunch in Dinard from a fixed price menu, which seems much more expensive this year; then Petra, looking at her maps and her book, says that they should drive southwards across the peninsula to the southern coast, where the sun will be warmer. They drive across to Vannes, and then to Guerande, and the salt-flats near the sea, and come to La Baule. It is a longer drive than John has remembered, and he feels irritated, handling the car a little clumsily, feeling outside the family conversation, which still has a note of resentment. Joanna wants boys, but she does not know how to get them; John remembers himself at this age, the sense of total solitude, and the desire for others. It is hotter in La Baule. The wind is blowing hard, the tide is up, the waves high; a French couple trying to launch a catamaran keep being thrown back on to the shore again. Under the concrete wall, a party of nuns sits. Their habits are streaming and blowing like flags in the wind, and they laugh uproariously at the grotesque shapes they make.

'Aren't there good shops here?' asks Joanna, who has some money to spend. They go into the town, which is expensive, and they find a shop where Joanna is able to buy a cheap necklace she likes. Along the street is a very good dress shop, to which Joanna draws attention. Petra looks, and checks it in her book. It is mentioned there, so she decides to go in. Joanna picks out a black dress that is slit down between the breasts. 'It's not your sort of dress,' she says. Petra immediately tries it on. She stands in the dress in the entrance to the fitting room. 'Dare I?' she asks. 'We are on holiday,' says John. 'I think I might,' says Petra, and looks at the price-tag; it is very expensive. 'You could get it for half that in England,' says Joanna. 'Oh, you couldn't get it in England,' says Petra. 'Go on, have it,' says John. 'We are on holiday.'

After the dress, they feel very conscious of money, being, as Petra says, the poor relations of Europe. So Petra checks the prices of hotels in the book, and finds them impossibly high; they decide to drive on to Pornichet, just along the coast. In the car, she looks through the books, and picks out an hotel, reasonable, well reputed. It is, when they get there, as she says: a pleasant place. They take the rooms, and John goes out to carry in the cases from the car. When he gets up to the room, Petra is standing there, in her pants, with the dress laid out on the bed. He looks at her from behind, at her bare shoulders, the part-bulge of her breast, the faint blueness of the little cave behind her knees, the flat line of her foot on the floor, the sag of her pants. She looks unformed, unshapen; he moves away from her, to the window. He thinks of the spastic children coming up the cobbled hill. Petra takes the dress off the bed and lays it in a careful ring on the floor. She steps inside the ring and draws the dress up her. She shapes it to herself at the bodice. 'Zip it up for me,' she says.

He goes across to her, from the window, and pulls up the zip; it catches her hair. She shakes her hair loose and goes to the mirror, examining the dress and herself. She pulls it about a little more, as if to give her body its distinctness. Her breasts jut. She is formed again. She says: 'Is it nice? Does it suit me?' John looks and says: 'I think so.' She turns and looks at him. 'You're not very interested,' she says. 'I do like it,' says John. 'I'll keep it on for dinner,' she says. In the dining room, a little later, they find Joanna already there. 'I think French fashions are behind the English ones,' she says when she sees the dress. 'You're both making me feel very good,' says Petra. They order the middle price menu, but it is rather a poor meal; the stew is coarse, and the wine a disappointment. Afterwards they walk down to look at the sea, but the wind is still high, and the sand stings their faces. They go back again to the hotel, and sit in the bar, drinking brandy.

'I'm quite tired,' says Petra after a while, 'I'm going to bed, don't be long.' John and Joanna stay talking; she is unhappy, she feels unattended to. 'I can't wait to be grown up,' she says. They talk for a good while, and then they go up to their bedrooms. In the room, the tiny washbasin light has been left on for him. The dress lies neatly on a chair. Petra is in bed, asleep, lying with her mouth open, her face tired. Beside the bed is the guidebook. Of course she is tired; they are both very busy people. He gets into bed and she does not stir. He lies on his side, his face away from her.

In the morning they get into the car again and drive to St Nazaire, to take the ferry across the mouth of the Loire to Mindin. On the ferry, beside their car, is a truck and trailer, labelled 'Les Chiens Volants'. 'Ses singes, ses colombes, ses pouces', says a bright poster. Once off the ferry, they find themselves in the last of Brittany, where it begins to turn into La Vendée. It is a region of small coast towns and fishing villages, economically fitted into the line of the landscape and seascape, which turn into simple resorts in the summer; the tourists come mostly from the French cities and the prices are really much lower, They come into piney country, and reach the small coastal town they are making for. They stayed here last year, and Petra has months ago, with her usual efficiency, booked pension arrangements for them. The proprietor recognises them, or affects to, when they arrive.

In the afternoon, after a slow pleasant lunch, they go down to the beach and lie there in the sun. Petra sits upright in her swimsuit, and talks to Joanna. John lies on his stomach and looks out toward the sea. This is an occupational coast, with a fishing port and a fish market. The sun has left red circles in his retina. Out on the sands, between the high and low water marks, stands a row of ramshackle wooden cabins, raised up on stilts which keep them above the level of the high tide. The stilts are covered in barnacles now the tide is out.

From the cabins, jutting out on all four sides, are long wooden poles with nets on. Petra has already looked them up in the book; they are called *pêcheries*. Something is happening; a group of men is walking out, their boots splashing in the wet sand and mud of the foreshore. They are carrying loaves of bread, bottles of wine, rugs, lanterns and nets. Three men go to one cabin, three to another, to stay there till the tide comes in and goes out again. 'I want to join the beach club,' says Joanna. 'Come on, I'll take you,' says Petra. 'Give me some money, I can do it myself,' says Joanna.

The next day the Partridges arrive. They have their own caravan, so they go to the campsite in the pines. The Bellamys are on the beach again when they arrive; Dennis and Pat and the two young children. Joanna takes the children to the Club Mickey, which has climbing frames and organised games run by youthful disciplinarians. The children can be left; they all gather up their things, and go and sit at the tables on the pavement outside the hotel. They talk about foreign drinks – their flavours, their prices, their alcoholic content. They remember a restaurant they all went to last year, somewhere just along the coast. They decide to go there for dinner. Joanna and the children join them, and she has to be persuaded to babysit, but finally it is settled; it was what they had done last year. 'I'm a year older than last year,' says Joanna, 'I think you might take me.' 'It's an adult treat,' says Petra.

So, a little later, the children are put to bed in the caravan and Joanna is left at the other end, under a lamp, with a paperback Kurt Vonnegut. Dennis has had the foresight to paint his headlights yellow, so they are going, the four of them, Petra and John, Dennis and Pat, in the Partridges' car.

The Café Breton is a seafood restaurant and is just as good as they remember it. They have an excellent meal, pleasant wine; it is not expensive. They drink their coffee, and then Dennis remembers something; they ought, as last year, to go and play miniature golf on the course that adjoins the restaurant. There is a hut, where you rent clubs and golfballs, and are given a scorecard. The course is lit by electric lights in shiny silver shades. The air is still warm, and you can see the lighthouse flashing in the dusk along the bay.

They split into pairs, Petra and Dennis, John and Pat. Each hole is a concrete track, with obstacles between the tee and the hole. The first one consists of a narrow house with a narrow doorway; the point is to get the ball through the house and into the hole on the other side. Petra plays first; but she is used to a larger kind of golf than this, though she doesn't, of course, have time to play much, and she hits the ball very much too hard. It overshoots both house and hole, and disappears into coarse grass. She laughs; 'Dans la nature,' shout two French boys, waiting to play. Dennis Partridge goes for the ball: Petra takes his and plays again. She manages better this time, and finally plays the hole in four. But Dennis beats her by doing it in three; it says on the scorecard that this is par.

They move on, and Pat Partridge and John play. Pat is a neat, well-made person; she does everything very precisely, and has none of that touch of angular clumsiness there is in Petra. She swings, the ball rolls down the track, rests neatly just through the house, waiting for her; she holes in two. John has much more trouble. His shots keep hitting against the house wall, so that the ball rebounds back to him again. The French boys, waiting, show impatience. Finally one of them comes over and shows John something on the scorecard. It is confusing; John can't translate; but Pat looks and explains. After three failed shots, you can take a penalty point and lift your ball to the far side of the obstacle. Even then, it takes him two more shots to hole the ball.

By the time they have done, the other two have already moved far on. New players have somehow come in between them. The course, with its wandering sequences and man-made hills, gives an artificial sense of distance. It is also crowded, so that it takes them a time to see, under the shiny lights broken by dark patches, where Petra and Dennis are. They are several holes on. Petra has taken off her woollen sweater, and hung it round her waist. She has brought the sweater for the evening chill; under it she is wearing the black dress. Her body looks angular and forceful, almost too powerful for what she is doing. Her hands are clenched on the club, her hair is blown. She hits the ball, somewhat clumsily; her breasts twist up as she moves.

She appears to be laughing. Pat and John attend to their own game. 'I wish I was better,' he says, 'I'm holding you up.'

'It's so easy, though, look,' says Pat, and she swings. The ball moves exactly again, the movement being light; gently it moves down the course, through the obstacle, nearly to the hole. When she has done, John tries, but he is again clumsy and slow. And so it is all the way round the course. By the time the two of them have finished the eighteen holes, it is completely dark. The others are not in sight. They hand in their clubs at the hut, and add up the scorecard. 'You've won,' says John, hardly bothering. 'I beat you,' says Pat, 'but what about them?' They walk back towards the restaurant. 'It's funny how involved you get in games,' says Pat, 'Even miniature ones.'

Inside the restaurant, they look for Petra and Dennis, but there is no sign of them. 'We'll wait in the bar and you can buy me a drink,' says Pat. 'I could look and see if the car's gone,' says John. 'Come on, buy me a Pernod,' says Pat. They go into the bar and sit by the window. In the clear, southern weather, you can see the paced bright flashes of the lighthouse; they illuminate the beach and the sea. The waiter comes, and John orders two Pernods. 'It's a very nice place,' says Pat, 'How did we find it?' 'Petra looked it up in her book,' says John. 'Petra's very good with her book,' says Pat. Out on the water there are flickering lights; they probably come from the wooden fishing towers. 'How do you get on these days, you two?' asks Pat. 'We're both very busy,' says John, 'We don't have a lot of time to notice. 'That's nice.' says Pat. 'What do you think they're doing?'

'I expect they're doing what they did last year,' says John. 'What about you?' asks Pat, 'Do you want to do what you did last year?' 'Actually, I'd really prefer not, thank you,' says John. 'I see,' says Pat; there is a faint tint of red over each of her cheekbones. 'Petra says I suffer from withdrawal symptoms,' says John. Pat looks at him, sad about the eyes: 'Why do people make themselves so solitary to each other,' she says. 'Do they?'

says John. 'Don't they?' says Pat. The waiter comes with their drinks on a tray, and leaves the slips in a saucer on the table. They drink the drinks and, perhaps half an hour later, perhaps a little more, Petra and Dennis come into the restaurant. Petra wears her sweater over the black dress. 'We didn't think you'd have managed to finish yet,' says Dennis, 'It's not your game, is it?' 'We just went and looked at the lighthouse,' says Petra. 'What were your scores?' asks Pat. They compare scorecards and it emerges that Petra has won, by one stroke. 'I think the loser ought to buy the winner a drink,' says Dennis.

'Look, what about Joanna?' asks Petra, 'I don't think we ought to leave her any longer.' So John pays the drink-slips, and they go out to the car. Dennis and Pat get in the front seats, and Petra and John in the back. There is a beachball between them. Nobody says very much. They park the car by the caravan, and Dennis goes and opens the caravan door. He stops in the entrance, and puts a finger on his lips. When they look, they see Joanna is asleep, over the Vonnegut, her head on the small table, her thumb in her mouth, under the lamp. She is hard to wake, and can hardly stand between them as they take her to Dennis's car. As soon as they get in, her head falls on John's shoulder, and she is asleep again. 'I'll undress her and put her to bed,' says Petra, when they get back to the hotel. John and Dennis sit on the empty unlit terrace for a minute, but there is no sign of service. 'It looks as though that's it for tonight,' says Dennis, 'I'd better get back. See you tomorrow. Nice to be together again.'

John watches the car drive off. The town gets very quiet in the evenings. He steps off the terrace and walks across the street. He takes the path down to the beach. The beach is very dark, and it is hard to see the lie of the sand, so he stumbles. But from time to time the lighthouse flashes, and he can see out to the glint of the sea, and the wet shine of sandbank. On the banks are visible the vague, misshapen forms of the fishing towers. Lights are flickering inside them. It is pleasant to imagine what is happening in those cabins. The men will be eating, drinking and fishing, lowering the big nets off the poles every so often, then drawing them up and pulling the catch into the cabin with their hand-nets. He starts to walk towards the cabins. He is into the sea. The moving water comes up to his knees, to his thighs. His suit fills with water. He turns and walks back on to the sand again, and then, in his wet suit, up the beach, back toward the hotel room where, he thinks, Petra will be lying in bed, on one elbow, looking things up in her book.

Composition

I

WE ARE, for the purposes of this story, in the courthouse square of a very small Middle Western town. It is a hot, sunny afternoon in the September of an old, tumultuous year, 1971. In the centre of the square stands the courthouse itself, a Victorian building of no distinction, with defensive canon at every corner. In front of the courthouse stands a statue, of a soldier, his rifle in a negative position, a Henry Fleming who has been perpetuated as he ducks out of the Civil War. On the copper roof of the building, gone green, a row of pigeons stands, depositing in some vague evolutionary gesture, quantities of new guano on top of the old guano. From a corner of the square there enters the one Greyhound bus of the day, which comes down from the state capital, two hundred miles to the north, where they keep all the money and the records of accurate time. The bus has aluminium sides, green glareproof windows, and a lavatory; it circles the square, slows, and stops at the depot, a telephone booth outside Lee's Diner. The driver, J. L. Gruner, safe, reliable, courteous, levers opens the door; steps unfold; down the steps there descends, into the literal level of reality, in a brown suit, carrying a mackintosh on one arm, his hair long, his face lightly bearded, hot, but in good order, a person, a young English person named William Honeywell. His feet touch the board sidewalk, crisp with pigeon dung. He does not look around, or move far. Instead he stands close to the aluminium flank of the bus, which coughs diesel fumes at him, for the engine is still running, as J. L. Gruner gets down and unlocks the flaps under which this William's luggage is concealed. J. L. Gruner has been William's guide and conductor for most of the day, virtually ever since that early morning hour when William arrived, on the Boeing 727, after a transatlantic and then a transcontinental flight, in what pleases to call itself America. It is J. L. Gruner who took William's ticket as he stood in the bleak bus station, amid the lockers and the bums, in the state capital, two hundred miles to the north; it is J. L. Gruner who, his face reassuringly reflected in the driving mirror, has driven him for four hours over rough concrete highways that flipped rhythmically under the tyres, unravelled straight ahead into the haze, flashing him past fields containing withered cornstalks and rooting hogs, past sorghum mills and Burmah shave signs, past the Wishy Washy and the Dreme-Ez Motel, to deposit him on this wooden sidewalk, here. 'Okay, pal, which is it?' asks J. L. Gruner. William points out his big Antler suitcase, his little boxed typewriter, with their new airline labels; Gruner puts them out onto the sidewalk. 'Thank you,' says William. 'Or righty,' says Gruner, then he climbs back into the bus and, from the operator's seat, clangs shut the big aluminium, or rather aluminum, for we are there not here, door. The diesel engine whirs; the bus moves, circles the square again, finds an exit, and takes off into the great American steppeland.

William stands, beside his luggage, on the pigeon dung, in the dust, in his brown suit, holding his mackintosh. He is there, here. This is his beginning. He sniffs the smell, tastes the air, of the town. It has a faded, dusty note, as if generations of farmhands have shaken out their coveralls in the little square. Around it are two-storey buildings in wood and brick. There is a J. C. Penney, a Woolworth, a Floresheim Shoe, a McDonald Hamburger, a gas station with a sign saying 'We really are very friendly' and no people, and seven parking meters. A big dog lopes down the gutter. A cat comes out of J. C. Penney. A person laughs somewhere in Lee's Diner. Somewhere out there Nixon is President. The marquee of the tiny movie house advertises *I Was a Teenage Embalmer*. The Pentagon Papers have appeared in the *New York Times*. A sign on the novelty store says 'Worms'. They are having a war in Vietnam. They are having a sale on hoes at J. C. Penney. William goes on standing; he is here, such as it is. Somewhere in this town, if it is the right town and not the wrong town, there is a state university; the university has many students and a library containing the papers of many famous writers, none of whom have ever lived here. At that university, if it is here, and not there, William will teach Freshman Composition, a course in existential awareness and the accurate use of the comma. But is it here? On the steps of the courthouse, in the sunlight, a row of elderly farmers in faded denim coveralls sits; they have been there all the time, watching William unblinkingly. William, one eye on his luggage left on the sidewalk, moves, crosses over to them. They inspect him as he comes: the suit, the mackintosh, the longish red hair. William stops before them; he says, to the oldest and so presumably the wisest, 'Excuse me, please.' 'What's that, boy?' asks the man, spitting into the dust. 'Do you know,' asks William, looking around, a mystification on his face, 'where I can find the university?' The man screws his eyes, thinks for a moment, spits again, and says: 'Didn't know it was lost, son.' His eyes glaze, cackles come from the others, and the courthouse pigeons drop dung around the outer edges of the encounter, plainspeaking America triumphing over fancy Europe.

William, standing there, knows himself. He is not a naïf. He has read widely in literature and profited emotionally from the experience. He has taken all the lesser drugs, has had two mistresses, and assisted one of them through a neurotic abortion. He has travelled as far as Turkey, has a good graduate student knowledge of structuralism; he has been hit by a policeman with a truncheon at a political demonstration in London, been in a sit-in, and written two pop songs. He has not been to America before, but has been Americanized, by cultural artefacts and universal modernization, and he knows it by image and by

137

instinct. He has read America in many books. He has a part-written thesis in his luggage, on the disjunctive city in contemporary American fiction, and he has liberarian intentions. He has even come here hoping to find a little bit more of himself, to extend his being beyond its present circumscriptions and circumference. He has existential expectations, based on self-knowledge and sex. But he knows he is resident in a very old story: only I myself am novel, he thinks, the experience is not. Nixon is President. There are the Pentagon Papers. The Vietnam war, against which he has protested, goes on. There are black ghettos, poverty programmes, corruptions and conspiracies; actuality is continually outdoing our talents. History is moving apace, and is everywhere; the simple literary redemptions are hard to sustain. He wants more, deserves more, than a replay of old fictions, a plain and simple reality. 'Great, thanks,' he says, and walks back across the street to his lonely baggage on the sidewalk. But what, he thinks, next?

'Hey,' shouts one of the other farmers, pointing down the street. About half a block down, in front of Sears Roebuck, there is a cab, with a sign on the side saying 'Schuler Taxi'; it was not there before. The driver sits inside and watches William unmovingly; he watches as he carries his heavy bag and his little case, the mackintosh over the shoulder, down the sidewalk. He watches, through the mirror, as William opens the rear door and lifts the luggage inside. 'Baggage goes in the trunk,' he says, when William is finished. 'In the boot?' asks William. 'In the trunk,' says the man. It is an ancient terminological game they are playing, thinks William, as he heaves out the bag and puts it in the binominal place, the rehearsal, a million times in, of a traditional, weary encounter; the lousy part is it also strains the back. 'Whar to?' asks the man, when William is back in the cab. William hands him the slip of paper that has been sent to him, back in England, stating his dormitory reservation, exhausted with dialogue. The man starts the cab, tours the square, strikes out into the hinterland. They pass the Astoria Motel, which advertises two for the price of one, and through a residential section where housewives sit on frame porches in mail-order sportswear. 'Whar ya frum, boy?' asks the man. Now there are stone houses with Greek letters over the doors, and young men lying outside them in Ford Mustangs, with their feet over the side. 'England,' says William. There are Victorian semi-churches, covered in red ivy, a large football stadium, a television mast. 'England, huh? Hoity toity,' says the man. There is a long low building outside which students in sweatshirts are throwing a frisbee in great arcs. 'Five dollars,' says the man, 'You'll like it here better.' 'Will I?' says William, finding currency. 'Good.' 'One time we had a mayor of Chicago punched your King George right in the snoot,' says the cabbie. 'You did?' asks William. 'That's history, that's an accurate fact,' says the man, staring incredulously at the quarter William has pressed into his palm as a tip, 'You can look it up in all them books you guys has got in that library.' 'I will,' says William, collecting up his luggage. A frisbee whizzes past his ear. 'Some of those fraternity boys,' say the cabbie, admiringly, 'they lay eight, ten girls a week. They get prizes for it.' 'Well earned, no doubt,' says William. 'Don't forget now,' says the cabbie, 'It's better here, so if you don't like it go back where you came from.'

'Ting,' says a voice, as William, carrying his bags, pushes open the door of the graduate dormitory and walks into the hall, 'Ting.' 'I've just arrived from England, fresh to teach Freshman Composition, and I have a room booked here,' says William to a small oriental student in a collegiate sweater, who sits in a small wooden armchair in a cubicle, reading Lemon and Reis, eds., *Russian Formalist Criticism: Four Essays*. 'Ting,' says the student, getting up and shaking his hand. There is a metal bunk bed, an armchair, a small desk, and a lamp on a snaky spiral support, which looks capable of wrapping itself around the arm as you write under its light (a minor symbol, a serpent for the American Eden), in the first-floor room this student leads him to. 'Fine, thanks,' says William. 'Ting,' says the student. William begins to unpack: his clothes, his medicines, his teaching notes, his small flute, his part-thesis, the leather toilet case given him, with tears at Heathrow, by the girl with the abortion. He sits on the bed. There is a knock at the door. 'Ting,' says the oriental student, 'I take you to where we eat.' But it is evening now: the sun has suddenly withdrawn, leaving a faint chill, and William has been awake for a ridiculous number of hours. He has culture-shock, jet-lag, a coffee hangover, the plasticized remnant of an airline meal knotted in his stomach. He says he will sleep. He finds a bathroom, with no doors on the stalls, and an Arab sitting on one of the bowls. He urinates, returns to his room, undresses, gets into the iron bed. There are a few brief, disorienting images in his head – of a girl in a caftan who sat across the aisle in the jet, of a man in the bus depot in the state capital who asked for a quarter and then, hearing his accent, raised it to fifty cents – such as travellers have to make them feel lonely; but they are purged by unconsciousness, and he is asleep, his red hair on an American pillow.

It is much later, in the middle of the American night, when he wakens to a curious noise. He gets up and, in Winceyette pyjamas, goes to the window. The landscape suddenly judders and explodes; the rural plain which stretches beyond the window is lit by a bright green glare. In it, white barns flash into existence, then expire. A torrential rain is falling. Blackness resumes. 'Cling, cling,' goes a noise. There is a strange hooting and a roaring. The noise, mobile, comes closer. On the right of the blank composition a slowly gyrating, long beam of light appears, its shifting angle casting itself first towards William, then away again. Another green flash lights up the fast-running sky; William realizes that this is abstract realism he is in, and he sees that the shrieking torch is his first American train. It grinds near; it says 'Cling, cling'; it passes hard by the dormitory. As it does so, a bolt snaps down and catches a power sub-station, mounted fecklessly on a pole across the street. It explodes with a flash and a roar. There is a scream, as of pleasure. In the flash, William has seen a human figure. On the grass below his window it stands, a fat naked girl, her legs wide apart, pushing up her loose large breasts to take onto them the impact of the rain. There is a knock at the door. 'Ting,' says a voice. 'Cling cling,' says the train. 'Who?' says William. 'You,' says a voice. 'What is it?' asks William. 'A visit,' says the voice. William goes and opens the door. The little oriental who met him stands there, in shortie pyjamas. 'Bill Ting, your counsellor,' he says. 'You must close wlindow. Water coming through floor into my loom downstair.' 'I'm sorry,' says William. 'Also, offplint of article for loo to lead. For English opinion. Source, *Victorian Studies*.' Another pleasured scream shrills from outside. 'Who wrote it?' asks William. 'Ting,' says Ting, 'On Charlotte Blontë.' 'Look, I'll read it tomorrow,' says William, putting the offplint on his desk, 'Goodnight.' He goes back to the window, to shut it. It is entirely black outside, too black to see the girl: the storm is subsiding. 'Okay, America,' says William to the dark world beyond the fly-screen, 'we'll let you know.'

William stands in a puddle and closes the window; but the truth is that, despite himself, he is at last impressed. He knows himself under the agency of divine comedians of a somewhat different stamp from those whose work he has always known, new gods with a fancier taste in apocalyptics, quite like those of the modern critics he reads. He is here. What will he do? He will teach freshmen composition, demonstrate the orderly economy of language, the complexities of *langue* and *parole*, cleanse the tools of speech and thought. He will teach wisdom, taste, cultural awareness. 'Ring,' goes the telephone. 'Ting,' says a voice down the wire. 'Rain still come in.' 'Leave me alone,' says William. He stands in the dark, thinking of the girl with the abortion, dark-haired, a little fat, someone he is not sure whether to remember or forget. It is an imperfect image: a photograph into which the light has been let. He stands in the puddle, he feels in a muddle. Somewhere below the typewriter clatters. He gets into bed, he puts down his head. The typewriter reaches the end of a line: 'Ping,' it says. He starts to weep, he goes to sleep.

II

'You seem to be a well set-up, morally earnest young man,' says Fardiman, 'The sort of person who takes literature seriously, and teaches it good. So why worry?' Outside the window, on the grass, blue jays screech offensively. A man with a leaf-collecting machine comes by under the trees, collecting a faint harvest from the first of the fall. Two dogs copulate over by the Business Building. It is a bright fall day; William can see all this from the screened wooden window of the office in Humanities Hall he shares with five other graduate assistants. He has a large desk by the window, a desk with inkstains in the drawers and a large, high-backed, swivel chair. William is grieving. He has been teaching now for just over a week, and has met all his classes, twice, in the Chemistry Building, his hands dangling loosely in the pedagogic sink, or absent-mindedly turning on the gas taps, as he stares outward at the massive ethnic mix of the faces before him. Overcoming timidity, if not terror, he has begun work; he has told them where his office is, writing a map on the board so they can all find him, and where the library is, and where they are; he has asked them to write for him the first theme on the official schedule, on the demanding topic of 'My Home Town'. Now these themes have come in, deposited in a pocket outside his office door; he is marking them now. Fardiman sits at the next desk, writing a report for the graduate seminar on Milton he is taking; he keeps a copy of the *Kama Sutra* on his desk and a jar of apple cake on the bookcase. William is chewing apple cake as he reads. 'I am,' says William, turning to Fardiman, 'I'm a devotee of Leavis, though I disapprove of his culturally right-wing position, and also his interpretation of *Women In Love*. I'm also into semiotics, and I'm somewhat influenced by Frank Kermode.' 'I was reading his *What's the Sense of an Ending?*' says Fardiman, 'It stirred me in the gut. It gives me faith in my own clerkly scepticism. Now *that's* what you could use some of, right now.' 'I've read and digested Roland Barthes and the *Tel Quel* school,' says William, 'I'm into Adorno and Horkheimer and revisionist Marxist aesthetics. I'm interested in alternative education. I've got a part to play. But, Fardiman, what's it all got to do with essays about "My Home Town"?' 'It's all phenomenological discourse,' says Fardiman, 'Writing degree about twenty below. It has a beginning, a middle and an end, not usually in that order, but this it shares with most modern literature. It adds up to the cumulative fund of words in the universe; and, William, we want those words *right*.' William groans; he pushes the theme he has been reading across onto Fardiman's desk, which, in the cramped space, is up against his own. The theme begins: 'The people which lives in my home town is good folks, bad folks, rich folks, poor folks, white and some black, go to church and not go to church, and many other things.'

Fardiman puts down his apple cake and, picking up a red pen, he looks at the theme. While he reads, William swivels his chair and stares again through the screened window. Blue jays screech. The leaf-collector with the leaf-collector collects the leaves. The dogs are separate and distinct. Along the pathway between Humanities and Business, so ironically juxtaposed, as if by some cynically literary architect, a procession begins. The bells have rung in the classrooms and the students pour along the paths, in bright clothes, the girls making cradles of their arms to carry their textbooks and notecases in. Some of the students, a distinctive group, the girls without bras, the men with long hair and Afros, go by with anti-war placards; there is a political demonstration that day. William has a sense of his pointless little face staring through the dark grilled screens at what they are doing. But he is here to read what they have written, which seems to bear no resemblance to what they are doing, to have no connection with these minds and bodies. 'It's not a great start,' says Fardiman, putting down the theme, 'But how would you have started it?' 'It's not *my* home town,' says William, 'There are all kinds of ways to start a piece about a town, if you want to start one.' 'Talk to him,' says Fardiman,

'Try to get him to do it more personally. But there's real potential here.' 'There is?' asks William, staring at Fardiman. 'Sure there is. This kid is a comma artist. I know it doesn't sound much, with the world the way it is, and *Tel Quel* the way it is, but those are real good commas.' William looks at Fardiman, who has marched on the Pentagon, and reads Illich, and will refuse to be drafted; and he sees no light. 'Don't be anxious,' says Fardiman, 'It's your task to take these self-satisfied, supersensual oafs and lead them, through the study of sentences, into becoming mature, questioning, critical, politically alert individuals like ourselves.' 'With better hang-ups,' says William. 'Right,' says Fardiman. 'Alternatively, I guess, you could move, yourself, in the other direction, and have fun.'

William looks out of the window. The trees on campus start to turn brown, orange, and maroon, in a brilliant fall display. The air grows colder. The leaf-collector collects many a leaf. William puts on thicker clothes, and goes out to the few student bars that serve the specially diluted beer that will protect them. He goes to the McDonald Hamburger stand, and to graduate student parties to smoke pot, and to political meetings. He writes letters home to the girl with the abortion, and washes his clothes in the laundry down in the basement of the graduate dormitory, shown the way by Ting. He eats Fardiman's apple cake and grades many themes. He stands behind his desk in the Chemistry Building, three days a week, and tells his students about Carnaby Street and the Portobello Road. He goes to the Teaching Round Table, where all the graduate assistants sit around a square table and discuss their problems, about grading themes, about flunking students who might be drafted, about why are we here, about the falling jobs market. Sensing an over-devotion to diurnal reality among his students, even the politically active ones, he tries to find his way to truth by perplexing them with complexity of fictions, reading them Nabokov, Coover, Barthelme, asking why writers write like that. 'Finks,' says one student, Miss Armfelt, an energetic little girl who interrupts his classes by asking him about their relevance, abusing Nixon, talking about the Third World, speaking for Women's Rights, condemning the conformity of the course, the uselessness of education, the corruption of grades, 'Escapers.' William likes his students, more than he likes most of his colleagues; the trouble is he is unsure how close he should get to them. Taking one or two of the co-eds on dates, he feels a vague inhibition, a guilt: the start of a professional conscience. He does not touch them; they stare at him. Once he asks Miss Armfelt, but she tells him dates are a fake ritual, part of the heterosexual conformity she repudiates. For safety's sake, then, William redirects his emotional ambitions; he has an affair with a graduate girl, also teaching freshmen composition. Strangely, it seems that some diminution of sexual attractiveness is an entry qualification for graduate school. Miss Daubernethy is not like the co-eds; she is tough and fairly charmless, a dark girl with a mole on her cheek, whom he meets in the basement of the dormitory, while observing one night the whirl of his socks and undershorts as they spin behind the thick bubble of glass, and to whom he makes all unwittingly, an obscene suggestion: for he asks, as they stand drinking Coke together, on the wet floor in the windowless room, smelling of washing powder and drying clothes, whether she could possibly sew a button on his shirt. 'Christ,' says Miss Daubernethy, staring at him in anger, 'I'm not a homemaker. I'm a graduate student. I'm not a woman, pal. I'm a person.' 'Of course, right,' says William, 'I believe in all that. I wasn't trying to rôle-type you, honestly. I'd have asked anybody.' 'Oh, sure. Anybody who's historically supposed to be seen around with a needle,' the girl said, 'like a woman. Come on, how come you picked on me?' William is aghast with his own guilt, glimpsing the darkness of his unconscious chauvinism. 'Oh God,' he says, 'I'm sorry.' It can of course only have one consequence: it is not very long after this – in fact later that night – that, person to person, with William abased, they are making love on the metal bunk bed in his room, while Ting goes ping below.

The winter outside the office window gets colder, and all is not well. Miss Daubernethy, who comes from Florida, is shrill, tastes of Listerine, and not quite William's ideal type, or the sort of person he would have picked in the free and open market. He knows, and fears she does, that she is a surrogate for the fancy, fresh, forbidden bodies in his classes, for the flashing legs and mobile nipples under sweaters, such as Miss Armfelt's sweater, that he finds himself staring at as he stands over the sink in the Chemistry Building, and talks about the use and significance of tenses. Miss Daubernethy is thirty, tight around the jaw, and has cramps because of the tension of her PhD orals. She wears long dresses to hide her legs, and has exhibitionistic tastes in lovemaking, liking to pleasure herself, by seeing herself or doing things to herself, which is spiriting at first, but somehow basically uncooperative, and not very easy in her or William's dormitory room, or in the back of her Willy jeep. She has an overhung bottom, stout thighs and there are more moles round her waist. There is an old myth in these matters to which William has subscribed: that American women have outrun the world in establishing an intense level of sensation for themselves in sex. William, having had too much of the over-domesticated British variety, feels that this should have its potential for him, its high compensations. Yet, with Miss Daubernethy, as the weeks go by, it seems not to. He touches and rubs and kisses, they move and wriggle and sweat, but the challenging athletics gradually acquire not the tone of an existential liberation, a Reichian fulfilment, but rather of a vulgarly inflated achievement, like trying to play a Beethoven quartet with ten musicians, for better sound. A certain fleshly exhaustion begins to come over William, and something more: I'm a humanist, he thinks to himself. As he sits in his office by day, writing B, and D, and F on essays, and noting at the end of them 'Shows improvement', 'This could be better developed', 'You get to the point too quickly', he feels unease, knowing that his own beginnings, middles and ends, his paragraphing and spacing, his use of the colon, will be similarly flatly measured by Miss Daubernethy's idealized grading system. The students get very anxious about these grades: 'Do you grade on the curve?' they come and ask, 'Do you give As for the best work you get from us, or do you only give them for, like, *Middlemarch*?' Miss Daubernethy in the dormitory room, lying across his armchair, feet splayed and apart, crotch high, raises a similar problem in standards: 'You're okay, you're as good as anyone I've had, to be fair, but you're not as good as the ones I'll get.' William grows haunted by these Joyces, Prousts, and Manns of sex. Back in the office, he tells the kids who come and sit in his consultation chair, 'It's not an abstract best. There are rules and good habits, which I'm trying to teach you. But it's a humanist affair, the best from you, the fullest insight out of you.' Back in the dormitory room, William, lying naked on top of Miss Daubernethy's desk, the sweat on his brow, and the inexorable large thighs dominant above, says: 'Do you think sex can ever become personal?' 'I want you back up higher and your knees more together,' says Miss Daubernethy, monstrous against the light, ultimately and in all a teacher. 'I want your adjectives spaced out more and your verbs more together,' she is saying, in conference in her office, in the light of the snaky desk lamp, when William comes by to fetch her for a meal – for they eat too – the following night.

The winter grows colder still, and all is worse. One night, in her dormitory room, while Miss Daubernethy paints her nipples with silver nail varnish in the light of the desk lamp, William, naked on her bed, finds a large sharp knife under her pillow. 'What's this?' he asks. 'You shouldn't have found that,' says Miss Daubernethy, and starts to cry. William feels a little twinge of terror: 'What were you going to *do*?' he asks. 'I don't know, I think I must be going lesbian. I can't tell you how the shape of a man's body gets me disgusted. I hate you *there*.' Then her nails come flying across the room and she is lunging for the knife. The door is locked but William turns the knob, flies out into the corridor. Happily he still holds the knife. There are long, long corridors back to his room, on the other side of the building. But William makes it in a hurry, seen only by Mr

Ting, a cool person, who stands contemplatively in the passage, evincing only a modest clerkly scepticism at the sight of his nudity, his knife, his panting terror. He locks his door and leans against it, feeling for the first time not the chance and arbitrary nature, but rather the utter precious sanctity, of his male equipment. Is this the lesson? 'You need to cut down your ending,' Miss Daubernethy, unchanged, is saying in her office next day, as William goes in, interrupting a conference, to ask for his clothes back. The clothes turn up in the garbage can in the basement, just by the washing machine where they had first met, back there when the weather was by no means so cold.

It is over, and William subsides into an extraordinary fleshy disgust, thinking over without pleasure the detailed, intimate construction of her body and sensing an ultimate deceit in what the flesh, with all its promises, actually contains. But it is not over, for Miss Daubernethy is omnipresent. She starts wearing sexy clothes, and appears by his side during the break in the Teaching Round Table, when they all stand in the corridor drinking Cokes, saying: 'It was nothing personal, William. It's not because I don't like you or anything. It was just because you're a man.' 'Anyone who's historically supposed to be seen around with a prick,' says William. 'That's chauvinism too.'

In the Victorian Novel seminar, on the very day he is due to read his paper on *Jane Eyre*, Miss Daubernethy comes into the class and sits beside him, though she is not enrolled for the seminar, being a medievalist. 'Any comments?' asks the professor, when he has finished. 'I just love your penis,' whispers Miss Daubernethy. 'Do we all agree about the symbolism of the blocked up window?' asks the professor. 'You can't have it,' whispers William. 'Narrative strategy?' asks the professor. 'I want to feel it inside me,' whispers Miss Daubernethy, looking heated. 'How do we relate this to the symbolic emasculation of Mr Rochester?' asks the professor. 'Now,' says Miss Daubernethy. 'Do you?' says William, looking around at the rest of the class taking notes. 'With or without me attached?'

At the faculty picnic in early December she appears round

the other side of a tree by the icy lakeside, holds onto his coat, and says: 'Funny dark things can happen, William. I was crazy. But I'm through it now. You have to be with me again, because I think of you all the time.' William looks at her, thinks of her disgust, and then of his, inspects the body with no appeal, the body which is supposed to render us everything. 'I'm really sorry,' says William, 'But I'm really way into celibacy now. I want to try that for a bit.' 'No,' says Miss Daubernethy, pushing him into the lake. Two deans and three fully tenured professors are needed to get him dripping out. He is taken back by a Swinburne specialist and put into his dormitory bed. In the following days his throat seizes up and, after two croaking classes, speech becomes impossible. He goes to the campus hospital and lies feverish between clean, antiseptic sheets, while beautiful white-clad nurses inject penicillin into his bottom. Sometimes, hot, he thinks he sees Miss Daubernethy peering in through his room window, but only Fardiman comes inside, bearing the *New York Review of Books*. When he is better, it is Christmas, the festive season, and the students have gone home; happily Fardiman is there, with his old Studebaker, proposing, for his family have gone east for the break to New York City, that they both go off on a healthy vacation together. They drive south, William's mind clearing under Spanish moss. They leave behind the cold and the snowfalls. On Christmas day he sits on the porch of a motel in the sunlight, watching pelicans, farcical birds, ungainly and unadapted, revelling in their own absurdity.

III

After Christmas, with only a little more of the semester still to go, the snow piles up on the window sill of William's office, from which the screens have gone, and there is a curious change of atmosphere in his classes. He has been, with his little English radicalism, and his fancy talk about fictions, a popular teacher, but now someone steals his nameplate from the door of the office, and the students come in to complain about grades he has been giving them. There is a politics about grades, but it is a curious politics. There is the problem of the draftees, which would have been simple (William has been putting brackets, and commas, in for them right through the course), were there not also, subjunctively, the problem of the girls, and the problem of the footballers, and the problem of the blacks, and the problem of the fraternity boys. 'What did she mean when she said she'd do anything to get an A?' asks William, as a girl who has plagiarized an essay, having submitted for him a copied-out article from *Reader's Digest*, entitled 'One of Nature's Wonders: The Mighty Bee', leaves his consultancy chair, right by his desk, and departs angrily from the office. 'She means *anything*,' says Fardiman, 'She'll use what she's got, and what she's got isn't in her head.' 'I thought that's what she meant,' says William. 'I wonder whether you could take a moment or two to talk to me about a few of my themes,' says Mr Krutch, coming in; Mr Krutch sits in the front row of William's class with his feet up on the teaching desk, sometimes with vaguely insulting messages – like 'Limey' – written on the soles. 'Sure,' says William. 'I wonder whether there's any rational explanation of the grades you gave them,' says Mr Krutch, 'Or whether you're just plain crazy.' 'I could be,' says William. 'Look,' says Mr Krutch, 'this theme was handed in by another guy to another teacher. He gave it a B, you gave it a D. How come?' 'Maybe you didn't copy it out very well when you were plagiarizing it,' says William. 'What do I have to do to get good grades from you?' asks Mr Krutch, 'Stand on my head? Play the piano with my ass? I'm just a nice, ordinary guy. I'm not so different than anyone else on this campus.' 'From,' says William, 'We did different from.' 'Tell him goodbye, and Happy New Year,' says Fardiman. An hour later the football coach is in to plead for Dubchek, who has submitted an essay called 'The Function of Criticism at the Present Time', an argument so complete that it even concludes with the name Matthew Arnold. Fortunately there is Miss Armfelt, who comes next, dark, intense, with no bra, a city girl. She has been getting As right through the course. 'Another A,' says William, handing her theme back to her with relief. 'So what?' says Miss Armfelt, putting her Mexican tote-bag down on the desk, and putting the folded theme, with William's red A on it, inside it, 'Grades are crap.' 'That's right,' says Fardiman, leaning back, 'Take Hester Prynne. She got an A, and look what happened to her.' Miss Armfelt looks coolly at him. 'Grades are repression,' she says, 'Grammar's repression. All true creativity transcends rules.' 'So does all true stupidity,' says Fardiman, eating apple cake. 'I wondered if I could have a private word with you, Mr Honeywell,' says Miss Armfelt. 'Sure, I'll go to the john for a minute,' says Fardiman, 'Since you're already getting As.' 'Oh, it's not about *grades*,' shouts Miss Armfelt after him, 'Screw grades.' When Fardiman has gone, she says: 'It's just a crazy thought. We were wondering – we is myself and Laura Ann Dix, she's my room-mate and she's in your section too, you know? – we thought you looked kind of bushed. We both enjoyed your classes. So, like to say thank you, we thought we'd ask if you'd like to stop round at our place sometime for a drink. And one thing we *won't* talk about is grades.' 'That's very human,' says William, 'Sure I'll come.' 'Tomorrow night around eight?' 'Fine,' says William. 'They're even crowding round the doors of the faculty john,' says Fardiman, when he comes back, 'Hoping to catch us unbuttoned.'

The next day William posts one set of his final grades on his office door and locks himself in. He can hear the students outside, reading the grades and banging on the door. He has been infinitely generous, a compromise between the system and his politics, but indignation is rife: 'We know you're in there,' voices shout. Towards evening he creeps out down the ill-lit hall and, his coat collar turned up, eats a hamburger at the hamburger stand, before going to Miss Armfelt's. He crosses the campus. Some black students, sitting-in in the computer block, have started a fire. Outside a dormitory, boys in red Ford Thunderbirds are shouting to girls to come away with them to the West Coast. William reaches the tree-shaded streets just off campus, with ploughed snow stacked on the sidewalk, and finds Miss Armfelt's place, a small basement entrance below a frame house. He taps on the door. 'Come on in,' someone shouts. Some freak music is on the record player. 'Hi,' says Miss Armfelt, wearing her swimsuit and sitting on an exercise bicycle in the middle of the room, pedalling busily, 'I'll be through in a minute.' Laura Ann Dix, whom William knows, sits on the sofa, next to a brown retriever, which growls at him. 'Stay, Fidel,' says Laura Ann. 'Fix some beer, eh?' says Miss Armfelt, peddling on, 'There's some in the icebox.' 'I'll get it,' says William. 'Let me, you talk to Ellie,' says Laura Ann. William leans against a bookcase and watches Miss Armfelt getting up real speed. 'You don't need exercise,' he says. 'I wish I had one of those exercise pogo sticks, with a pedometer on it,' says Miss Armfelt. 'And another one for the dog?' asks William, 'Why do you need exercise?' 'It's for the bodily pleasure,' says Miss Armfelt, 'Hey get me a cigar, will you? Right there in that box, Mr Honeywell.' 'William,' says William, getting a cigar and slipping it between Miss Armfelt's pert lips. 'How's that for symbolic action,' says William. 'They're illegal Havanas,' says Miss Armfelt, 'I guess it keeps *him* in business.'

'How come we have so much light?' says Laura Ann, bringing in the cans of beer. She switches lights out and others on, leaving a paper Japanese lampshade hanging low over the end of the sofa, and a tiny intense-light desklamp on the coffee table. William picks up a matchbook and lights Miss Armfelt's cigar. 'Get one,' says Miss Armfelt. 'She'll be through in a minute,' says Laura Ann, 'Come and sit on the sofa with me.' William sits down. 'Doesn't it drive you crazy, teaching this crazy course?' asks Laura Ann. 'It wouldn't, if all the kids were as bright as you.' 'I look at you sometimes, standing there, and I keep thinking, what he must be thinking! But you never get mad.' 'I really would just once like to see you really let fly,' says Ellie Armfelt. 'It'll happen,' says William. 'But you must have such a good level of consciousness,' says Laura Ann. William laughs and says: 'I'm a stranger. Maybe what sounds commonplace to you doesn't to me.' 'Oh, but the things they tell you,' says Laura Ann, 'They make up things because they think you'll believe it.' 'He knows that,' says Ellie, 'I keep wanting to interrupt, but I say to myself, he knows that.' 'I loved the way you put down that WASP kid who was talking about dates,' says Laura Ann. 'What's that?' asks Ellie. 'Oh, she was saying she gave a boy her right breast on the first date, and her left breast on the second date, and he said, it was funny, what happens on the third, don't you run out of breasts?' They all laugh. 'We really enjoy your classes. You're the most interesting teacher I ever had.' 'You haven't had him,' says Laura Ann. '*You* haven't had him,' shouts Ellie Armfelt. Laura Ann laughs, and then pushes her face against William's. He kisses it. Miss Armfelt suddenly gets off the exercise bicycle and disappears into the kitchen space. Laura Ann surfaces out of William's arms and says: 'What are you doing, Ellie?'

'I just had a great idea, let's have some tequila,' shouts Ellie. Laura Ann's face pushes back into William's. 'She'll be a minute, let's have a first date and a second date.' William's hand goes in under her blouse and slides up over her right breast; she presses it into her and he feels the fluttering stir in his palm. 'Wait,' she says, and pulls off the blouse. Her brown body is under the light from the Japanese lantern, and William feels at last the waning of the physical aversion that Miss Daubernethy had left with him. His hands run up her, and then a voice says: 'Me too,' and there is Ellie Armfelt by him, swimsuit off, naked. William feels a splendid, relaxed sense of benison, of plurality of gifts. The record player switches over to Beethoven. Now Laura Ann is out of her skirt and her hands are on his body, pushing aside his shirt. Ellie Armfelt is working on the trousers. 'I thought,' says William, 'you were lesbian.' Miss Armfelt leans over Laura Ann and William and hugs them together, kissing both their faces. Laura Ann is pulling his body round to reach it with her mouth. Ellie Armfelt puts a breast against his face. William can hardly see, but he knows there is another girl in the room. The impression is so hazy that it almost drifts past him.

But there she is, near the bicycle, holding up a square black box. 'Who's that?' asks William. 'That's our other roommate,' whispers Ellie, 'She's in your class too.' The flashbulb goes off, leaving a glaring residue of light in William's retina, showing him, vividly, the breasts against his face, like the breasts of the fat girl he saw on the grass in the electric storm. She was graceless; he has an instinct of the gracelessness of these bodies too, but the shudder is coming up him. There is another flash of light, and another, and another. The girl with the camera comes nearer for a moment. She says, politely, 'Why, hi, Mr Honeywell,' and then she goes away.

IV

There is an envelope, almost expected, lying under the door of William's office when he gets there early the next morning. He has slept well in his dormitory bedroom, post-coitally tired, and then, waking up towards dawn, has thought of this, getting up soon after the light came to come over and check. But they have been up early too. He carries the envelope, with his name on it, the handwriting recognizable from themes, to his desk. He opens it up and takes out the single Polaroid print, with its whirl of bodies and its central, naked Honeywell, and then the sheet of folded theme-paper, with its long message. It says:

Dear William,
    This is to thank you for last night. Oh boy are you a swinger. It really was a good scene. Take a look at the photo. Isn't it great? It was taken by a friend, Delise Roche, who shares our pad too. I guess you saw her when she stopped by. She's a really keen photographer, and a friend. Please remember. This is all part of the fun we have had, and a wonderful way of us all remembering it for all time. It was a swell evening, and I know I will always want to remember it. I hope you will come around again, 'for a drink', I mean it, you're really welcome. Next time we ought

154

to make it a foursome. I mean, you really ought to meet Delise. She's a really good friend of Laura Ann and I. You will know her, she's in your Comp. class too, a different section than us. A great kid with a problem. Her problem is that she has been working really hard 'for the cause', active in Civil Rights, anti-war, Women's Lib, etc. and has just not made the grades. Like me, she thinks grades are crap, though I guess her parents would kill her or something if she flunked out of college. Anyway we need her around, on the political front, etc. A great girl. Photography's her bag right now. She says a photograph is truer than words, and I guess she's right. It's typical of her that she takes these photographs of us just for fun, and for keepsake. Not to do anything with them. Show them to anyone, I mean. What grade are you giving her in Comp, William? Hey, you have a great body, William. See you maybe?

    Yours with affection, really,
      Ellie.

William sits at the desk. He scratches at a body bite and reads the letter through carefully, twice more, trying to penetrate it. It is a crisp and beautiful morning, and through the window he can see the sun bringing out red glitter on the new snow that has dusted the campus, in the small hours after he got back to his room. An innocent morning. The fire seems out now in the computing complex. He stares at the photograph, with its sticky surface and falsified colours, at the image of himself from outside, alienating, gross, yet retrieving the doings already hazy now in his head. There is a footstep out in the hallway. A key turns in the lock. 'I already opened it,' shouts William. 'My,' says Fardiman, coming inside in red earmuffs, 'And I thought I was early.' 'I couldn't sleep,' says William. 'I've got some more grades to turn in,' says Fardiman, hanging up his coat, 'I've been reading themes all night. I'm so tired. I start to think the way they do. In unattached subordinate clauses. Like this.'

'Can you bear to read one more?' asks William. 'Only for a real friend,' says Fardiman, sitting down at the desk and taking off the earmuffs. William throws the photograph and the letter onto the stack of papers on his desk. 'Look at the photograph first,' he says. Fardiman looks, and whistles. 'You should make the sex magazines with this one,' he says. 'I like it, but I'd question whether you can count it in your list of publications.' 'It was taken by a student,' says William. 'Well, I like the way the guy has got this bicycle wheel in the foreground, to give perspective.' 'Now the letter,' says William, 'Read it carefully, for tone.' 'For tone, heh?' says Fardiman, automatically picking up the red pen from his desk, and making marks as he goes through the document. When he has finished he says: 'Well, William, I think it's got a lot of tone. I told you if you taught these kids properly they'd learn to write relevant prose.' 'You did,' says William, 'What do you think it means?' 'Well,' says Fardiman, 'We could have a graduate seminar on this one. Indeed it's better than *Moll Flanders*. If read at the level of innocence, she likes you, William. She's a sentimental girl, given to reminiscence. If read for irony, with the methods of the New Criticism, hunting for paradox and ambiguity, I'd say she's got you. It's a rhetorical technique called blackmail.' 'How do we determine which?' 'I have a feeling it's one of those occasions where the intrinsic approach fails us. Where we turn to contextual factors, like are there more photographs.' 'I think she took four,' says William. 'Of course, they may not all have come out,' says Fardiman, 'but that would affect my reading of the text.' 'Yes,' says William, 'Fardiman, am I in a bad position?' Fardiman looks at the photograph: 'It looks quite a good position,' he says. 'With the university,' says William. 'Oh, with the university,' says Fardiman, 'That depends what you want to do, in the future. These are permissive times.' 'This permissive?' asks William. 'What are your career plans?' asks Fardiman. 'I'd like to stay on here a couple of years, and get my Master's, and then take a university post, if there are any around then. Here, or in England. I've been thinking about it a lot. I like teaching.' 'William,' says Fardiman, looking at Honeywell in despair, 'why pick a future like that at a time like this?' 'No?' asks William. 'No,' says Fardiman.

William sits for a minute, and thinks. The sun is coming up over the snow, and the early students are going to eight o'clock class. He says: 'You really think if she sent these photographs to anyone, I'd be in difficulties.' 'There's still a professional code, especially for guys without tenure,' says Fardiman, 'If she sends them to our Department Chairman, I'd think your chances of a renewal next year, or a good reference on your placement file, sort of low. Like around zero. If she really papers the town, and sends them to the Regent and the President, it might be wise to have a booking on the next flight home. On the other hand, if she keeps them in her purse, and looks at them occasionally, with a fond smile for the teacher she once had, then you'll have a sweetness following you for the rest of your days.' 'I suppose I could, at a pinch, argue that I'm human like everyone else,' says William. 'What kind of an excuse is that?' asks Fardiman, 'The plea of the rogue throughout the ages.' 'It could happen to any of us,' says William, 'I didn't really do anything. It was all done to me. And it happens all over, Fardiman.' 'I know,' says Fardiman, 'But you got caught.' 'I could tell the whole story.' 'Then all four of you would get fired. You could run away and make blue movies together.' William sits and stares at his desk, at the list of grades he has given. He inspects the list; Delise Roche has a D. Not even an F. Just a D. 'Fardiman,' he says, 'How will it end?' Fardiman looks sadly at him. 'I'm sorry, William,' he says, 'You have to write your own ending.' 'Do you think,' says William tentatively 'I should raise Miss Roche's grade? We raised grades for the draftees, for the blacks. She's been working for them.' 'I would never advise it under any circumstances,' says Fardiman, 'But my mother, that old fiend, my mother would raise Miss Roche's grade.' 'I'd never do it at home,' says William. 'You'd never do *that* at home, would you?' asks Fardiman, tapping the photograph, 'I guess we all do things away from home we wouldn't do at home. And since most of us are never at home we're always doing things we would never do.' 'Fardiman,' says William, 'if I do it, and keep my job, I wouldn't feel fit to keep the job I was keeping.' 'I said you were a well set-up, morally earnest fellow,' says Fardiman, 'and they always get screwed. Of course, we could be screwing ourselves.'

William looks at Fardiman, wondering. 'We're complex people,' says Fardiman, 'that's our training. We're always reading for necessity, design, structure, plot.' 'It's quite a plot,' says William. 'But are we missing innocence? Maybe it's contingent, not necessary, as Kermode would say. Maybe this letter's a pristine, guileless thing, all this while. A statement of modern love.' 'Can it be?' asks William. Fardiman gets up from his desk and goes to his jar of apple cake. 'We find it hard to believe. I mean, what's personal now? In bed my wife is a political agent, a minor functionary for the woman revolution. My kids rip off cookies from the refrigerator and call it an anti-capitalist gesture. But people *do* do loving things.' 'But how do we find out?' 'Well, how do we? Do we really know about ourselves? You could go and see her.' 'These grades go into the office at nine,' says William, 'then they go in the computer, unless it's all burned up.' 'There's always another computer,' says Fardiman, 'I'm sorry, William, I don't think you can know. Here we are: we've read Leavis and Kermode, and *Tel Quel* and Marcuse. We're lost souls on the historical turn. But, we say, we know how to read. Then here's a text, offering two worlds, one glowing with fleshy promiscuities, one tainted with the harsh corruption of interest, okay, radical interest, and what happens? We can offer multiple interpretations. We can see it psycho-linguistically and socio-linguistically. We can find the apocalyptic figure and the low mimetic type. We can note its thematic constituents, like Delise, photography, politics, grades. We can observe in it the post-modernist or the McLuhanite emphasis on the visual as opposed to the verbal or linear mode, right? We can read it as Sontagian erotica. The only thing we can't say is whether she got you round there to try a bit of Sontagian erotics herself on that nice British body of yours, or to shake you down for a safe passing B for this Delise. We can't *read* it, William. Or, in a phrase, penetrate the literal level of this reality.'

And so there sits William Honeywell, who came here on the Greyhound bus and stood in the courthouse square, in his high-back swivel chair, looking out at the snow. It has been the coldest night on record in this little Mid-Western town, with its rich folks and its poor folks, its go to church and its not go to church two hundred miles south of the state capital, where they keep all the money and the record of accurate time. On the literal level of William's reality, it is seventeen minutes past or after eight, and his grades are due at nine. Can there be a knock on the door, Miss Armfelt come by to say that it is all for love? He sits and sits, staring at the path between Humanities and Business. Fardiman, with a red pen, marks.

V a

There is a knock at the door. Fardiman goes and opens it. 'Happy New Year,' he says to whomever is outside. 'Is Mr Honeywell there?' asks a voice. 'He's gone to Chicago, Mr Krutch,' says Fardiman, 'the Windy City.' 'I have to see him about my grades,' says Krutch. 'Come back another day, when once more he's not here,' says Fardiman. 'There's someone breathing back there,' says Krutch, 'He's there.' 'No, there's no one breathing,' says Fardiman, 'If I let you in here, you wouldn't see anybody, but I won't. You've got to learn to take words on trust.' 'Oh, *sure*, Mr Fardiman,' says Krutch, unconvinced. 'Goodbye now,' says Fardiman. William breathes: he reads, and then rereads, the letter. He takes up the red marking pen from his desk. From under the letter he takes out the computerized mark-sheet. He runs his eye down it, finds a name and, with the pen, he makes a small alteration. Then he picks up the letter, tears it, and throws it into the wastebasket. 'How about keeping the photograph?' asks Fardiman, 'A sweet reminiscence.

159

Something gained, however momentary.' William reaches in his pocket and brings out a matchbook. It has the name of a motel in Saratoga Springs, NY, 12866, on it. William stares at it, for he has never in his life been to Saratoga. Then he recalls that he picked it up in Miss Armfelt's basement apartment, to light her cigar. He strikes a match on the matchbook, closing the cover as instructed, and puts the little match to the photograph. It flares, with a smell of chemicals. 'You must come back to New York City and meet my mother,' says Fardiman, coughing in the polluted smoke.

Vb

There is a knock at the door. Fardiman crosses the room and opens it. 'Mr Honeywell in?' asks a voice. 'He's gone to Chicago,' says Fardiman, 'Hog butcher, stacker of wheat.' 'I need to talk to him right now about my grades,' says the voice. 'Try again some other time, Mr Krutch,' says Fardiman. 'There are papers rustling in there,' says Krutch, 'I know he's there.' 'It's the wind,' says Fardiman, 'The local mistral. I'm all alone. Okay?' 'I don't know whether I believe you, Mr Fardiman.' 'What's truth?' asks Fardiman, 'What's lies? What are fictions? Where is the literal level of reality? You just go away, huh, Mr Krutch.' 'Metaphysician,' says Mr Krutch, and goes. William releases the papers he is holding; he reads, and reads again, the letter. He takes up the red marking pen from his desk. He goes carefully through the letter once more, making professional markings on it. He underlines the phrase 'a really good friend of Laura Ann and I' and writes 'error in case'; he underlines the phrase 'a different section than us' and writes 'Not a comparative: different . . . from'. On the bottom he writes: 'You get to the point too slowly' and then 'Two errors carrying full penalization: F.' From his desk drawer, he takes a clean envelope and addresses it to Miss Ellie Armfelt, at her apartment address. 'Sell me a stamp, Fardiman,' he says. Fardiman, marking, reaches in his back pocket and pulls out his black wallet. 'Have it on me,' says Fardiman, and then, 'Let me go down the corridor and mail it. That guy could still be waiting out there, puzzling through the metaphysics.' Fardiman goes, and William sits at his desk, and looks out of the window.

Vc

There is a knock at the door. Fardiman steps across and opens it. 'Oh, hi,' he says. 'Is Mr Honeywell there?' asks a voice. 'He's gone to Pittsburgh,' says Fardiman. 'Oh, I'm sorry,' says a voice, 'My name's Krutch. I just wanted to tell him he's the best teacher I ever had. I really learned from his course. I didn't understand it, but it was really good, you know what I mean? It's funny, there are some teachers who just make everything seem really interesting. I mean, I'm a dull, ordinary guy. I got these terrible grades from him. I may flunk. But who cares? That's not what matters. I'll never forget being taught by him. You know?' 'I'm sure he'll be really glad to have that message,' says Fardiman, 'I'll tell him when I see him.' 'You won't forget?' asks Krutch, 'I mean, if a guy's great, he ought to be told, right?' 'Right, Mr Krutch,' says Fardiman. 'Oh, and a Happy New Year,' says Krutch. 'And to you.' says Fardiman. William reads, and then re-reads, the letter. He takes up the red marking pen from his desk. He takes up a clean sheet of paper and begins writing. 'Dear Ellie,' he writes,

> I can't tell you how good it was to get your letter. It was under my door first thing this morning, when I arrived, just what I needed to hear. I'd been wondering all night, with the snowstorm going on outside my window, just how you felt, you and Laura Ann. I mean, it could have been something just casual. Like *Blow Up* or something – did you see that great film? What it meant to me was a breaking down of distances, a real getting close. How these artificial roles, teacher and student, block out real relationships. I accept

your invitation, who wouldn't? I'll be round tomorrow night (I have a paper tonight to finish for my graduate course; I wonder what grade I'll get!). Certainly I'd like to meet Delise. She's right, of course; photography is better than words, as involvement is better than analysis, life better than writing about life. And you're right too, about grades being crap. In fact that whole academic factory atmosphere is crap too. Petty research by petty minds evading everything that's real and alive. Well, you're alive, and you've taught me something. Do you know what your letter made me do? Burn my grade sheets I guess that's the end of my contract, but who cares? What kind of life is that? I wanted to write songs anyway. Don't take too much exercise before I come. Do you know what I'm doing? I sit at my desk, in a high-back swivel chair, looking out at the snow. I have an incredible, fresh sense of reality. It's a really crisp, beautiful morning, and out through the window I can see people walking in all their peopleness, and the sun bringing out red glitter . . .

'Hey, William, William,' says Fardiman, marking, 'what's all that stuff you're writing?'

Dodos Among the Elephants

What with the Indian thing and globalism mattering so much nowadays, it isn't surprising that Angus Wilson's middle-class dreadfuls should be covering a rather wider landscape. So now, after *As If By Magic*, though before *Kipling*, a scrap pulled out from his forthcoming collection, *Mrs Weenie, Giggling, Meets the Rajah, And Other Stories*.

SERENA WINSOME knew as clearly as anything that the whole evening was going to be spoiled. She sat in the loo, on the pink tufted candlewick of the seat cover, fighting back the little hot tears and trying to be stiff-upper-lipped about what had happened. Of course it had to be today, what with the committee meeting that evening and all her hopes pinned to it, that her father chose to arrive, in his usual sudden way, bursting in on them both while they were having afternoon tea and scones and leaving Michael to pay the untouchable who had carried him up on his back from the station. Michael had been a dear boy about it at first, only blinking a little when the spray of spit that Father always emitted when he spoke fell on his lapels, and really quite letting himself enjoy the beguiling charm that the old man could still produce when he talked about the houseboat parties and the Simla season. But she could see the annoyance wrinkling Michael's forehead when father had insisted that the poor boy buy his wristwatch, and it really was too much of the old man to take his trousers off like that, exposing those senile, wrinkled legs, to show them the holes in his underpants. Serena felt a hot blush of shame run across her face, and she knew from Daddy's cross expression that he had noticed. Of course he didn't say anything, but instead turned to Michael and began on one of his interminable stories, as much to annoy her, it was obvious, as to impress Michael with the famous Plumb charm.

He was really impossible, and she didn't know who should be humiliated most: Michael, who was after all only related to the old man through her, or she herself, even though it was

Michael who had told him that the house was his to use when he wished. She tried not to get steamed up about it, but it was no good; you couldn't forget all the other humiliations like this, and the 'Committee of the Deccan Foxhunt' was just the one group of people who wouldn't stand his airs and graces for a moment. They were all people of real rank, not ones who had been lifted up by the war like Daddy, who although he pretended to be of an old army family really came from a family of innkeepers in Chesterfield. Serena could have wept with annoyance, but it was no use. Perhaps the old man would be too tired to want to take drinks with a crowd of total strangers – though past experience told her that you couldn't count on that for a moment. Still, she could try. She dabbed her eyes, touched up the mascara in the loo mirror, and went into the kitchen looking as bright as she could manage. Krishna, the old eunuch servant, was spreading mango chutney on the Bath Olivers. 'Krishna, I want you to make sure that the drinks you give to the Daddy sahib are as weak as possible,' she said, 'Except he'll probably want something horrible that we can't water down. Like Green Chartreuse.' 'Wery good, memsahib,' said Krishna, his high voice sympathetic; he really was an awful brick.

Back on the verandah Daddy was singing 'The Boy I Love Is Up in the Gallery', to Michael, who seemed to be listening quite attentively. The old songs *were* lovely, and it brought a gasp in Serena's throat, even though she'd heard him do this thousands of times before and anyway tried not to be sentimental about things. But then he started talking about his dicky heart and wanted to show Michael his athlete's foot, and of course you had to start feeling stern with him again. 'Daddy,' she said, 'I hope you won't mind but I've got a committee meeting this evening . . .' 'Jolly-o,' he said, 'What's it all about? Probably I can sit in and lend a hand with an old man's wisdom. . . .' 'I thought you might like a rest,' said Serena, 'The fan's on in your room and one of the servants can massage you if you'd like that.' 'Serena was always an old chump, even as a child, weren't you, lassie? If there's anything I really fancy it's gassing away with Serena's pals. Are they la-di-da?' 'I suppose you'd say so,' Serena said. 'All the better,' said Daddy, rubbing his hands and winking over her shoulder at Michael, 'Nothing like a bit of class, I always say, So long as it's white class. It is white, isn't it, lassie?' Michael laughed and said, 'Oh, it's white all right, though I've no doubt the old committee's had to rig the votes a time or two to keep it that way!' 'Oh, Michael, how could you?' said Serena, feeling mocked; trust Daddy to touch on the one sore spot that Michael, in his liberal way, had about the committee.

'Actually,' Michael was saying, 'Serena's really been terribly clever about this committee meeting and we're going to have pegs with it to keep it informal.' Serena could have cried when he said this; if there had been any chance at all of getting Daddy to go away, it would only have been by pretending it was all going to be terribly private, though even then he thought nothing of gatecrashing anything, however constitutional. That was why he had never got anywhere in India; you'd think being British he could have done all kinds of things, but everyone could see from the start that he just didn't care, and it always counted against him. She'd always told him he wasn't the India type at all, and could probably do quite well for himself back home now Britain had gone democratic; but though they'd twice given him the boatfare home he had spent it on drink and probably on immoral girls in the bazaars, and was still in the country giving the people who had stayed on a bad name. 'Ah, drinkies,' he said. 'I wondered when that question would come to the fore. You can't send the old boy away now you've told me that. It wouldn't be *comme il faut*, would it, laddie?' 'Quite so, sir,' said Michael.

Krishna waddled in, his legs apart, and beat the brass gong in the doorway. 'Wisitors arrived, memsahib,' he said. 'Ah, good-oh,' said Michael. The only thing was to put on as brave a face as possible, and Serena went over to the gilt-framed mirror in the wall, one of her 'bits', and put the cyclamen back on her lips. She saw in the glass the little blobs of moisture that always gathered on her heavy eyelids when she got a bit worked up, but she was determined not to let the strain tell. 'Now, Dad, I'm counting on you to put on a really good show,' she said, 'And no taking your clothes off like last time.' 'Count on me, lassie,' said the old man, 'I'll have them rolling in the aisles.' 'I'm sure you will, sir,' said Michael. Forcing herself, Serena lifted the venetian blinds and watched the trishaws unloading in the drive. There they all were; it seemed hard, looking at them, all dressed up to the nines, to think that the Union Jack wasn't still flying on Government House. Old Miss Bickerstaffe-Ogmore, who really deserved a medal for the way she managed to keep the hotel running on about a tenth of its former staff (it was said she blacked the guests' shoes herself, and at her age!), was being lifted up the steps by a handful of bearers, who were carefully shading her scrawny flesh from the pitiless sun. The Colonel, who still, she saw with approval, was managing to keep up his old custom of wearing the fresh rose he'd always had flown in daily from his son's nursery in Surrey, had recovered marvellously from his tiger-mauling and was climbing the steps himself. It was wonderful the way he managed to make one leg do the work of two. And Miss Adela Quested, who had had that bit of trouble with the Indian boy all those years back and now had virtually to live in retirement away from the hordes of research students who were always pursuing her, looked a treat in her puce chenille. For some reason she had forgotten to remove her gardening hat, and her clay pipe always struck Serena as a little *outré*, but you had to admire the way she could still join in all the fun.

'My dear, what an utterly delightful house,' said Miss Bickerstaffe-Ogmore as they all flooded onto the verandah, 'Is one permitted to smoke in it?' Serena accepted the familiar friendly malice in the same spirit it was offered: 'Oh, I think we can be indulgent just this once, seeing as how it's the committee.' 'I say, I spy a stranger,' said the Colonel. 'Yes, I'm afraid it's terribly unconstitutional of me,' said Serena, 'but I thought you'd permit me to smuggle in an intruder – seeing as how it's just me old dad.' 'By Jove, Serena's papa,' said Miss Bickerstaffe-Ogmore, 'How very fascinating. They don't feature one another a bit, do they, Adela?' 'Don't mind her,' said Miss Quested, 'She's quite a clown, really.' 'No offence meant, none taken,' said the old man, 'Mind you, there's one thing my daughter here and self have in common. We both love putting on a bit of a jamboree.' 'Yes, Serena's jamborees are really quite something,' said Miss Bickerstaffe-Ogmore. By now Krishna and the other helpers had brought in the drinks and bits. 'Do dig in to the tipple,' said Serena. From the word go everyone seemed to be enjoying themselves. The old man was being his comical best, making fun of everyone and being a marvellous mimic, and Serena began to feel a bit ashamed of her forebodings. After all he could be really good fun when he wanted to be. He kept moving from group to group, saying funny things like 'Fine words butter no watercress' and 'How's about you and me moseying over to the window and rubbernecking at the view, partner?' and then he went out of the room and came back wearing a sari. 'You like I do saucy belly-dance?' he said to Miss Quested, who could hardly keep her eyes dry. 'He really ought to be on the stage, your dad,' said Miss Bickerstaffe-Ogmore. Serena stood to one side and thought that they were, despite their dreadful eccentrics, really a very gallant company. It made you believe that there was something worthwhile just about being English. Michael came and stood beside her. 'Enjoying yourself, duckie?' he asked. 'I think it's one of our best,' she told him. 'See, they all love him,' said Michael, 'Nothing to have worried about at all.'

Michael's reassurances cheered her further and she went elated into the kitchen to see to the second helps. She'd never seen the Committee members enjoy themselves so much for years. When she went back, the old man was standing in the centre of an admiring crowd. 'All the problems of inter-racial living have been grossly worked up by these professional sociologist chappies,' he was saying, 'While they've been arguing, we lads and lassies on the ground have been living out these problems, and solving them. The answer's simple enough – just stick up for the values you believe in and no matter what colour a chap's skin is he'll respect you.' Serena had been hearing this stuff since the year dot, but it impressed the Committee members, and the Colonel got so excited that in attempting to pat the old man on the back he toppled off his one leg and fell on the floor, pulling down Miss Quested in a desperate attempt to save himself. The others crowded round and, as Serena watched in horror, began to try to pull the Colonel up. 'All I can say,' said Miss Bickerstaffe-Ogmore, 'is that someone has been damnably careless.' Then she too slipped in the puddle left by the Colonel's spilled drink and was on the floor with the others.

All her worst premonitions had been fulfilled! Serena felt the tears rise and could have fled from the room in utter disgrace, but at that moment Krishna was at her side whispering that two policemen had called to arrest the Colonel for molesting a Hindu boy in the cantonment. And as if that wasn't enough, Miss Quested's clay pipe had somehow set fire to the puce chenille. Michael, in his quickwitted way, picked up the drinks pitcher and poured it over her. And then outside a sudden screaming began. The old man hurried to the window. 'I don't think we can help,' he said, 'It's a nasty business all right. Two of the bearers who brought Miss Bickerstaffe-Ogmore. They can't have seen the elephant until it was right on top of them.' Lost in the obscene horror that had come out from nowhere and engulfed her, Serena stared at the whole unreal scene. Then she noticed the crowning humiliation: her father had taken his trousers off again and was using them to bind the livid burns that had started up on Miss Quested's legs. She gave in and ran upstairs to her bedroom, her heels pattering absurdly on the tiles. On the bed she loosened her girdle and gave way to grief. The scene in the room was etched on her mind – the tumbled bodies of the Committee on the floor, the screams outside, and Father's naked buttocks – and awful, retching sobs welled up to rack her fat body. After that, what hope was there that she would be made chairman of the Committee? But her sense of duty told her she must pull herself together. She pulled her girdle straight and went to the mirror to repair her ravaged face. Then, putting on a gay smile, she went downstairs. A few of the old songs and it would all be right as rain again. No one was going to say that Serena Winsome's jamborees weren't a thundering success.

An Extravagant Fondness for
the Love of Women

Strange, I thought the other day, when some persecuting critic explained to me that all modern academic novels were forged out of putting together C. P. Snow's Lewis Eliot with Kingsley Amis's Jim Dixon – strange that neither of those two distinguished novelists actually recorded the occasion. Happily I was wrong, as this extract shows. I won't say which of the two did it, though the fact that it comes from a forty-volume *roman-fleuve* called *Staircases of Disputation* may be a clue to some.

A WARM FIRE burned in my grate, its flicker illuminating the book-lined walls, as I sat in my Cambridge room that evening in the early sixties – I am usually either sitting or eating when I begin a chapter. My fire, my leatherbound volumes, my warm body in the armchair formed a little pool of civilization, though through the medieval wainscoting the draught from outside struck cold. Below, in the wintry courtyard, tourists with plastic cameras walked clumsily on the lawns, or kicked against buckets in the narrow Tudor passageways; being, however, from a lowly background, I felt this quite excusable. I could hear their murmurs of veneration for the ancient college, and realized how they would envy me my traditional rights and comforts, could they see me sitting there with the tray the gyp had left me, on it a decanter of nuts and a bowl of sherry. The rain rattled my windows. The leatherbound tome on my lap struck cold, or warm, I hardly remember which; after all, this is fifteen years ago. The book was a study of the Martyrdom of Polycarp, an old and well-loved interest of mine; and I was so deeply engrossed that I did not notice the step on my staircase, until someone knocked several times, with heavy knuckles, on my oak door.

'Come,' I called; and I looked up to see Dixon enter. The fire was, as I said, warm, the books radiant in its glow; but Dixon's entrance brought in the draught and wet of the weather outside, which struck cold into the room, and I hastily bade him shut the door.

'Well, wotcha, old sock,' he said, taking his place before my fire (not his fire) and warming his youthful, fleshless buttocks impetuously, 'I suppose this is what you call studying, then. Do a lot of that, do you?' As he spoke, his eyes flickered enviously over my ample chairs, my seventeenth-century tapestries, the rows of diaries, the volumes of briefs, the scientific notes, the political memoirs that betokened my eclectic interests; and his features assumed an expression which bore, I noticed, an extraordinary physical similarity to that of Dame Edith Sitwell.

'Do be seated, Dixon,' I said, and Dixon sat down. He was a young man of thirty-five, though from his youthful manner many thought him younger; however, I happen to be remarkably good about knowing the right age of people. He had been elected to a college fellowship only a week or so previous, and in somewhat mysterious circumstances. One of the fellows, a man with a taste for the untoward, had proposed the name of L. S. Caton, an eminent medieval historian, who was, however, we were warned, travelling abroad. Though none of the Fellows had met him, his name had, after the necessary disputation and colloguing, the familiar backstairs struggles and flagrant sexual innuendos always invoked in a college election, been selected; but at the start of term, on Caton's expected day of arrival, Dixon had appeared instead. His claim that Caton was the pseudonym under which he published his many bulky monographs had not convinced some of the older Fellows, struck by his utter want of accurate historical knowledge; but naturally they had said nothing to him directly, preferring to bicker and calumniate in small groups on the bends of staircases, where the air struck cold. Other fellows had taken the view that his tendency to confuse the events of the twelfth with those of the fifteenth century had a simpler explanation: Dixon had confessed that he had taught once in a provincial university. I myself had not taken sides, as is my custom, and had already talked to Dixon occasionally in hall. Within days, though he was in character and spirits my direct opposite, we had formed a relationship. He clearly liked and respected me, while I regarded him with that amiable, rather contemptuous distance it is always pleasant to adopt towards a willing protégé.

So it had gone on, though from the start Dixon had mystified me. He struck me oddly, as a man curiously uninterested in power. Jago had told me that he had seen in him an extravagant fondness for the love of women, and it was probably this propensity that corrupted his natural instincts. He had avoided our cabals, remained unspeaking during our gossip, and had taken a negligible part in our recent poisoning attempt upon the Provost. On the other hand, my gyp told me one morning, when he drew my curtains and cut me my first cigar of the day, that Dixon was in the habit of scraping acquaintance with working-class barmaids from the suburbs who served beer and other brews in the local hostelries, and of escorting them along the tree-lined walks beside the Cam, where the air struck very cold indeed, and whence their faint giggles and occasional cries could be heard even in the Provost's Lodge. He was, I supposed, a man who suffered from the frets of sensual love, who 'let the heart lead the head', and who dangerously lacked the subtlety to conceal his tastes, for I had heard discussions of his conduct on several evenings over dessert in the combination room. It was, however, hardly my business to warn or to criticize; and, in any case, if a man is not prepared to accept and take on his own terms every Fellow of the college, he is hardly likely to acquire enough material for a *roman-fleuve*.

'Sherry,' I said, looking up at Dixon.

'I'm all right.' He produced, with a lithe movement, a small can of beer from the pocket of his turd-brown anorak and, from another of his many pockets, drew out a metal bottle-opener of the kind then recently introduced to facilitate this new fashion in drinking. With this, he succeeded in penetrating the circular container, and put it to his lips. It was not one of the more expensive or better reputed kinds of beer and he gulped it inattentively.

'I'm not disturbing you, am I?' he then went on, 'I see you're

177

only reading. The kind of bloody boring stuff us chaps have to do to pretend we're up to something, eh, Lew?'

'One tries to keep up,' I said.

'Actually,' said Dixon, 'I hoped I'd catch you in. I wanted you to know that last evening I was accorded one of those there signal honours. In the election after dinner I emerged victor. I'm now captain of the darts team down the Feathers.'

'You know how delighted I am. Perhaps you'll allow me to present a bottle this evening, and record the occasion in the wine-book.'

Dixon sometimes gave the appearance of brashness, but I could see that he was taken right aback. He gave a shy, somewhat diffident smile. Down below in the court someone walked towards the chapel, whistling a passage of *Carmen*. Dixon seemed affected by this, and, as if to draw attention away from his embarrassed gratitude, he snatched up a small eighteenth-century alabaster figurine from my mantelshelf and crossed to the window. After a moment's pause, he opened the window, so that a draught of air struck cold to my chair, and hurled out the precious object. The throw was evidently accurate; outside the music ceased, and a sailor's oath reminded me that Crystal had promised the Duke of Edinburgh as his guest at the feast that evening. Dixon pulled down the window, giving the rain something to rattle against (it had had to stop for a second or two) and came back to the fire (which had kept going throughout).

'With increasing years has come wisdom, Lew,' he said smiling down at me, and twanging his braces inconsequentially, 'One learns the art of not getting caught. Or even of getting others caught. Bloody Beethoven.'

'Bizet,' I said.

'Oh, so-so,' he replied. Then, collecting himself, he said: 'But I haven't come just for that small triumph. I've come, Lew, for your support. You see, I'm a fresh eye here, and I probably notice a number of things about this place you older blokes would miss. I've never been a straight academic. I've always detested books, something of a barrier in this racket. I can't do research, and libraries give me dandruff. As for this sherry bum, and gyp bum and Martyrdom of Polycarp bum, it gets on my, you know, wick. Then I've spent some time outside the academic world. In fact I worked as a personal secretary in London until I was fi . . . until I resigned, I know you've spent some time sodding about in the corridors of powers too. You see now why I've come to you.'

'Men do,' I said, inhaling, unobtrusively, the bouquet of my glass of Montrachet. I wondered what it was, apart from my natural gift for eliciting the most profound of confidences, that made Dixon speak to me. All men seek for power, I thought, and those in universities do little other. But what was Dixon seeking? His appearance suggested that he had no aims, which made me, of course, suspicious; for me, that meant he had every aim. His guileless face, the absence of any air of deception, made me conscious of all the possible deceptions such a pose could conceal. Was he after the Provostship already? Or was it rather my work on the double helix, a part-time preoccupation of mine, later taken further by others? I answered him non-committally; after all, you never get anything out of me until the twelfth chapter, and then not a lot.

'Port?' I said.

Dixon replied comically, claiming that port always sent him running for the lavatories, clutching at his bowels. He was, I saw, a man unfinished, a man unpretentious because he had not realized his pretensions; I admired him for it. But then, with a decisive gesture of his feet, he came suddenly to the point.

'Look, I don't know whether you've spotted this yet, Lew, but there's one thing gravely lacking in this college. Something I think I could give a little assistance with. It's something that every sound society requires, and I think we should act decisively and together, old sock.'

He stood there gravely, dressed with subfusc taste in anorak and jeans, waiting for me to encourage him to go on.

'Go on,' I said.

'It's tail, Lew. Women. I've looked around carefully, and all the Fellows here are men.'

We are a small college, and it took me only a moment to hurry mentally through the thirteen Fellows, calling each vividly to mind. They were – you're sure you don't mind when I hold the action up to tell you things like this? – from a mixture of subjects, and they revealed that mixture of natures one finds in any sodality. There were the grave and the gay, the deceitful, the likeable, the noble, the weak. Four of them lay dying, in unutterably painful circumstances; two were now held in prison, bearing treason charges with stoic endurance; at least one was an adulterer, another a blackmailer, a third an arrant political opportunist. They made a varied group, like any other group of people drawn together by profession or interest. Yet I quickly saw Dixon's point; various they were, but one thing was theirs in common. All were men.

'Claret?' I said. I felt, with my deep experience of people, I understood Dixon now. Like so many men, he had fallen in love with the college, and wanted to give himself to it entirely. It had won his dedication, his faith. He came from a lower middle-class background, and he had expressed radical sympathies to me in secret, sympathies that I recognized from the struggles of my own one-time youth. There was nothing in his heritage or history that could have prepared him for anything like this; none the less, faced with its medieval grandeur, with the feudalism and simplicity of its life, with the possibility of escape from the overweening century we live in, with the opportunity of stimulating company from men like myself, he had yielded himself heart and soul. The college offered a draught of certainty in the lonely anguish of mortal personal life.

'It's not just that,' he said, 'It's the lavatories. Not enough to go round. Something nasty's going to happen one of these days. Of course, the place really wants pulling down.'

'Nuts?' I said.

'And you,' he said, 'And, now we're speaking frankly, well,

it's a case, Lew, of under which king, Bezonian, if you catch my meaning.'

'I think I know four people we could get on our side,' I said to him, 'Then come dreary weeks of bargaining and colloguing . . .'

'I don't see why we shouldn't put a match to it now.'

I have always been excited by young rebels, and found them often quite as natural company as merchant-bankers, statesmen, international scientists, judges. It was hard not to yield to his young enthusiasm, his appeal to the future, but the spirit of intelligent compromise which has made all things to all men asserted itself.

'May I propose to *part* of it?' I said.

Dixon smiled. 'Beer?' he asked, offering me a can. Then, allowing his lower lip to droop forward and raising his arm loosely in the air, as if depending from some imaginary branch, he did a gibbering ape imitation around the room.

The air struck cold as, some little time later, Dixon and I went out into the court. In the further corner stood one of the latest additions to the college, a wing built during an access of wealth in the middle nineteenth century, and now given over almost entirely to freshmen, though the Bursar's rooms were there too. It had little architectural merit, and was evidently rather jerry-built, for the flames spread through it from end to end as soon as we tossed our matches into the petrol. The fire flickered brightly on the Tudor stone of the old quadrangle, forming a bright pool of warmth, though further away, of course, the cold struck colder than ever. After the last ember had died and the last scream faded, I returned to my rooms to wash off some of the dirt deposited by the evening's adventure.

I felt uneasy and a thought depressed. Perhaps I had let my hot–cold imagery take me a mite too far. Further, I felt that I had fallen under Dixon's spell, been taken further than by nature I would wish to go. My gyp had left me a pitcher of water, laced with rose petals, and as I slopped it in the bowl I caught sight of my features in the mirror. An idea struck me.

If I loosened up my clauses, let my dialogue dangle a bit, and twisted my plot into a grimace, I could make my style exactly like Kingsley Amis's. I put it to the test. 'Filthy grass-eating codpiece,' I said to my features. 'Toad-faced hanger about ladies' lavatories,' I continued. The image stared stiffly back and then suddenly yielded; and a moment later, when my gyp came in, I was doing a gibbering ape imitation about the room.

A Jaundiced View

Among our leading novelists, some are prolific, some less so. There must be many readers of Miss Iris Murdoch who live in fear of a fallow year, when no more than one novel by the author drops from her pen, leaving them with long empty evenings to waste. The following extract, from a new work called *The Sublime and the Ridiculous*, is designed to cater for this eventuality, by having many characters, some of them hardly used at all, who can – under fresh titles like *The Necessary and the Contingent* or *The Many and the Few* – be put through fresh sexual permutations by bereft readers on rainy days.

'FLAVIA SAYS that Hugo tells her that Augustina is in love with Fred.'

Sir Alex Mountaubon stood with his wife Lavinia in one of the deeply recessed mullion windows of the long gallery at Bishop's Breeches, looking out at the topiary peacocks on the terrace beyond. In front of them the fountain, topped with statuary in which a naked Mars played joyously with a willing Venus, gently coruscated, its tinkle audible through the open windows. The scene before them was of order and peace. They could look down the park at the mile-long drive of lindens, the colour of jaundice; to one side, away from its necessary order, stood one dark and contingent cedar tree. Beneath it their older daughter, Flavia, could be seen from the window, sitting on a white wooden seat, in her unutterable otherness, her pet marmoset on her shoulder, her cap of auburn hair shining like burnished gold on her head. Nearer to the house, in the rose garden, their younger daughter, seven-year-old Perdita, strange, mysterious and self-absorbed as usual, was beheading a litter of puppies with unexpectedly muscular and adult twists of her slender arm. Her cap of golden hair shone like burnished auburn on her head.

Alex turned, catching sight of himself in the big, gilt, rather battered cupid-encrusted mirror that soared over the mantel. Mortality was there in the darkened eyes, but most of what he saw there, the solid, round face of a man of principle, pleased him exceedingly. His book, a philosophical study of Niceness, was almost complete; in its writing Lavinia, his second wife, had proved the perfect helpmeet and companion. No one lay dying upstairs. He looked around at the familiar objects, the Titians and Tintorettos, glowing in their serried ranks with jewelled beneficence, the twined, golden forms of bodies twisted together suggesting a radiant vision of another world. In cases stood the Sung, cups, the Ting plates, the Tang vases, the Ming statuettes, the Ching saucers; these last must, almost certainly, go.

'Who says whom tells her that who is in love with whom?'

Lavinia, her arms full of lilies, did not turn. 'Flavia,' she said.

'And are they?'

'They think so. I don't think they quite know.'

'But at least we know. About us,' said Alex lovingly. He looked out of the window and saw Perdita staring strangely up at the house; and suddenly, involuntarily, he recalled again that experience of utter freedom he had known for the first time when he and Moira LeBenedictus had lain naked together in the Reading Room of the British Museum, after hours of course; he, as a senior civil servant, had been entitled to a key. Other moments came back: Moira walking through Harrods without her shoes, Moira on the night they had boxed together on the roof of St Paul's Cathedral, Moira threatening him in the Tottenham Hotspurs football ground at midnight with her whaler's harpoon.

Two miles away, in the bathroom at his house, Buttocks, Sir Hugo Occam laid down his razor. He walked through into the bedroom where Moira LeBenedictus lay. She was his good towards which he magnetically swung. She lay on the bed, gathering her hair together into a cap of black.

'Are we acting rightly?'

'I think we are,' she said.

'Oh, Moira.'

'Come, come, Hugo,' she said. From the alcove, Leo Chatteris, a spoiled priest, long in love with Moira, watched them in protective benediction. Could he surrender her? The pain was so much he knew it was right.

'Do we?' Lavinia had thrown down her lilies and now stood facing Alex. 'Alex,' she said with sudden passion, 'I have resigned from the presidency of the WI.' The words struck a sudden chill over him, and he knew that the shapeliness and order about him were about to be violated. 'I am in love with Fred.'

'You can't be,' said Alex, speaking without thought, absorbed in his own misery, 'Augustina is in love with Fred, Hugo is in love with Augustina, Flavia is in love with Hugo, Fred is in love with Flavia, Moira is in love with Fred, I am in love with Moira, and you are in love with me.'

'No, Fred . . . Hugo . . . Alex rather,' said Lavinia, her voice trembling, 'I'm afraid you have it *all the wrong way round*. I am in love with Fred, you are in love with me, Moira is in love with you, and you utterly missed out Leo, who is as unutterably particular as anyone else, and who is in love with Moira.'

'But how, why?' Alex murmured, his hands over his face.

'It's one of the wonders of the world.'

'All right,' he said, 'Here we go again. Will you call them, or shall I?'

*

'Do be careful of the Gainsboroughs,' said Alex to the men, 'And I do think the Renoirs ought to have a van to themselves, and not be put in with the fountain, which is liable to wet them irreparably.'

Already seven of the thirteen furniture vans had been filled, and were on their way to Buttocks, where Moira was awaiting him. Bishop's Breeches, descending through the female line, stayed with Lavinia, but most of its exquisite contents, including some singularly heavy statuary, belonged to Alex. He stood in the noble portico, feeling the familiar, loved house around him, so fit for free characters to live in, and knowing he must leave soon, for the last time. The heavy van lumbered away down the drive, beneath the yellow of the lindens, towards the North Lodge. He turned to go back into Bishop's Breeches, and then heard a strange splintering noise. He walked towards the drive, passed under the deep yellow lindens. A very dove-grey Rolls was parked at the side. 'I'm afraid there's been a rather nasty accident,' said Fred Tallin, getting out, 'Your first van ran into my first van. There's stuff spilled all over the road. We can't tell whose Titians are whose. As for the Sung and the Ting and the Tang and the Ming and the Ching, I'm afraid all that's gone bang. Awful business, this packing. How the deuce do you pack up a herd of deer? Lav all ready for me?'

'She's in her room, holding daffodils,' said Alex.

A flotilla of pantechnicons was turning in by the West Lodge and coming up the other avenue. 'I say, that's funny,' said Fred, resting his very white hand on the bonnet of the very dove-grey Rolls, 'Those vans aren't mine. Mine are from Harrod's.'

'They're not mine, either,' said Alex, 'You don't think Moira's got it all wrong? She did know I'm going to Buttocks, not her coming here to me?'

'It rather looks as if not,' said Fred, 'In any case, I thought Buttocks belonged to Hugo.'

'Moira told me it belonged to Leo, who had given it to her,' said Alex.

'Very funny girl, Moira,' said Fred, 'Did she ever show you her sarcophagus?'

A horn blared behind them, and they both turned. There, on the gravel in front of the house, stood another row of pantechnicons, which had evidently come in from the East Lodge, and drawn up unnoticed. 'I say,' said Fred.

'Now whose . . . ?' began Alex, but his question was quickly answered. For now Flavia came running from her white seat by the cedar, the marmoset chattering after her.

'Have these to do with you?' he asked.

'Dear Hugo,' said Flavia. She put her arms behind her and

suddenly released her hair, which fell across her shoulders and down her back like a shower of gold.

'Flavia,' said Alex. Then he stood spellbound. For the unused gate at the South Lodge had been swung open, and up the drive came another line of vans.

'We live in a realm of startling coincidences,' said Fred.

They stood and watched as they saw a figure, bounding with joy, running to meet the vans. It was Perdita, strange and mysterious, her puppies forgotten.

*

Sir Alex Mountaubon stood with his wife Lavinia in one of the deeply recessed mullion windows of the long gallery at Bishop's Breeches, looking down the mile-long drive of lindens to the tightly locked gates at the bottom. The trees, the colour of jaundice, stood in their necessary order; to one side, beneath the dark, contingent cedar tree, their daughter Flavia sat on the white wooden seat, unutterably particular, while in the rose garden Perdita, still strange and mysterious, was twisting the neck of Flavia's marmoset. 'You know, Lavinia, I'm glad matters have reverted to normal,' said Alex, 'I know it's philosophically wrong, and I'm afraid we've done little for the plot. Am I wicked to say it?'

He leaned forward and, putting his arms round Lavinia, gently loosened her hair. His book on Niceness was now complete, and Lavinia was proving a perfect proof-reader. Lavinia turned her face and then, her arms full of roses, she smiled at him. 'No, it's marvellous,' she said, 'I love you, you love Moira, Moira loves Fred, Fred loves Flavia, Flavia loves Hugo . . .'

'You missed out Leo,' said Alex.

'To hell with Leo,' said Lavinia, 'I don't care how unutterably particular he is. There is one thing that worries me, though, Alex. Why is it that, when we sleep with all these people, they're all either titled or in the Civil Service?'

189

'I don't know. I suppose you might say it's a condition of our world,' said Alex, looking around the gallery. Only a few gaps on the wall among the Tintorettos revealed the ravages of the last days. 'However,' he said, as they both turned and looked out at the Mars and Venus sporting in stone on the fountain, and then, further beyond, the deep yellow light under the lindens, 'I do know this. Love is a strange, mysterious and wonderful revelation of others. But, for people in our station in life, it's really far too much of a bother.'

Tough at the Top

Of course, up at the top of the pile, things have been changing for the realist hero too. Mr Braine's Joe Lampton, for example, has had to keep on raising his sights persistently, in the Balzacian mode. And, in case you missed *The Lampton File*, *The Day of the Lampton*, and *The Joe Memorandum*, here's a recent page from the *histoire*.

I DIPPED INTO the pocket of my suit – it was an eighteen-ounce quince-coloured safari-style barathea, and cost me seventy-nine pounds from the best boutique in Leddersford – and offered her a John Player Special. Then, when my Braun butane flickered, I turned away from the wheel, and looked straight into her Mary Quant face. 'Aye, things have changed,' I said, in the flat northern accent I use when I'm with very expensive people, 'You've got to have progress, haven't you?' Laetitia, Marchioness of Salop, *was* expensive; you'd only to glance at her to see that. Her body was like that of a pet cocker spaniel fed on Lotameat, fine, trim, shining, well-brushed; and you could tell at a glance that everything around her was dedicated to keeping it that way. She put her hand lightly on my wrist, touching my Omega digital; I could smell the fresh scent of her Badedas. 'Say progress again, Joe,' she said, 'I just love your round Rs.' 'I like yours too, love,' I said.

Beneath us the tyres crackled; we were doing a hundred and thirty. Luckily we were in a car, her new, milk-white priority-built Jensen Interceptor. She'd thrown the keys at me as we got in; I couldn't help noticing, as I grovelled on the gravel for them, the vanity number plate, POSH 1. I'd met her only that lunchtime in an old haunt of mine, the Trolls Bar at the Batley Trattoria, but, sitting next to her in the Jensen, it was as if already our relationship had matured to a fine old glow – the way a good Stilton does, if you pour a couple of bottles of Cockburn's port into it. We sat there with our self-retracting seatbelts on, and already I think we both felt that we were something more than lovers. Not that we'd made love yet; but looking at her I knew she had that in mind, just as much as I had. The whole thing had just burst on us, like a nuclear explosion. Place and people had been just right: an atmosphere you could savour the way you do a Wills Castella, wine-lists with silk tassels, waiters in Gestapo uniform, and a good modern group, called Turd, playing a rhythm that set even forty-five year old pulses like mine bouncing. The Sheik I was with – I'm an oil man now – was a tough nut to crack, but I'd just got him to drop his barrel prices by two-thirds; and I was feeling good, the way you do after making love, except of course I'd got all my clothes on. We sat at the bar, drinking rums and peppermints (the Sheik had agreed to change his religion too), talking to Enid, the topless barmaid, when I happened to glance at the mirror behind the bar.

It was then the fireworks started. She'd come in at the door, and was just sitting down on one of the purple toadstools that are part of the décor, when I spotted her. I knew at once I had to have her. It's a feeling I get now and then. She'd sprayed something on her hair that made it look as if she'd iced it. The trouser suit was Yves Saint-Laurent, I could see at a glance; the label hung down in front, an oversight, obviously, on the part of the maid, a nubile Asian girl who stood beside her, holding the Afghan hound. As I looked in the mirror, I could imagine that trouser suit and the silken blouse beneath it falling from her, revealing the shapely body beneath, muskily scented with *parfum*. 'Excuse me, Sheik,' I said, reaching in my pocket and taking out my nickel-plated Dr Feelgood badge, which I pinned to my lapel. Then slowly, showing my good profile, I walked across the room towards her and sat down on the opposite toadstool. 'Haven't we met before, love?' I asked. She looked up at me, her green lips pouting. 'Possibly,' she said, looking me up and down, 'Weren't you at Wragby one weekend?' 'Wragby?' I asked. 'One of Connie Chatterley's little bashes,' she said. 'Oh, possibly,' I answered, 'I never forget a face.' 'It's hardly faces one remembers from Wragby,' she said, with a laugh, 'Dear old Connie, I really must ask her sometime how she manages to keep her staff so well.'

It began, quietly, simply, like that. Moments later we were walking together towards the Interceptor; fortunately the Sheik, the Asian maid and the Afghan dog all seemed to get on terribly well together, and made no complaint at all when we suggested that they go off and spent the afternoon out of the story, at the Leeds Palace of Varieties. Soon we were away from the grimy slate roofs of the city and driving through dense country, on our way to her place, which she told me was called Veblen Hall. The speedometer was at a hundred and forty. In the fields cows stood, strange bags under their hindquarters; Laetitia explained to me that they were full of milk. The wind blew in our hair, more in hers than mine. 'Progress,' she said, copying my accent tenderly, 'And you're it, are you, Joe?'

'I am, to be frank, yes,' I said, 'I know what I want and I get it.'

'And what do you want, Joe, *mon petit chou*?' she asked, poking a finger in my ear.

'Laetitia, Marchioness of Salop,' I said, pressing my foot down on the accelerator.

'You're brutally direct, aren't you?' she said, running her hand through my hair, 'I see now what makes you so attractive to women.'

'There's also the ceaseless amoral vitality,' I said, 'You'll notice that in a minute. Are we nearly there?'

'Another ten minutes,' she said, 'We've been driving through the estate for the last hour.'

'And the Marchion?' I asked, 'Will he be at home?'

'Who, you tensile brute?' she asked, staring at me with bright, amused eyes.

'Your husband,' I said.

'Oh, Derek's in the Bahamas having a sex change. He'd do anything for me. Would you do anything for me?'

'I'll see,' I said.

'Oh, Joe,' she said, 'Do stop the car.'

'Why?' I asked.

'We're here,' she said, 'This is the drawing room.'

A quarter of an hour later we were sunning ourselves on the terraces at Veblen. The estate was Capability Brown, with trees organized down to a perfect lake. Deer roamed in the woods. A group of eight musicians sat in the top of an elm, regaling us with two of Beethoven's late quartets. Two gardeners with aerosols were spraying some bushes green – Laetitia explained that they'd been discoloured by the sun – and occasionally peasants from the estate cottages, especially chosen, she told me, for the luxuriance of their forelocks, came by and touched them politely at us. Around the fountain, where stone dolphins spurted, a group of naked Moroccans were playing volleyball. There was also an admirable display of dahlias. It was the experience of a lifetime. I've been in a lot of places, known a lot of pleasures, but the luxuriance of the scene outshone them all.

Do you like it, Joe?' asked Laetitia, swinging her hammock near to mine, and looking with limpid eyes at my face, her expression showing the expectation of a woman who hopes to have pleased her man.

'I think you've got it very nice,' I said, 'Laetitia . . .'

'Ssshh,' she said, putting her finger to her lips. I looked around and saw why. Two beautiful servants in Pompadour headdresses and shepherdess costumes stood there, one beside each of us, offering us drinks in frosted glasses. 'Well, cheers,' I said, raising the bubbling wine to her as she sat smiling opposite me, 'And here's to the two of us.'

'That will be all, Millett; thank you, Greer,' she said, and the two girls bobbed and then vanished, with that practised skill in self-effacement that only truly professional servants possess.

'And now we're alone,' she said, 'Tell me, Joe. Have you ever drunk Babycham nude in a heated swimming pool filled with Chanel Number Five?'

'I don't believe I have,' I said, 'but I'm game for anything with you.'

'Come, *ma petite aubergine*,' she said, rising to stand invitingly before me, 'Let me take you.'

'Where is it?' I said.

'In the bedroom,' she said.

She led the way through the great house, through the hall where Titians hung, up the great stone staircase to the master bedroom. It was a room of splendour, the walls covered with ornate mirrors, the ceiling rich with cut-glass chandeliers, the bed covered in a cloth of damask. Everything seemed chosen to give pleasure.

'First the Babycham,' she said, opening a Louis Quinze escritoire to reveal, inside, a modern drinks cabinet, 'And now we're alone, tell me what stirs in that unrococo, frank mind of yours?'

She stood in front of me in the green trouser suit, holding the glass. The drive, the setting, the drink were all combining to stimulate my desire. 'There's nothing like wealth to make a woman truly beautiful,' I said.

'Why, Joe!' she said, 'I shall call you Sensualdo.'

'Do,' I said. Her eyes stared at me like inviting pools. Her hand, with the drink, was held out to me. I bent forward and brutally, with both lips, I kissed her fingers.

'Joe,' she said, 'you're so irreduceably real. A man who knows where he's going. Takes what he wants.'

'Yes,' I said, and, reaching forward, I began to unbutton the trouser suit. Underneath was the fresh skin, flawless and alive.

'Wait,' she said, 'You'll crush that fine barathea suit. Let me take your jacket off.'

She slipped the jacket from me and then, with a quick movement, unloosed her own green suit. It slid from her like a skin. Underneath she was naked and very beautiful. Behind her was the damask-covered bed. She drew me gently towards it. 'Oh, Sensualdo,' she whispered, 'come to me.'

It was just then, as I was about to slip off my trousers, that I heard a faint noise, rather like a giggle. It seemed to come from close by, somewhere behind the bed, outside the room. I turned and threw open the door in the wall beside the bed. Outside, down the long corridor, hung with El Grecos, I saw, fleeing, the eight musicians, the two gardeners, the naked Moroccans, and Millett and Greer. Only three peasants remained standing on the reverse side of the two-way mirror, politely tugging their forelocks at my appearance.

'Sensualdo, where are you?' she called.

I returned to that marvellous, flesh-coloured body, lying there so invitingly on the bed. 'A while ago,' I said, 'I spoke of my amoral vitality. But there are some lines I draw. One of them is viewerism. Where's my jacket? I'm off.'

'But why, Joe, why?' she whispered.

'Our mores are not compatible,' I said, and took my jacket from the chair.

'Very well, Joe,' she said coolly, pulling on a denim peignoir; then she was gone. I should have known, I told myself angrily, as I walked down the drive, permissiveness has gone too far. I stared back at the great house behind me, then walked on, through the trees, towards civilization. It took me three hours to reach a bus-stop. And it was then, when I felt in my jacket for my Cardin pigskin wallet, that I realized I'd really been had. The wallet, the Braun lighter, the John Player Specials, the Omega digital, even the Dr Feelgood badge; every one of them was missing.

Last Things

It has been widely noted that the recent fiction of Miss Muriel Spark has been concerned with those two crucial enterprises, fiction and death, and that somehow this has been making her novels shorter and shorter. The following, then, is not an excerpt from, but the entirety of, her newest, shortest, and most deathly work, *The Nuns of Terminus*.

'I HOPE you are both keeping an extremely careful eye on the weather,' says Sister Felicity, who is small and fat, with a shrewd mouth, 'It is perhaps the commonest way available of procuring our downfall.'

'I can't think of any reason why it should be,' says Sister Mercy, who is famous for being stupid, and for getting the weaker lines of dialogue, and who will die, in distressing circumstances, rather closer to the beginning of this story than any of the others.

'Felicity is right, of course,' says Sister Georgina, still one of the novices, but taken up by Sister Felicity for her cunning: she is reputed to have worked for the Political Intelligence Department of a certain Foreign Office during the war, 'It is a question of sustaining an adequate level of probability. Even a simple change of barometric pressure can lead with unbroken logic to a chill, and a chill to bronchial pneumonia, which in turn can have fatal consequences without disturbing at all what people are pleased to think of as the normal order of things.'

'That is why Sister Georgina urged you to put on your thickest shoes,' says Sister Felicity, walking on with her quite long stride.

The three nuns, black like crows in the habit of their order, walk, on the grass, under the trees, up and down, round and round, in the private and unseen grounds of this rigorous convent, notable for its chastity, in an unnamed northern country. It is, for the moment, a nice day. The sun is shining in an apparently pleasant way on the grass, on the leaves of the trees, and the barometric pressure, while subject to sudden fluctuation in these parts, is recorded as steady and fair in the newspapers that will, on the following day, have so much to report, in long black columns of type, about these lawns, these trees, this famous and rigorous convent. Inside the cold stone buildings, just visible over the wall, the other nuns are even now performing the appropriate observances. The Prioress, in her white habit, is looking at her watch and noting, so that she will be able to report tomorrow, when it all comes out, the extent of Felicity's absence. But, at this moment, she is not alarmed. Felicity's absences are famous. She has been at this convent longer than any other nun, and her shrewd tongue and her authoritative manners have won her exceptional privileges, privileges now as ritualized, in their way, as the Vespers and the Complines, the duties and observances, that the reporters will record for their columns, the television crews film for their audiences, in the weeks of publicity that are to follow.

'The real torment,' says Sister Georgina, drawing Mercy away from a large puddle which has appeared before them in the path, 'is to know that there is a hand at work, yet not to know where and when it will choose to reveal itself.'

'I don't think I want anything more to do with this plot,' says Sister Mercy suddenly, putting her hands to her face, and bursting into tears. 'I'm not even sure there is a plot,' she cries, looking at the other two.

Sister Felicity stops abruptly, and looks at Mercy, appraising her with her judging brow. 'I'm sorry, my dear,' she says, 'I am afraid you have very little choice. It is the way of things to be necessary, when *we* wish them to be contingent. But this you know, from your faith. There is little any of us can do about it, except take every intelligent precaution. That is why Sister Georgina has brought a sunshade, as I, you see, have brought my umbrella. Of course,' she adds, 'the best thing of all is just not to be her type.'

A small white cloud appears in the blue sky above the trees in the convent garden.

'I think Felicity should notice this cloud,' says Georgina.

'I have already noticed it, my dear,' says Felicity, walking round and round, up and down.

'If one were to leave and go somewhere else under another name,' says Mercy.

'I very much doubt if that would work, except in the most exceptional circumstances,' says Felicity.

'But what circumstances?' cries Mercy.

'If, perhaps, one were being saved for something,' says Felicity, 'You must understand, Mercy, I have been in a novel before. I know what it's like. It is extremely uncomfortable, unless one manages to stay entirely peripheral to the main line of the action, and not to draw attention to oneself in any way. I have always thought,' she adds, drawing Sister Georgina from the vicinity of a large overhanging branch on an old tree, 'that the best way is to be a member of the servant classes, or to be asleep in another room most of the time.'

'It *has* been done,' says Sister Georgina, 'There have been some who have escaped. One was called Golly Mackintosh, who conducted herself with very sensible restraint, I thought, in remaining out of Italy entirely over the period when that English film-actress had such a bad time.'

'Which actress was that?' asks Mercy.

'Felicity will know her name,' says Georgina, 'She is stupendously well read.'

'Annabel Christopher,' says Sister Felicity, 'There was also a sickly looking man in a plane and a hotel who was wise enough to confine himself to the minimum of conversation with Lise.'

'Who is Lise?' asks Sister Mercy.

'She is in another by the same hand,' says Sister Georgina, 'A woman of great linguistic abilities, but I'm afraid the effect of that sort of cleverness is only to get oneself noticed.'

'I think it would be unwise to say much in front of Mercy about what happened to Lise,' says Felicity, 'I fear they are much of a type. Am I mistaken, or is that cloud growing darker? I'm sure we'd be wise to return as quickly as we can to our offices.'

Under the trees, at the very end of the garden, the three nuns turn. 'I wish we could get ourselves into the hands of Mr Fowles,' says Sister Mercy, as they walk back in their dark habits, 'He's much kinder, and allows his people an extraordinary freedom of choice.'

'We understand your feelings,' says Sister Georgina, 'but it's a very secular judgment. In any case, you'd find with him that what's sauce for the goose is sauce for the gander, if you understand me.'

'I think not,' says Mercy.

'One would almost certainly find oneself being rogered by one of his libidinous heroes,' says Felicity, 'At least our context here is not particularly Freudian.'

'It could be interesting,' says Mercy.

'I have never myself taken any pleasure in the sex part,' says Georgina, 'It is all right at the time, but not afterwards.'

'I think I could put up with it,' says Mercy, 'I expect one could enjoy it a great deal, if one was prepared to become famous at it.'

There is a sudden burst of lightning from the darkening cloud above the trees, causing Mercy to fall inert to the ground. The other two nuns, in their black habits, kneel beside her. In a moment they rise, their faces solemn. 'It was lucky she murmured something sensitive just before she passed on,' says Georgina, looking down on the recumbent body, which before the night will lie in the chapel of the convent, the composed and stupid face staring sightlessly up at the nuns who file by and, later, at the police inspector who finally orders the autopsy.

'I am afraid we were not paying sufficient attention,' says Felicity, 'We had dropped our guard.'

Georgina breathes hard, as if fighting off inevitable tears. 'It is not very kind of Miss Spark,' she says, 'And it is hardly as if Mercy were a full protagonist.'

'Come,' says Felicity, 'I think we should sit over there by the wall and be quiet for a while. If there were no dialogue, there could be nothing to incense her.'

The two nuns, in their black habits, walk to a corner of the garden that is treeless and, putting down the sunshade, putting down the umbrella, they seat themselves, backs against the wall, at a place that, in tomorrow's papers, will be marked with a stark X. They look across the bright trimmed green of the turf, beyond the crumpled black corpse, to the columns of trees, the once again blue sky. In the blue of the sky appears a white plume rather like a feather, the trail of an aeroplane that carries many travellers from homes to meetings, from holidays to homes, travellers who will read with surprise in their next day's journals of the events that unfolded, apparently without connection, below them.

'Even she could hardly want to push coincidence too far,' says Georgina, inspecting the plane with some anxiety. 'Surely her critics would begin to talk.'

Felicity, too, looks at the plane. 'I think you may be right to see a hand,' she says. 'And I am afraid the critics themselves are not entirely innocent in these matters.'

'I had not known there could be others,' says Georgina.

'You have not heard of a Professor Kermode?'

'I had not thought of him in this connection,' says Sister Georgina, 'I thought he was usually in America.'

'The Atlantic may be a substantial stretch of water, Georgina,' says Felicity, 'but it is not an outright barrier to intellectual intercourse. I think we should go in.'

But Sister Georgina is still looking at the plane, with its many travellers, and glimpsing, with a growing horror, the silvery piece of metal, a part of a wing perhaps, a piece of a wheel, that has detached itself from it and, twirling, changing in shape but not in direction, angles down through the air towards the treeless corner of the garden. She rises and runs, her gaze fixed in the air. The aeroplane part whistles in its descent and falls harmlessly into an adjoining field. Felicity rises, in her black habit, and runs to Georgina who, looking upward, has stumbled over a croquet hoop, inadvertently left in the grass, and fallen to the ground. 'You were lucky, Georgina,' she says, 'You might well have been dead.' But a closer inspection reveals the truth; the fall has clearly been a heavy one, for Georgina, in fact, is.

For a moment Sister Felicity stands there, in her dark habit. She looks at the two crumpled bodies that lie in the grass, in spots which, tomorrow, will be staked around, and examined intently by many policemen. Then, in a sudden movement, she disappears behind an adjacent bush. 'She's caught me,' she shouts, in seven languages. There is a sound as of cloth ripping: a white coif flies above the bush and falls some distance away on the grass. A short while after a figure appears from behind the bush, in familiar street clothes, a dress of slightly more than miniskirt length. The shoes are perhaps heavy, and the blackness of the material of the dress duller than would suit most people's tastes. The figure rapidly crosses the grass of the convent garden, walking not towards the buildings but away from them, towards the high wall that shuts out the diurnal world beyond. And now the figure reaches this high stone wall, climbing it with agility and some speed. It gives a last glance to the garden that will be in so many newspapers, and then disappears from sight.

Later Felicity will do many things. She will fly to Africa, to Canada, to South America. She will hunt tiger in India, and take a small canoe down the Amazon river, through disease-infested waters and snake-inhabited swamps. She will climb precipitous mountains in the Tyrol, where sheer drops overlook green and church-filled valleys far below. She will die, in New York City, in the year 2024, at the age of ninety-eight, of benign old age. She will lie in bed at the last, and look up, and say: 'What did you want of me? What have you been waiting for all this time?' But I don't feel that it's my business to go around answering questions like that.

Voluptia

Voluptia, the recently published fifth volume of Lawrence Durrell's *Alexandria Quartet*, appears to have caused the critics considerable perplexity, since the character of Voluptia, Darley's 'charming brainstorm of negritude', does not appear at all in the previous four volumes. In fact it is quite clear, on careful reading, that no violation of the space–time continuum of the sequence occurs: Voluptia is in fact physically composed of parts severed or amputated from other characters in the previous books.

IN MY MIND, I was thinking. Alexandria, Queen of Cities, gathered round me as if it were a violet dusk. Mauve clouds like sheared seaweed filtered across the sky. Somewhere, over boxes of nougat, ambassadors wrangled. I scratched a love bite on my shoulder and gazed down at my pallid body, clad in its tartan underdrawers, stretched out before me, a long, sad groan of fate. O, how lonely I felt. I called Ali, in my best Greek, to bring me a nectarine of Scythian *krash*. I was so subtracted I forgot he was deaf, and probably knew no Greek anyway. But he KNEW, even as I held up a finger which hung in the velvet air like a tendril of verbena.

Then Voluptia was there. She laid a hand over my ears, and whispered softly. I could not hear her. I gazed upon her dank lips, rubbed with old kisses, those obfuscating osculations suspended there, recalled on the instant she reappeared. That her words were endearments of love (L-O-V-E) I was sure. Then, with a brisk chattering snatch of laughter, she sat: as delicately as a mushroom on the green sward.

'Darley!' she whispered.

'Voluptia!' I murmured.

'Darley!' she said.

Then I noticed she had lost her nose! I stared spellbound at the hole like a fox's hide which lay gaping between her eyes. A long moment wound itself away; I knew she would tell me. 'I've had a tiresome day,' she began. Ali came in with my *krash*, and I signalled one for her in my second-best Greek. 'First,' she whispered, 'let us drink to . . . love!' 'Life!' I said.

She arranged herself into a pattern of Byzantine order, her clothes fighting for their colour with the grass. 'I lost an ear this morning,' she uttered at last. 'Hamid cut it off in pique. Then the left eye Memlik dashed out at lunchtime, because I wouldn't take him on Mountolive's spider-shoot.' But it was still the nose that took me by surprise. I looked at her, trying to fathom the labyrinths of her silence. What can I give you, I cogitated with myself, but sympathy? (As Pursewarden – the devil – wrote: TO ALL WHO SUFFER SHALL COME . . . SUFFERING.)

The heat popped and eddied in my eardrums; I watched lazily as a bead of sweat formed on the skin of my baggy, shapeless hand. 'Let us make love,' I outspake at last, 'even on a punt, even on Mareotis, which by now must be the colour of gunmetal, the texture of boiled offal. Now!' I feared that she would feel unwanted.

'No,' she responded, vivid in grass, 'I must tell you the story, and without obfuscation. There are three versions so far, as many as there are persons, and there might be more if we wait. If we have time to wait. You see, it is so cruel, not really knowing WHY!'

'Yes,' I muttered. My heart was drenched in brilliants of violet love. But before she could even begin her first explanation, there was the sound of footfalls, many footfalls. Scobie dashed in on us, his glass lips blubbering. Behind, the soft-footed Ali beat out his lighter yet fundamentally arrogant note. He stood protective as Scobie, disagreeably abnormal, spoke in a tottering voice.

'Sorry, Darley,' he said, avoiding looking directly at the nipples on my chest, 'but I've got to cart Voluptia off to chokey. She's been interfering down in the circumcision booths. There've been complaints.'

Voluptia, to give her credit, resisted.

'YA SCOBIE,' I yelled, 'are you sure you're not under the influence?' After a moment he nodded, closing his eyes. Then musingly he *loquitur*: 'Sometimes the mind strays further than life allows. It is easy to excuse, but one's duty is in the end to judge. Alas, our pitiless city demands . . .'

Voluptia rose. I glanced at her warningly. There was a terrible *mêlée*. I became another person, utterly different from the person I'm usually talking to. In the frantic struggle, Scobie sweated, and Voluptia had her foot pinned to the floor by a Bimbashi's dagger. I was aghast!

Then she had all her clothes pulled off. UNDERNEATH SHE WAS DRESSED AS A MAN! 'Voluptia! Scobie cried out, his voice stark, nude. 'She eschews definition,' he finally said. Voluptia, wax pale, moaned on the note of a distant sirocco. Then she broke from Scobie's grip and her lips touched my ankle. She murmured, brokenly, half a dozen lines from Cavafy, their spirit untranslatable. Scobie watched and uttered: 'Sex speaks rapidly between unbridgeable cultures.' Then Scobie took her, not as a lawgiver takes a lawbreaker but as a dragoman leads a spirited horse. 'Allah be praised!' said Ali by dumb-sign as he left with his prisoner. Prisoner! (As Pursewarden writes: we are all prisoners.) I heard her go, soft-footed to the last.

'Another Scythian *krash*,' I signalled, my head askew on my shoulders. Mareotis grinned back at me under the puce moon. I felt almost sick. Alexandria! Her voice came again from below, swept up on the hot airs of the city. '*Chéri*!' she cried, and I could sense the vibration of those firm slanting breasts, 'We must all go back.'

Sweaty, my tartan undershorts clung coldly to my alabaster thighs. Again I was lonely. I wanted to press someone's elbow, but there was only Ali; and after some thought I simply pressed my own. Outside smugglers drove past in old cars; somewhere, over boxes of nougat, ambassadors still wrangled. A smell of decay, the smell that goes indeed with perfection, came up from the city. Excited, my nostrils quivered. For then it came to me, throbbingly out of the desert, over Mareotis, over minaret and palm, through the circumcision booths, through the pierced cheeks of the demon dancers, straight as a glinting arrow through the musk and maze of what we think of as reality. As Pursewarden said: Love is a four-letter word! In a feeling of exultation, I rubbed my hands together, thankful that, despite the company I mixed with, I still had them to rub.

Room at the Bottom

Realism's not playing on a very good wicket, nowadays; but there's still a writer or two with social concern enough to look at the language, just what's happening. As fair reminder, then, here's a brief fictional item that somehow got omitted from Alan Sillitoe's collected chronicles of the vigorous anarchism of Nottingham working-class life.

THE HUGE GREEN Nottingham trolley-bus circumnavigated the roundabout of Canning Circus, its rod-like poles hissing as they crossed the centripetal nexus of overhead wires, and pulled up at the stop. A group of lads from the factory, on good money nowadays, got off, laughing, shouting and saying their tatas. Eustace Seaton stared wistfully at them and then stepped on, with great arm-swinging strides, up the gradient of the Derby Road, only wishing he could afford the fourpenny fare into Radford. A javelin wind was daggering into him, and an evening rain made an oily shine on the pavements. Home seemed miles off, but Eustace stumped on, his feet feeling like great lumps of pig-iron at the bottom of his legs. He walked past pub doors out of which came draughts of beer and smoke smells, but with his pockets as empty as boggery it was no use thinking of stopping. Under the street lamps drunks mumbled in the gutters, celebrating the start of the weekend binge, and swaddles walked in and out of the pawnshops. It was a tiring, uphill walk, but at last Eustace knew that he was getting there when he saw that the policemen were at last walking about in pairs. 'Hey up, goodnight, lads,' he said, as he passed a couple; it gave him a happy feeling to know that he lived in a stable, responsible society where, impartially, the interests of all good men were so carefully protected.

Now he was there. He walked down the street of back-to-backs, feeling round him the life he knew so well. The roofs of the outside lavatories were flushed red in the post-meridional glow of the setting sun; the fog-dragon of night was beginning to slink between the steaming chimney pots. Kids he had been at school with, swum in the canal with, now on the machines at Player's and the Raleigh, were unloading crates of pinched fags and tools from the sidecars of motorbikes. The family on the corner, two years in arrears on the rent, were doing another flit, all their furniture, and several other people's besides, stacked up on creaking barrows, while a crowd of ragged-arsed kids tagged behind. On every doorstep housewives threw plates at hire-purchase collectors, and the white faces of the army deserters peered up at him through cellar gratings.

He turned along the twitchell towards the back door, and clobbered through the yard. His brother Arthur was sitting at the open back bedroom window, rifle in hand, taking potshots between the houses at the distant figures of bailiffs as they passed back and forth on the Derby Road, an everlasting source of annoyance to the Seatons. 'Hey up, me owd duck,' he shouted as Eustace came along the twitchell, vomiting into a convenient jug; Eustace suppressed a frisson of irritation at the uncouthness of his kinsman. 'Bagged owt?' asked Eustace. 'Nowt,' said Arthur, ''Ere, there's that owd biddy down t'twitchell as towd on me to the bobs. I'll notch her in the buttock.' Leaving his brother to it, Eustace stuck his head in through the back door that led into the tiny kitchen, overheated by the large fire used for mashing tea and making dough for wads. Whenever he did this, he was always struck by the way the Gissing-like natural-ism of the ambience was mitigated by a Lawrentian vitality; he felt that again now. Vera Seaton stood at the table, scraping jam onto a buttie.

'Hello, our mam,' said Eustace.

'Look, 'ere 'e is, then, daren't show his bleddy face round t'door,' said Vera Seaton, 'Where in the name of boggery 'ave yo' bin, then, eh?'

'Well, our mam,' said Eustace, 'I 'ardly like to say. I've been up the university, and they've accepted me to tek a degree i' classics, our mam.'

Vera looked at him scornfully. 'This is a fine bleddy thing, this is, innit, then?' she said, 'I don't know what Seaton'll say. I expect he'll bat your bleddy tab for yo'. We've never 'ad a bleddy layabout in the family before.'

''Ow is our dad, our mam?' asked Eustace, easing off his steaming shoes.

''E's in a real lather, and no mistake. Our Brian's come 'ome from Swansea and 'e's brought a black lass with 'im. Seaton towd her she'd 'ave to sleep up in't loft wi' the deserters 'cos she's so mucky. You'd better tek care what you say, our Eustace, if yo' want my opinion.'

There was a thunder of footsteps on the stairs, and the door from the hall shot violently open. Seaton stood there in his braces, breathing heavily, his face inflamed to the colour of puce. It was at once apparent to Eustace, a delicate lad, always sensitive to atmosphere, that his father was, as so often, a trifle out of sorts. 'Ere, was it your 'eavy boots woke me up, then, when I'm trying to get a bit of shuteye?' he asked thick-voiced in the doorway.

'They can't have bin, our dad,' said Eustace, 'They've never bin upstairs.'

'Don't yo' cheek me, yer young bogger-lugs,' exclaimed Seaton, 'And look at that bleddy clock. What time do yo' call this, then? Fine bleddy time to come 'ome, innit? We've bin sitting 'ere for 'alf an hour, peein' ussens to 'ave us snap, and yo' comin' in this late.'

'Well, I'm sorry, our dad,' said Eustace, 'but I 'adn't no money left for the trackless, cos I'd spent it all buyin' these books about Spinoza and Descartes and 'umanistic rationalism, our dad, and so I 'ad to leg it 'ome, and it took me a long time.'

'Leg it 'ome?' Seaton dissolved into black anger. 'Yer silly loon-faced young mardarsed bogger, I've towd yo' once if I've towd yer fifty times, get on the bleddy trolley and when they want the fare, tell 'em yo're under five.'

'But, our dad, I'm eighteen.'

'Well, tell 'em it's the bomb, sharpshit; tell 'em yo're a mutation. Yo' bloody look like one to me.'

'I don't like telling lies, our dad.'

'Well, yo' gret soft thing,' said Seaton. 'Yo' allus was the mardarse. Right from a nipper. When all the others wor on probation for nickin', all yo' wanted to do with yer bleddy sen was go to the grammar school and read Theocritus on pastoral.'

Vera, pouring hot water into the teapot from the range, looked up. ''E's a bleddy disgrace, our dad, that's what 'e is. 'E's bin up the bleddy university fer an interview.'

'The bleddy blackleg, 'e ain't, an he?'

''E bleddy 'as.'

Shades of vermilion crept over Seaton's face. 'Ah'd niver 'a thowt it. Ah niver 'a thowt a nipper o' mine ud end up wearin' a bleddy white shirt and goin' up the university. Look at thysen. Tha hasna' even the shame to blush.'

The door was kicked open. Arthur stood framed in the space, an open bottle of Shippoe's Ale in his big fist. 'That swivel-eyed get's niver going up the university, is 'e, then, our dad, eh?' he asked.

Seaton sat down brokenly in the chair in front of the fire, and poked the coals with his foot. 'I thowt I'd brought my lot up right,' he said, 'I thowt I'd towd 'em to niver join owt.'

'And yo' bleddy did, our dad,' said Arthur, 'It's our Eustace, he's niver been right. 'E wants a right bat across the tab, that's what 'e wants.'

'No, Arthur,' said Vera, 'Yo' let 'im be, and perhaps he'll come to his senses before it's too late.'

Brian came into the room. His sultry Eurasian mistress followed him in a silk dress. 'Hey up, our Eustace, my owd lad,' he said, 'I want you to meet Mimi.'

'Don't talk to him,' said Seaton, ''E's a bleddy crime, 'e is. 'E's gone in wi' them.'

'He wor allus the same, even at school,' said Brian, kneading Mimi's full Chinese breasts as he spoke.

'I wain't forget that business wi' Phyllis Batty,' said Seaton.

'What wor that wi' Phyllis Batty?' asked Brian.

'She got in the family way, and then it turned out our Eustace wain't responsible.'

'Look, stop meggin', the lot of yo', and come and sit down and eat your snap,' said Vera. A steaming hot plate of bacon and beans was put on the table. The Seatons sat down and soon were enjoying the feast. Only Eustace sat sullen in the corner.

'Nay, you can't blame the lad,' said Vera, ''E's the runt o' the pack, he's bin brought up soft wi' all this bleddy affluence. I mean, look at him, e's niver 'ad to do 'is own pinchin' and scrapin' like yo' two big uns. 'E's not 'ad your advantages.'

'Well, I'm not sittin' down at the same table wi' *'im*,' said Arthur.

'It's all right,' said Eustace, 'I'll take a tuffy wi' me up to me room.'

'When I was 'is age,' said Arthur, 'I 'ad seven girls i' pod and wor going' wi' a married woman.'

Anger burst into Eustace's brain. 'All right then,' he said, 'Gi' us me coat, I'm off.'

'Where are yo' going, Eustace?' asked Vera.

'I'm bleddy leavin' 'ome, that's where I'm goin',' said Eustace. He ran out of the house, clobbering down the yard and into the dark, rain-soaked street, past the beer-offs and the chip-boxes, running he didn't know where. A neighbour passed him, being wheeled home on a barrow from the Star and Garter. In dusty, ragpatch back gardens, people he'd known since he was a snot-faced toddler were burning their rentbooks. A feeling of sudden loyalty daggered through him. He remembered the beatings they'd given him, the times they'd pinched his pocket money as he dragged his welly-booted legs off to school. He went out onto the Derby Road. The headlamps of cars coming from the illuminated boneyard of the city below stabbed into his eyes. A train stormed through the darkness somewhere, and the Council House clock chimed out its chronicle of time in Slab Square. He had no idea where he was going, what he was doing. But then a trolley going towards the town came along and he ran to the stop and climbed aboard. He went upstairs and to the front. A notice said: DRIVER BELOW: PLEASE DO NOT STAMP FEET. The conductor, a whippet-faced youth, had followed him, and stood by his side. Eustace felt in his pocket, and suddenly remembered; he had no money. The thought would have shamed him an hour ago; now it delighted him. 'Me fare?' he said, looking owlishly at the conductor, 'I've already gen it yo'.'

'You han't, then,' said the conductor.

'I bleddy 'ave,' he said, remembering Arthur's motto: lie till you're blue in the face, and you'll always be believed, sooner or later, 'I gev it yo' at the bottom of the stairs.'

The conductor looked doubtfully at him, then turned and went away, along the top deck and down the stairs. When he had gone, Eustace turned, a big exultant smile on his face.

'I've done it,' he cried to himself, 'I've grown up at last. I'm socially mobile downwards. Keep your bleddy grant.'

He lifted his feet and suddenly, wildly, the metal floor began to resound to a frantic tattoo from his boots.

'What's goin' on up there, then?' shouted the conductor.

'Yo' shut your cake 'ole, surrey,' Eustace cried, 'I'm all right. I'm a bleddy socialist anarchist at last.'

Fritz

The prolonged silence of J. D. Salinger still raises an uneasy shiver or two in those forty-year-olds who, weary for a moment with the constant round of divorce and wife-swapping, hark back to their college days, when they had the Glass family saga to serve them as an ongoing testament of the path to ultimate truth. It's happy news, then, that the sequence is not quite ended, as the following item, culled of course from the *New Yorker*, shows.

THERE ARE PEOPLE in this neighbourhood who think that, for my role and status, I'm a rather fancy writer, so let me say right now that I wouldn't like you to run off with the impression that, in inditing the matter that follows, I'm trying to rustle up some kind of *prestige* for myself, for chrissake, or putting myself forward as some primitive-chic virtuoso of the typewriter. Quite *au contraire*; I'm light-years on from that ego trip way of writing, and have been ever since we moved out of the Bronx. My wife Gudrun, who's screeching out there on the porch at this very spot in time, wanted me to consign this little unpretentious sub-*Festschrift* to the basement furnace, and I'd have done it too, goddam it, with no loss to the spirit, had I not come round to the posture that silence in an incipient, unpublished writer is actually the really phoney angle. I mean, Beckett wrote first, didn't he, not to mention one other guy whose name is on everyone's mind; I can be silent later. Anyways, I figure I have real existential responsibilities *vis-à-vis* all those ex-kids out there, graying with inflation, who keep scanning the *New Yorker* for some message, however blurred and faint, from what the campus critics – primitive I may be, but I did take one hotshot year of Freshman Composition – call the Salingerian mode of being, and are getting zilch, right? No, I've been all through this, thought by thought, in encounter group, on the can; and in brutal frankness I'd better say that, if you don't want a blow-by-blow self-psych running to forty pages, and it's in that loose tradition I'm operating, then you'd be wise to acquiesce. If, that is, you really want the story.

Though, come to think of it, I'm probably way off base in calling this a story at all, when the literary genre it most resembles is, perhaps, that of the snivel. Still, if I read the *Zeitgeist* and Philip Roth aright, the confessional mode is all the rage again this fall, and since I'm industrious, uptight, and don't get to poke too many women too often, its topic is not self but others. In fact, I've no serious doubt but that the younger members of a certain family who used to live way up there on the fifth floor of this very building in which, in my own time, I'm pounding these keys would probably accuse me of writing scurrilous poppycock; and I'd better say right out that if I knew what words like that *meant* I'd probably be way out front there agreeing with them. The reason I don't know what words like that mean is that I didn't get the education; okay, I went to high school, and that framed document up there on the wall is an M.Sc diploma, but how does that rate against the achievement of guys who were glossing the subtleties of Spinoza to the listening millions at age eight? The tone there isn't, let me note for the close readers, envy; I've no time for those hangups, and I guess there's a natural justice at work in the universe that put those towering intellects up there on the fifth floor, while I pass my days stoking a furnace down this crusty basement. It's the same justice, I guess, as that which entitles those guys to record themselves high by high and low by low in practically whole issues of the *New Yorker*, while a schmuck like myself has to narrate himself into business from way down the very bottom.

But enough social reflection; I hope this proem has by now gone on long enough to titillate even the doziest reader into curiosity, however sparse or minimal, about who (whom?) I am, so let's at least not delay *that* revelation any further. Well, *amigos*, Fritz Pitz is the name, and if that doesn't immediately hook you then let me explain fast that my sole claim to word-space in this saga is that I'm super in the Manhattan apartment block that housed the family of renown several times cited infra, and who passed, in this neighbourhood, under the name of the Glass menagerie. But to the substantive data, which is, I'd like to make clear, in no way mystical or concerned with the higher mind-blowing, or at least none of mine. I've been around; I spent some time in Japan and the Oriental countries while on active service in Korea; I've been out on the West Coast a couple times; altogether, then, I've been exposed to the transcendent sufficiently to know by now that karma, suttee, nirvana and the sound of one hand clapping isn't exactly *my* cup of *sake*. In any case, who wants to know about the spiritual traumas of a *janitor*, for chrissake? No, it's the business of some to freak out with an Upanishad; and of others to be neat and tidy in the hall, keep stairwells clean, know who's in and who's out, who's alive and who's dead upstairs, put out the garbage, filled as it is with pilgrim-type knapsacks, and so let's not confuse things. However, there do come moments when even a supernumerary super, a figure all too normally cast into roles of narrative redundancy, does have uses; and I'd like in all temerity to propose that a situation where a writer writes himself into a corner and then leaves his characters in uncontrolled riot half way up an apartment building is one of them.

The truth is, I'd been keeping an eye on those Glasses for some little time, monitoring the anxieties from upstairs, even before anything really happened. I don't want to sound like I'm super at the Waldorf-Astoria or something; but the fact is ours is a fairly elegant kind of apartment building – I guess we have our marquee dry-cleaned more times than any other block here in the East Seventies – and most of the tenants are a bunch of nice, comfortably-off old ladies who pass the day pricing the goodies at Altman's and then triple-lock the door, put in the Flents, and slip the Luger under the pillow as soon as twilight falls. The building may be oldish, by current values, but I'd say categorically that it's not unfashionable; the area's good, the place affably urbane, the muggers clean, and all in all it does constitute, well, a 'distinctly Manhattanesque locale', as I caught one of *them* referring to it in only three of the million or so words of text they've managed to generate up there on the fifth. In general, then, our people are not of a kind that impinge insistently on a poor old super's consciousness, and an amiable live-and-let-live atmosphere prevails, to the satisfaction of most. And I must say, in all conscience, that when Bess and Les Glass first appeared here, all those years back, before their family had gotten to any size, they appeared utterly consistent with the general ethos; just a couple of good troupers, with polite bearing and respectable countenance, who cheered the heart a little just to look at them. No, it was later, when the kids started to press on into puberty, if you'll pardon my French, when they'd made it on the radio, and a certain high-toned solemnity pervaded their style, that the Glasses got to be, from a super's angle of vision, a somewhat insistent presence. I still remember the time, this is way back in the Forties, before Gudrun started piling on the weight, when she watched a couple of them – maybe it was Franny and Zooey, or Buddy and Waker, or Seymour and Raise High the Roofbeam, Carpenter, but, anyway, a couple of them – coming into the lobby, back from one of their broadcasts, and she said: 'You mark my words, Fritz Pitz; it's a wise child that knows it's a wise child.' Or something to that general effect. Anyways, this was when the trouble started.

Now, as I've indicated earlier in these jottings, I'm a simple janitor; so you'll have to bear with me if I find it hard to verbalize with sufficient finesse just what it was made me wonder what in hell was going on up there. I guess what I'm trying to say, in my inadequate, associative, *Tristram Shandy*-ish way, is that, though the Glasses kept themselves very much to themselves, and there were a lot of them with a lot of selves to keep themselves to, there was a certain . . . conspicuousness of lifestyle that titillated the attention. To take one tiny exemplum; I'm no prying sneak, but I did have to go into that apartment regular, admitting, in later days, doctors and psychiatrists mostly, and while it's the business of the tenant and the tenant only to determine how he furnishes his own place, well, there's furnishing and furnishing. I mean, you only had to go in there to feel a certain material amassing, or what Henry James, if in a somewhat other context, called a solidity of specification. The crap they had in there, well, you wouldn't believe – a concert grand, televisions, radios and phonographs in such profusion as to suggest an obsession with the spoken word, a ping pong table, enough ordinary furniture to fit out a small hotel, and a whole lot of other stuff it takes *some* writers two whole pages of text to describe. Add a load of books the New York Public Library must have been ravenous to get its hands on and it wasn't hard to guess what it was that kept cracking the ceiling of Mrs Dalassio's apartment, three floors down. Talking of cracked ceilings, it was some time earlier that the family used to put on those late night vaudeville routines that drove old Mr Seligman, on the fourth, into Payne Whitney. The song items he could take – in fact if there was one thing poor old Seligman delighted in it was a steady diet of 'Abdul Abubul Emir' sung through seventy verses by cracked children's voices – but the soft-shoe shuffles had a way of vibrating paintings off his walls that, I fancy, helps explain the sour attitude toward burlesque he evinced in his later days. But, returning to the décor, guy I knew had a nice little decorating contract for all the apartments in the block. Most tenants had their places done every two, three years (with Mr Seligman the necessity came up a mite more frequently); it took him *twenty* before he could coax a commission out of the Glasses, and then they nearly had his business tottering. It was a fixed rate contract, and seems it took him weeks to get through their place. Three days, it took, to get into one room, the haunt of a dame who fell into long-term bouts of sobbing the moment his brush was poised over the emulsion. Then, when he gets started, turns out that every wall in that place, from floor to ceiling and vice versa as well, is covered with photographs – and photographs of guess who (whom)? Untouchable photographs of themselves; he has instructions to paint *round* them. In fact, then, if I had to sum up the entire ambience in a word, you know what word I'd say? Solipsism is the word I'd say, and no goddam mistake about it.

It wasn't only the photographs. I mean, they thought Nixon was hooked on technology, right, but those guys, years before, had that apartment wired up from one end to the other with telephones, telephones everywhere, and all they ever did was call up *one another*! And the same would apply even if the one they wanted was dead. That's right. Okay, he's dead, but this is urgent, connect me. Another thing: did you ever come across a family that spent the largest part of its waking hours in the goddam *bathroom*? Their sleeping hours too, for all I know; I do know they had to come downstairs to go to the toilet. And, further to my point, they almost never went out any. Unless they went off for a bit to acquire some college credits, or take the lead in some play, or publish the best book of poems to arise in the West this century, or get married for a day or two, some self-sacrificing activity of that *timbre*. Of course, sure enough, they'd be back in a day or so, right up to the fifth, in the bathroom, looking at the photographs, on the telephone. Except there was this one thing, and this is what got me most of all. Just let a little *kid*, I mean, one little kid, you know, in snowboots and earmuffs, get out there on the street, playing some game, and it was like the rush to the lifeboats on the *Titanic*; I mean, they'd all be out there, all seven, eight, nine of them, talking to this little kid. Then it would be straight back, up the elevator, into the apartment, and, seconds later, *clacketty-clacketty-clack*; they'd all start burning up the typewriters. I guess even a writer needs a little experience of life. And that's how they were. Well, as they say down the block, the family that plays together stays together, but, well, I mean, for chrissake, in some *arrondissements* I know they'd call a lot of this stuff kind of, well, you know, crazy.

But back to the spot, such as there is; there's one thing I've been persistently silent about, and that's the breakdowns. The way I see it is a man's breakdown is his own business; I know all about the modern dilemma, and a cursory reading of Heidegger, Sartre and R. D. Laing has made even me, an ordinary guy, *au fait* with the realization that we dwell in an age of anxiety. The other tenants, many of whom only got up from bed in order to lie down again on the couch of some uptown psychiatrist, showed a similar tolerance, though it has to be said that a psychotic fit in a thin-walled apartment block has a more public dimension to it than the party in question cares to think. But I guess our attitude was that in some way those kids weren't just doing it for themselves; they were having their breakdowns, in a sense, for all of us. We'd got used to the sound of sobbing out of there, and the murmured Jesus-prayers, the high-toned wails; perhaps we'd even come to like it. At any rate it was Gudrun, my wife, the fat old biddy, who noticed the difference first. She heaved herself up from the old rocking chair – a kitschburger wicker thing we bought in a Macy's sale for a snip – out on the porch and came to speak to me about it. 'Fritzie, I just ain't heard a peep out the fifth one whole week,' she said, 'I think you better go up there and check things out.' Creep that she was, she was right; I knew I'd better get up there, if ever I was to have something to write about. Anyway, what follows now is an exact reproduction from a cheap diary, bought for 39 cents in a popular store a few days before Christmas in the year preceding the entry, the exact date of which I propose, sheerly for the purposes of mystification, to suppress. The entry is written in thick hand-writing and black ink, and is of a type that writers – especially *some* writers – love to reproduce verbatim:

Abruptly and very quickly, I went to the door of the apart-ment and, with a passkey, manipulated the bolt to the unlocked position. I entered the hall, attending to the such-ness of the environment. No sobbing, no Jesus prayers, just utter, perfect silence, with the cleanness of unbroken ice. I looked into the kitchen. A tomato sauce bottle, the top off, stood on the table. It was very beautiful; I felt unbearably happy. I went from room to room in the apartment. Each of the bedrooms was occupied by one of the Glasses. They lay silently in their beds, in apparent good health, not mov-ing, as if in a state of listlessness. Finally I entered the room in which Buddy, in green socks, was lying, in a posture similar to the others. I said: 'Anything wrong, bud?' He replied: 'We appear to have lost touch with our narrator.'

Well, of course, I'm talking about way back, now; there hasn't been a Glass round here for ages. I guess this was some kind of crisis for them. Certainly right after this Buddy quit writing altogether, cashed his royalties, and went into the macrobiotic fennel business on a commercial scale. Not long after, Franny took a McDonald's Hamburger concession in Des Moines, Iowa, married the Buick dealer on the adjacent lot, and got a blue rinse; friends who have seen them report them a groovy couple with an open marriage. Zooey stayed on at the apartment a while, calling up on the telephone at one end of the place and then running to answer it at the other, but after a couple of months he took off too and, after a spell financing blue movies, opened a Zen Archery range for singles in Sarasota, Florida. Seymour, being dead, has been harder to keep track of, but no doubt he's around somewhere. Life has calmed a lot, around this distinctly Manhattanesque locale, and the only worrying thing is the phone calls. They come from some guy in New Hampshire or somewhere; and he seems to have been calling for, like, *years*, looking for the tribe. I tell him what I know. He's nice enough, and always asks, from apparently altruistic motives, how my old biddy is getting on. She's sitting rocking on the porch righ now, watching the TV. They're showing the new set of Watergate hearings – some kind of spin-off from *Godfather II* – and it's sure doing her good to know there's some decent corruption left in the world. She has that goddam set on all day, to tell the honest truth. The fact is she can hardly move out of her chair these days, with varicose veins like a subway map and so much blubber it needs power equipment to move her. I try, in all compassionate humanity, to like the old sack, but there's one legacy that's been left around here by our late tenants, and that's a taste for the goddam *truth*. So I'll say right out I really hate her guts. There were many other details I wanted to put in to give this tale contingency and obliquity but, inconclusive or not, I'm going to leave it there. There are garbage pails in profusion to empty, and looks like we're in for another noisy night from this guy Rojack, who moved in on the fifth, complete with wife and German maid, after the Glasses dropped their lease. Oh, one thing, though, before I go; any of you college kids out there know what an Upanishad is?

On Yer Bike!, or,
Look Forward in Togetherness

Speaking of the Fifties, I went the other day to a local end-of-the-pier theatre specializing in revivals – frankly, it has little access to anything else – to see a hole-and-corner remake of John Osborne's *Look Back in Anger*, the play that had us all topsy-turvy in 1956, raging against anyone we could lay our hands on. It has to be admitted that, given the way the world has gone, it has not worn as well as it might have if we had all listened to its message. I saw, of course, exactly what needed doing to it – keep the good old nostalgic atmosphere, and the great clothes, but give it a positive, warm, entrepreneurial message. And, if you want Andrew Lloyd Webber in the package, make it a musical like everything else.

SCENE: *Realism, of course. A large outhouse in the garden of an old slum property in an English provincial city. Post-war neglect by the landlord and the droppings of passing crows have added something scabrous to the already prevalent odour of decrepitude. Here live* RUDOLF WINTHROP *and his wife,* MIMI, *daughter of* SIR WILKIE STANDISH, *a former colonel in the Nineteenth Hussars who was retired on a pension after mistakenly bombarding Gibraltar during the Suez campaign. Unbeknownst to all present, the outhouse is also used as a meeting place for the local cell of the IRA, which gathers weekly for readings from the plays of Brendan Behan. To the rear runs a British Railways branch line to a nearby glue factory, and a small goods train should pass back and forth during the action.*

RUDOLPH WINTHROP, *newly expelled from a provincial university for tunnelling from a convenient sewer into the showers of the women's dormitories, and now a vendor of low-grade curiosa at a stall in the town's marketplace, is seen using an electric iron, as the curtain rises, to expunge all the non-traditional elements from a recording of the Modern Jazz Quartet.* MIMI *has her back to the audience; she is breast-feeding her babies (triplets).*

RUDOLPH: It's no good. I can't stand it. The war was going to change all this. It was going to be better. Now it's worse.

I'm a kind of new culture hero
I'm the angry, the beatnik, the bum

I start all my values from zero
And take all events as they come
I suffer from boredom and anomie
I don't feel in touch with a group
I've no analyst who'll make a man o' me
Oh brother, am I in the soup.

Cho: Call me angry, call me beat
I think the world is just a cheat.

I'm starting from scratch, ontologically,
And though people say I don't care
I've come to my standpoint quite logically
Reading Sartre and Carnap and Ayer.
I suppose I'm a touch Wittgensteinian
With a heightened sense of the absurd
I break down the world and begin again
Analytically weighing each word.

Cho: Call me Kierkegaardian *angster*—
Though you think I'm just a gangster.

MIMI: You'll disturb the babies, Rudolph.

RUDOLPH: Women! They're all the same! Have you ever seen anyone die? Then you're a virgin.

MIMI: Three times hostess to parthenogenesis – this cannot be common. I must write to the *Lancet*.

RUDOLPH: Until you've seen someone die. (*He picks up one of the babies and flushes it down the toilet.*)

MIMI: Oh, God, not again.

RUDOLPH: I'll pour the tea. Later we can play cows and grasshoppers. Or bees and asphodel.

MIMI: Rudolph! At last I have taken from you more than I can bear.

When you burned down my parents' manse
And stopped up every drain
At all the houses of my friends
I did not, then, complain.
I knew not then, alas, that I
Should live to see the worst.
In a class-geared society
Milk does not go in first.

RUDOLPH (*raving*): You upper-class women are all the same. Cannibals, feeding on a man's vigour. Well, social mobility is no longer a crime. (*Slavering.*) I've had enough. I'm going to my room. (*Exits gibbering. A moment later the rattle of a typewriter shows he is up to no good there.*)

MIMI (*crying*): I should never have married. Hypergamy is unbecoming to both parties.

Oh, mummy said, to get your man
You've got to read your Betjeman

Yes, I was the girl in the Wetherall coat
And the thick Jaeger jumper, not allowed yet the vote,
But in other ways fully endowed and mature
Knowing all about life (as a keen televiewer).
My shoes came from Dolcis, my values from *Vogue*
I read Nevil Shute and not Christopher Logue;
I went to the tennis club every fine day
And I went to find *him*, not to drink squash and play.

I was dull, I was dim, I was daft, I was green,
My perfume was half *Ma Griffe*, half Germolene.
I was soft, I was silly, and gauche, I was grim.
On the back of my Vespa was room just for him.
He'd be rich, he'd be county, and handsome, and tall,
Then he came, and he wasn't – he wasn't at all.

(*During this song* Sir WILKIE STANDISH *has entered un-noticed. He is a true Edwardian (pronounced Edvardian) and consequently the bugbear of 1950s English letters. Decked out nattily in tweeds (pronounced toeeds), he now greets* MIMI *with affection.*)

MIMI (*throwing her arms around him, no small toss*): Daddy!

SIR WILKIE (*in hushed tones*): Where is he?

MIMI: He's in the next room, writing his novel.

SIR WILKIE: Gad, Mummy and I thought he was a bounder, but I never thought he'd sink that low . . .

MIMI: Daddy, I'm so miserable. The glow has gone out of our marriage. It's not a bit like it was in the good old days.

SIR WILKIE: Ah, the good old days! Beating off the screaming tribesmen with our polo sticks under the blazing sun!

> Oh, those were the days, yes, and those were the ways
> I wish that we had them again,
> The sun always shone, they should never have gone,
> And it never once, then, seemed to rain.
> Everyone knew his place, all the ladies had grace
> And a gent was a gent was a gent;
> The stout British lion the world had his eye on—
> And if *we* sent a gunboat, it went.

(*He goes into a soft-shoe routine, then pulls himself together.*)

> But quick, I've come to take you away. We must pack. Isn't there an old bag of Rudolph's around here somewhere?

MIMI: Oh, you heard about her too.

SIR WILKIE: Wait! Perhaps there is a solution. (*He reaches into the interstices of his Norfolk jacket and produces a copy of* McCall's, *an American family magazine devoted to the gospel of 'togetherness'. It falls open at a much-thumbed article entitled 'Forty-nine Ways to Make Your Marriage Really Work', and giving a list of hints guaranteed to spring-*

238

clean anyone's wedlock) Read *that!* It worked wonders for Mummy and me.

MIMI (*blushing*): Are you sure I should, Daddy? Is it nice?

SIR WILKIE: Naught in there that could bring a mantling flush to a maiden cheek. After all, *McCall's* does have a family readership. Remember its motto: 'The family that prays together stays together.'

MIMI (*reading*): 'Kiss your wife on the back of the neck once every day.' 'Go for walks together in the pouring rain.' 'Make your husband an especially good dinner every time you crash the car.' I see it all now. *Our marriage was not a partnership.*

SIR WILKIE: Knew we'd soon sort this little thing out.

RUDOLPH (*re-entering furiously – he is rendered neurasthenic and twitching when forced to remain offstage, hearing someone else speaking, for any length of time*): Ah, I thought there was a funny smell around here. So they dug *you* up again.

SIR WILKIE: By gad, you young whippersnapper, I'll thank you to stop making jokes about my being dead.

RUDOLPH: My daddy-in-law's so nostalgic,
He lives all his life in the past,
Though he's getting quite old and neuralgic
He thinks that it always will last.
Oh, he lived in the garden of Eden
But Sir Anthony played his cards wrong,
And the garden of Eden wants weedin'
And the past just can't last very long.

SIR WILKIE: I know that I'm just an Edwardian
When all of the world knew its place.
My life was once rather a gaudy un,
And I think the new world's a disgrace.

You could ride in the old first-class carriages,
And the people there were quite first-class,
Now we get these hypergamous marriages—
Oh, things *are* in a terrible pass.

MIMI: Oh, my husband's a mine of hostility
And he's definitely not of my class,
But as long as he keeps his virility
I'll let his vulgarities pass.
My father's an old sado-masochist,
He approves of the lash and the birch:
He tells me about all the things I've missed
But I'll leave the old chump in the lurch.

MIMI: Listen, Rudolph, doesn't it seem to you the glow has left our marriage, that what's missing is *bonhomie, Gemütlichkeit*?

RUDOLPH: Ge what lick height?

MIMI: Mut, Rudolph, mut. You have all the fun, pulling funny faces, getting hot and angry. Well, I'm tired of slaving my fingers to the bone over a hot cove. I want you to read this.

(*She hands him, reverently, the copy of* McCall's. *The stage fills with men from the Gas Board, who have come to read the gas meter, which is upstage, covered by the Panamanian flag (to reduce taxation), and with IRA men, singing*:

In a class-geared society
Milk does not go in first;
Of all the social crimes there are
That surely is the worst
For class mobility is all
And he who slips is curst
In a class-geared society
Milk does not go in first.

CURTAIN

ACT II

SCENE: *The same, one week later, but with print curtains, flower arrangements, candelabra and all the trappings of those old Batchelor's Soups advertisements.* RUDOLPH *and* MIMI *are finishing dinner; they smile at each other.*

RUDOLPH: Darling, what a wonderful dinner. I've always wanted to try ferret.

MIMI: And real Irish sherry in it, too, hic.

RUDOLPH: Good old Elizabeth David. Great Scott, it's nine o'clock. Time for me to buss you on the back of the neck again. That is, if you really want me to.

MIMI: Oh, I do, Rudolph. It seemed rather dirty at first, but I'm growing to like it. Isn't life wonderful?

RUDOLPH: Thanks to the women's magazines.

MIMI: Yes, thanks to *McCall's*.

> Oh, we went for walks in the pouring rain,
> And we nursed each other to health again.
> I've bought a car and we crash it often,
> My husband's ire with food to soften.
> And we kiss each other on the neck
> Whenever we feel our life's a wreck;
> We devote ourselves to togetherness
> Whenever we feel our life's a mess;
> We devote ourselves to Gemütlichkeit
> All the day and most of the night.
> Our wedlock's the finest you've ever seen
> Thanks to a women's magazine.

RUDOLPH: Now off to my typewriter.

MIMI: Rudolph, I sold it . . .

RUDOLPH (*suddenly beside himself, which makes two of him,*

a sad prospect for everyone): Are you mad? How is an artist to live without a typewriter? Nobody wants artists. It means you starve. (*He yatters on in this vein for several minutes.*)

MIMI: I bought food with it, Rudolph. I love to eat; we always used to eat, back at home.

RUDOLPH: I'm sorry I lost my temper. It's this infernal anger, clawing at my mind.

MIMI: I read today there's a new organization called Angries Anonymous. As soon as you feel it coming on you just telephone, and John Osborne comes out and talks to you till you get over it.

RUDOLPH: I'll call them today.

MIMI: And I was thinking. I'm tired of these dreadful old provinces. I'm through with low ambition and casual labour. Rudolph, let's get on our bikes and go to London.

RUDOLPH: But I've always loved the provinces.

> Ah God, to see the branches stir
> Across the moon, at Manchester,
> To smell again the river-rotten
> Effluvient from the dyeing cotton.
> Oh take me back to the L. S. Lowry-
> World where life is rich and flow'ry,
> Back to the land of Wilfred Pickles
> And good old Northern slaps and tickles,
> The girls are sweet, the chaps are pally
> And not too far away's the Hallé.

MIMI (*waving* McCall's): Remember togetherness.

RUDOLPH: Let me finish.

> But all of that is too disturbin'
> For a man so clearly urban.

Provincial life is much too cloistered,
I must be wined, dined and oystered,
Drinking all the latest drinks,
Slinking all the latest slinks . . .
Live among the high society,
Conduct myself with impropriety,
Kiss the girls with such a merry air
Pinch them on their London derrière.

Yes, we'll go.

MIMI: I knew you'd understand.

RUDOLPH (*a gleam in his eye*): Mimi, you're a wonderful woman. Let's play earthworms and antelopes.

MIMI: Or wolves and carrion.

They begin their favourite game. The gasmen and IRA men enter and sing with a will 'The Bells of Hell Go Ting-a-Ling-a-Ling' and Brendan Behan steps up from the audience as

THE CURTAIN FALLS

picador.com

blog
videos
interviews
extracts

www.ingramcontent.com/pod-product-compliance
Ingram Content Group UK Ltd.
Pitfield, Milton Keynes, MK11 3LW, UK
UKHW040640280225
455688UK00002B/38